beyond the sanctified

Sevens Prophecy Series

Book Three

beyond the sanctified

AMALIE JAHN

BERMLORD PUBLICATIONS

Whispering Hope, song lyrics written in 1868 by Septimus Winner.

ISBN-13: 978-0-9910713-5-7 (BERMLORD)
ISBN-10: 0-9910713-5-2

Library of Congress Control Number: 2017909568
BERMLORD, Charlotte, North Carolina

First Edition, July 2017

Typeset in Garamond
Cover layout by Amalie Jahn
Author photograph courtesy of Mary Ickert of Mary L. Photography

For Grandma,
my greatest supporter, life-long fan,
and best storyteller I know.
Thank you for always believing in me

Acknowledgments

Heartfelt thanks go out to:

Alton Jeffords, for your help with the Belizean translations and for all the work you do with the Oceanic Society to preserve Turneffe Atoll for generations to come.

Patrick Hodges, for stepping in during the eleventh hour. You're an amazing friend.

Fans of the Sevens Prophecy Series, for hounding me about when this final installment would be finished. Thanks for keeping me honest.

Fellow #NaNoWriMo authors who encouraged me during the month of November to complete the first 30,000 words of this manuscript. Didn't make it to 50,000 until well into December but at least you forced me to start.

And to my family, for sharing my successes and pulling me through the rejections. I couldn't do it without your love and support.

Also by Amalie Jahn:

The Clay Lion Series:
The Clay Lion
Tin Men
A Straw Man

The Sevens Prophecy Series:
Among the Shrouded
Gather the Sentient
Beyond the Sanctified

beyond the sanctified

CHAPTER

1

AKANTHA

Friday, October 14
London

Akantha heard the chains rattling inside the wall, alerting her to the meal. They'd been feeding her using this pulley system for several days, and she'd given up trying to get their attention. She snatched the new plate of food as soon as it appeared in the wall niche. This time it was a fish filet and cooked vegetables. For days, she'd sent flames up the chute, hoping her show of power would hasten her release, but no one had come to get her. At one point, she'd returned her plate engulfed in flames, but the meals kept arriving at regular intervals regardless of her provocation, so she'd given up.

She had no memory of how she came to be in the stone room, without windows or doors. There was a hatch in the ceiling but she couldn't jump high enough to reach it. Her last memory of the outside world was at Patrick's estate where she'd been given a room with a bed and something called a television. She'd spent hours watching the pictures flash across the screen and was even beginning to learn some of the language that was spoken in her strange new world. She liked it there. It wasn't hot like in the jungle and there were no bugs biting at her skin. She was grateful to her deliverer, Patrick, for bringing her to his home and considered him a friend. Especially since he hadn't even punished her when she'd accidentally set a corner of her room on fire the week before.

He'd taken her out a few times, around the city he called London, to places where she could set fires. They'd snuck away together in the middle of the night without her interpreter to abandoned places where he allowed her to light as many fires as she liked. Once, when a man crept unexpectedly from the shadows and caught her burning things, Patrick allowed her to set him on fire as well.

She'd thought perhaps they were going to set fires again on the night she was asked, via her new interpreter, to join the other gods downstairs. This was the first time she'd been with them all at the same time, as part of their group. She liked them much more than she had ever liked anyone in her tribe. They didn't shun her or throw rocks at her; they treated her with respect and kindness.

In the sitting room, she was offered a flaky food shaped like bread, which she was surprised to find was sweet and delicious. So much better than any tortilla she'd eaten among her people.

But no, she had thought, correcting herself. *These are my people now.*

After she finished eating the sweet treat Lillian called a 'pastry,' one of Patrick's servants began passing around a tray of beverages in tall, silver mugs. By the time he reached Akantha, only one remained and she plucked it greedily from the tray. The last thing she recalled before waking up on the floor of the stone room was the pleasant warmth of the liquid on the back of her throat as she swallowed it down.

She'd spent days going back and forth in her mind about whether one of the members of her new tribe was responsible for her imprisonment. Some moments she was convinced Lillian or the brutish-looking man was to blame; other times she was convinced of their innocence. Today, she was certain they could be trusted. If Patrick believed in them, she could too. They'd given her no reason to believe otherwise. She just couldn't wrap her head around what had happened or why.

She was still finishing her vegetables, wondering how to escape, when she heard a sound she didn't recognize. She realized it was coming from above her head and glanced up in time to see the ceiling panel lifting open.

Javier appeared in the opening and beside him was her interpreter, Irene.

"Akantha," Irene called to her in her native tongue. "We've been sent by Patrick to rescue you." Javier lowered a ladder into the room. "Climb up quickly! The time has come and we need you! The prophecy is about to be fulfilled."

CHAPTER

2

LANYING

Friday, October 14
Shanghai

Lanying mindlessly thumbed the edge of the folded sheet of paper in her pocket as she glanced out the window of her family's high-rise apartment to the courtyard below. Fog hung densely in the air making it almost impossible to distinguish kin from acquaintance as the last of the mourners exited the building. Her parent's hushed voices drifted in from the kitchen where they were cleaning up from the wake, and she was alone in the room with her grandfather for the first time since his passing earlier in the week. She turned to him now where he lay in the casket which barely fit against the back wall of the tiny sitting room. The smell of incense permeated the space nearly making her gag, and as she approached him she took the paper from her pocket, focusing on the printed characters, still unable to bring herself to gaze upon the pallor of his face.

"If, in the dusk of the twilight,
Dim be the region afar,
Will not the deepening darkness
Brighten the glimmering star?
Then when the night is upon us,
Why should the heart sink away?
When the dark midnight is over,
Watch for the breaking of day."

After the initial shock of his death subsided, Lanying made the conscious decision not to allow herself to become mired in her grief. She knew now, more than ever before, it was imperative that she remain steadfast where the prophecy was concerned. Her eyes scanned the second stanza of *Whispering Hope*, the song her grandfather sang to her during their last moments together. She'd printed out the words of the century-old Christian hymn the night he died, hoping to garner some meaning from the lines, but even after rereading them dozens of times over the past days, she'd learned nothing of his motives. She refolded the sheet and slid it into the pocket of her navy pantsuit, the one her mother purchased for her to wear during both the wake and tomorrow's funeral. Her mother, of course, wore black, as she was the daughter of the deceased. But as the granddaughter, Chinese tradition stipulated she wear blue clothing instead. She felt uncomfortable in the garment; too formal for the familiar relationship she'd shared with her grandfather. Theirs was a bond of love and respect and shared confidences. Stories of an ancient prophecy, the keepers bound to protect the truth, and the seven light and seven dark psychics poised to usher in a new world.

Now, however, the bond between keeper and psychic, between grandfather and granddaughter, was broken, and Lanying was alone.

Night was falling and the room grew dim with only a narrow strip of light creeping beneath the door from the kitchen. Somehow the darkness made it easier for her to steady herself, gripping the edge of the casket with trembling hands. She looked down at him now, finally forcing herself to say goodbye.

"Somehow I'll keep going," she told him. "Somehow I'll figure out a way to usher in the light." She touched his cheek, felt the coolness of his skin against her own, and said a silent prayer for his soul.

Back in her room, she heaved her rolling suitcase out from beneath her bed and opened it to reveal the items she'd already begun packing for her upcoming journey to the United States. She didn't know what purpose it would serve, traveling across the Pacific to be with the others, but she knew staying in China was not an option. Her parents knew nothing of the prophecy or her part in it, and with her grandfather gone, the people who understood her best were the other members of the prophecy. They were her family now. As soon as Salomon was able to make the trip, she would go as well.

She rearranged the handful of items in the suitcase. There was a bound book of notations explaining the origins of the prophecy from her grandfather's trunk, the routing numbers from the bank accounts established by the keepers which she had used to transfer money to Salomon in Kamina, and her grandfather's favorite wool cardigan sweater. She slipped the sheet of song lyrics from her pocket and placed it into the luggage beside a scanned photograph of Yekaterina Malinov which had arrived via email from Thomas the day before.

The young woman was a striking beauty with delicate Eastern European features and dark, soulful eyes. Staring at the photograph now, Lanying wished she'd been given a vision of this girl before her death as it would have helped to confirm Thomas and Mia's suspicions that Kate was, in fact, one of the seven light psychics. She felt certain it was no coincidence that she'd had visions of both Thomas and Salomon prior to confirming their positions within the prophecy, but without any definitive proof to substantiate their suspicions about Kate, all they had to go on was instinct.

It was this same instinct that led Mia to the newest member of the light psychics, a man named Jose with the ability to heal using the power of therapeutic touch. The story of Jose's introduction to the group, conveyed by Mia and Thomas during a middle of the night phone conversation, left no hesitation with regard to his belonging.

"He just touched Jack's gunshot wound with his hands and the flesh healed right in front of me," Mia had explained, unable to keep the awe from her voice. "Can you imagine having that sort of power?"

Lanying couldn't and admitted as much to her friends. In fact, in light of Jose's gift, her own ability to remotely see into other people's lives felt rather inadequate for the battle ahead. Even if she could somehow discover the location of the dark psychics, how would she be able to help keep them apart to prevent them from fulfilling the prophecy? She certainly wielded no sword. And yet, she'd promised her grandfather she wouldn't lose faith in her path or her abilities. She would carry on for him. And for the other's - especially Salomon who needed something positive in his life after witnessing the horrific slaughter of his tribe.

Both emotionally and physically overwrought from the burden of the unknown and her grandfather's two-day wake, Lanying returned her suitcase to the floor and slumped onto her bed, not bothering to pull down the duvet or change out of her formal attire. She curled herself into the fetal position, resting her head on her arm, and wished her grandfather was there to tuck her in the way he'd done when she was a child. Her eyes were heavy and as she gave in to sleep she was spirited away.

She sensed immediately that she'd traveled a great distance. Perhaps further than she'd ever been before, in or out of a vision. She was surrounded by cerulean water, in the center of what appeared to be a balmy, equatorial island, complete with the requisite coconut palm trees and rocky shoreline. On the far side of the island was an outcropping of rustic, green-trimmed buildings, perhaps half a dozen of various sizes. Behind them, storm clouds gathered at the horizon.

She was alone but for one other woman who somehow looked both older and younger than her. The woman was cooking in a large stock pot which hung over an outdoor fire pit behind the largest of the buildings, a thatch-roofed palapa. She stirred the contents of the pot with a large wooden spoon, more tool than cutlery, and Lanying watched as she brought a taste to her lips, hesitantly blowing on the broth. Seeming satisfied with the flavor of the dish, she set down the spoon, but as she wiped her hands on her floral apron, rain began to fall. Lanying expected the woman to cover the pot or hurry inside, out of the sudden deluge, but she didn't. She didn't move at all. Instead, Lanying watched in rapt fascination as the woman simply closed her eyes and raised her palms skyward. The rain began to pull back from around the fire pit as if she'd unfurled an invisible umbrella over the space. Raindrops fell in sheets along the periphery but no longer threatened the fire or her meal. She began stirring the contents of the pot once again.

Lanying caught movement from just inside the closest building and drew in a breath when she saw a small girl with plaited hair and a brightly colored dress appear in the doorway. She was favoring her right foot which appeared to be wrapped in a primitive dressing.

"How di fut be?" the woman said in a dialect clearly rooted in English but shaped by other influences as well.

The girl lifted her head, cocking it to the side in order to hear over the rain. "Aarite."

The woman nodded at the girl's foot. "Yeh, yah needs tah stay aff a dat fut if yah wah get betta. And how di boy, bway? Did yah breda stay outta trubba tday?"

The child bowed her head and shrugged her shoulders in lieu of an audible response. She avoided making eye contact by tracing lines in the sand with the big toe of her unbandaged foot.

"Yuh tell him he needs tah stay weh from di neighba, bway. Yah hang witt di daug, yah ketch di fleas."

Lanying smiled then, recognizing the adage about catching fleas from lying with dogs. She listened intently as the exchange between the woman and the child continued a few moments more until a foreboding looking man appeared in the doorway behind the girl, bringing their conversation to an abrupt end. From the expression on the woman's face, she was surprised to see him and the rain immediately began falling onto the fire causing it to sizzle and hiss.

His apron was covered in what appeared to be blood and fish scales, and he brandished a fillet knife casually in her direction. "Yuh out ya playin' tricks gen, Donescia? Yuh betta watch out or somebedda gonna lock yah up witt di rest of di nuts." From the way he laughed and carried on, Lanying could tell the two were not friends.

The woman, Donescia, stepped away from the fire, avoiding eye contact with the brute as she covered her pot and disappeared around the far corner of the building. As soon as she was out of sight, Lanying was tugged from the beach, and a moment later, found herself curled atop her bed once again. She lay there, motionless, paralyzed by too many emotions and too much pain. The memory of her grandfather's words cut through her.

"Time is growing short," he'd said just before his passing.

She had to believe this island woman was yet another of the seven light psychics brought to her through visions – first Thomas, then Salomon, now Donescia.

CHAPTER

3

SALOMON

Monday, October 24
Kinshasa, DRC

Salomon waited. He'd been waiting outside the US Embassy in Kinshasa since before dawn, sitting stooped against the eight-foot-high wall separating Congolese soil from the American soil guarded within. He was the first person in the line of roughly a dozen men waiting to gain admission. The solitary palm tree did little to shade him from the rising sun, and he was grateful when just after seven o'clock, the gate creaked open and he was ushered inside.

As he made his way through the security checkpoint, he was hesitant to surrender his folder of required documents to the officer. Laying them on the conveyor belt along with his wallet, the stack of papers felt heavy in his hands as if the fate of the world rested within them. In many ways, it did.

After successfully passing through security, he was ushered into the consular section of the embassy where he met briefly with his designated passport officer. He was prepared to be grilled about his reasons for securing the visa to the US but the interview was pleasant and succinct. Where was he going? Why was he going there? When did he plan to return? With little fanfare, Salomon received the officer's stamp of approval and was directed to the cashier where he paid his fees and was handed his three-month visa to the United States.

Out of the air conditioning and back into the heat of the African city, Salomon stood just outside the embassy clutching his visa to his chest. Sweat beaded on his brow as he considered what to do next. He'd been so sure over the past week that the US government would find some reason to deny his visa that he hadn't allowed himself to plan past his appointment time. After the pain of losing his family and most of his tribe, he could not allow himself to hope. Hope was for the naive. Now, though, with his visa secured, it was time to travel to America.

It was time to gather with the other light psychics and fulfill his destiny.

Not far from the embassy he found a cyber café where he procured a station and immediately contacted his best friend, Marceau, via Skype.

"Well?" the man answered, his wide expression speaking to his anxiety.

Salomon held the visa up to the camera. "I'm going to the US," he said proudly.

Marceau smiled, and while Salomon knew the smile was sincere, he couldn't help but notice the sadness pulling at the lines of his friend's face. He was wary of sharing any information about the prophecy with Marceau because he was unsure of how he would respond. Instead of risking condemnation, Salomon had allowed his friend to assume his sudden desire to leave the country was a direct result of the attack on his village. That he saw the United States as a place of refuge. A place where he could heal his wounded spirit. And while Salomon was sure his time away would help to ease the pain, he knew he would not return to Africa until he could do so having fulfilled the prophecy. He was sure only the fulfillment of the prophecy could end the poverty, war, and famine of his native land.

"It's only a three-month visa, though," Salomon continued, hoping to address Marceau's underlying sadness. "So don't worry. I'll be back before you know it."

Before disconnecting, the men spoke a bit more about how the remaining relocated members of Salomon's tribe were getting on in their new communities and made arrangements for Marceau to drive Salomon to the airport once his travel was secured. After a heartfelt goodbye, Salomon wasted no time making his second call of the morning, this time to Lanying.

CHAPTER

4

PATRICK

Monday, October 24
Pakistan

Even with his vast network of connections, it had still taken several days for Patrick to work out the logistics of securing his passage through Pakistan to the remote location where they'd successfully tracked down the seventh dark psychic. Initially, the plan was for all six of them to travel immediately to Pakistan, not wanting to waste a moment of valuable time which might give the light psychics an edge, but once the man's specific whereabouts had been determined, it became clear that passage for all of them would be far too difficult. And far too dangerous. At that point, there had been some debate about sending Wesley to collect Saif Naeem, the man they hoped was Number Seven, but in the end Patrick decided he didn't trust anyone but himself to make the journey.

Now, as he rode in the back of the heavily armored van beside two armed escorts through the Federally Administered Tribal Area of western Pakistan, he'd begun second-guessing his decision. The tribal areas were generally not considered a tourist destination and for good reason. Crawling with terrorists and other militants, Patrick had been thoroughly warned about people living in the region who were more than willing to cause trouble to foreigners.

"There's little that can be done to help you if you get into trouble," Javier had warned before his departure. "Don't expect the British Embassy to come to your rescue either. You're going to be totally on your own out there."

Lillian had also voiced her concern. "What if this man doesn't turn out to be one of us? And what if something happens to you along the way? Then what?"

Patrick tried putting Lillian's fears out of his mind as he adjusted his headcover and glanced at the armed Pakistani guards on either side of him. They were both built of stone, their muscles pulling at the seams of their shirts, and although he was grateful for their protection, there was still a part of him that hated being reliant on anyone else. The other members of his hired search party included a driver and a translator, both Pakistani, who he used for communication purposes. So far, however, his conversation with them had been limited, which didn't upset Patrick in the slightest. A destination had been communicated to the driver and payment had been negotiated, to be delivered only upon Patrick and Saif's safe return to Islamabad. These men were a means to an end, not people he sought to engage in an intellectual exchange. He was growing irritated, however, by their incessant guffawing over what he assumed was a mockery at his expense, as the men kept giving him sideways glances when they thought he wasn't looking.

As the truck lumbered forward along the cratered Khyber Pass, one of the oldest known passes in the world, once been an integral part of the ancient Silk Road, Patrick did his best to ignore his traveling companions and instead focused on the task at hand.

His return to London from his forced respite in South Africa had been a triumphant one. That he'd had the foresight to use the resources at his disposal to investigate potential leads in Pakistan was celebrated by all. Even Eshanti and Wesley were forced to admit they'd been mistaken about the importance of the paintings and congratulated him on a job well done. Patrick thought of this now, as the van lurched over the rough terrain, unsettling his stomach as well as his nerves. He alone had orchestrated the discovery of each of the six dark psychics. He alone would be responsible for ushering in the age of darkness.

He alone would lead the new world order.

That was, as long as he was able to return safely to London with Saif.

What he knew about the seventh and final dark psychic came from Lillian, who was able to bilocate to the man's location in the northwest province of the country near the town of Landi Kotal. Although she remained safely hidden for a number of hours, choosing not to communicate with the man, she observed him living with what seemed to be his extended family in a dilapidated two-story stone building on the edge of a partially abandoned rail line. It appeared to her that he was a smuggler dealing mostly in hashish, weapons and consumer electronics. Initially, Patrick didn't love the idea of allowing a common criminal into his inner circle, but when Lillian described his ability, he quickly changed his mind.

"He takes broken electronics and demonstrates to his buyers that they're in perfect working order using his power to control electricity. They purchase the defective merchandise none the wiser and Saif pockets a hefty profit."

"And what happens when these buyers discover the scam?" Patrick had asked her.

"He eliminates them, I suppose," she told him. "I watched him electrocute a man from across a room. Pulling sparks from the air around him, collecting them into a solid ball of electrical power, and throwing them at his adversary, killing him where he stood."

Patrick was typically most impressed by cerebral abilities, more like his own, but he had to admit, channeling electricity was something to be admired. What he was now concerned with, however, was his own safety.

Which is why he'd brought along Akantha, who was on the floor of the van across from him, dressed as a typical Pakistani man. She was adorned in a loose-fitting cotton robe and pants with a traditional Pakol and scarf around her head. Her brutish stature assured that no one had given her a second look with regard to being female. Some had, however, been intimidated by her threatening demeanor, which was the entire reason she'd been brought along in the first place.

Since releasing her from the dungeon of Javier's castle, Akantha had been particularly devoted to him. He'd increased the frequency of their outings, and with his own respirator for protection against the smoke, allowed her to burn portions of abandoned buildings and homeless people at will several times a week. During these special times, they'd established something of an unspoken rapport with one another, and it was as if she already understood her place in the new order as his right-hand man.

Her role in this particular mission had been explained to her before they left British soil. She was to protect Patrick. She was to protect herself. She was not, under any circumstances to harm Saif, although she would be permitted to use her abilities to restrain him if necessary. For everyone's sake, he hoped it wouldn't come to violence and that the final member of their group would join them willingly.

He looked across the van at Akantha now, her head bouncing along as the van jerked over rocks and ruts. He pulled a water bottle from his satchel and rolled it across the floor to her. She picked up the bottle without hesitation and nodded a gesture of thanks in his direction.

Her smile was the last thing Patrick remembered as the van came to a screeching halt and he was thrown to the back of the vehicle where his head slammed into the solid steel door.

CHAPTER

5

THOMAS

Monday, October 24
Baltimore

Thomas felt Mia slip into bed, pulling the covers askew and warming the space beside him. He opened one eye just enough to confirm it was still dark outside before he rolled over and gathered her into his arms. Her hair was still woven into the tight braid she wore for work but a loose end tickled his nose as he breathed her in.

"I didn't mean to wake you," she whispered. "I was trying to be quiet."

Her back was to him so he couldn't see her face, but he could tell by the tone of her voice it had been a rough night.

"It's okay," he said. "What time is it?"

"Just after five," she said, finally turning to face him.

Dark circles appeared beneath her eyes and her brow was furrowed, pinching across the bridge of her nose. He let his fingers trace her jawline down her neck to where a fresh bruise swelled at her collarbone.

"What happened?" he asked when she involuntarily winced and pulled away.

She sighed. "I got hit with a crowbar. Luckily the bastard missed my head."

For the millionth time, Thomas wished Mia had his ability to avoid danger instead of just being able to see if someone was good or bad. In her line of work, everyone she went up against was bad and being able to sense who was actually coming after her would have been a far more useful gift.

"Nothing's broken?" Thomas asked, unable to tear his gaze from the bruise.

"Only my pride," she said. "Wouldn't have happened if Jack would've been there…" She trailed off, testing the sensitivity of the contusion with her own finger. Thomas didn't like Jack being on paternity leave any more than Mia did. At least Thomas knew Jack would protect Mia at all cost. He didn't know a thing about this new guy, Brandon, who she'd been partnered with until Jack came back.

"It'd be nice if Jose was around," he said, more to himself than Mia who was struggling to stay awake. She murmured a half-hearted agreement as her breathing slowed. Minutes later she was sound asleep.

And Thomas was fully awake.

Careful not to disturb her, he crept out of their bedroom, which was really his bedroom they now shared. On Saturday, they'd attended Mia's roommate Chelsea's wedding and on Sunday Thomas, Jack, and Mia's father, Carlos helped Mia move from the girls' apartment into Thomas and Mildred's house. He wasn't surprised she was now sleeping while he was wide awake, as their opposing schedules were going to take some getting used to on days when Mia worked the night shift.

With several hours to kill before his nine o'clock Fundamentals of Musical Theory class at Towson University, Thomas pulled on a pair of jeans and a hoodie and padded downstairs to the kitchen. His latest obsession was searching the internet for insight into the whereabouts of potential dark psychic Lillian Hall and her known associates. What they knew about her could fit inside a thimble, but Thomas had a hunch she was connected to the prophecy in some way.

She needed to be. She was the only lead they had.

After booting up his laptop, he scanned the page of notes he'd devoted to her. He'd discovered in his sleuthing that Lillian was born in Texas to a Langford and Beverly Hall. Langford Hall came from old oil money and was written about with some degree of regularity in periodicals like *Forbes* and *Barron's*. Although he found Lillian's name on a class roster at Texas A&M University, her name did not appear on any alumni list which led him to believe she had never officially graduated. She seemed to disappear from public record after that with the exception of the Interpol arrest report Mia discovered in the police database and the YouTube videos of her online. Since there was nothing beyond an arrest for the high-end artwork, Thomas and Mia assumed she had never been found guilty of the crime. Whether or not she actually committed the crime was another matter altogether. But the arrest itself was enough to give Thomas hope that she was one of the dark psychics they were searching for.

To that end, Thomas was now focused on running facial recognition on the people who were with her on the handful of YouTube videos showcasing her abilities. There were four videos, and Lillian could be seen in each of them biolocating to two different places at once. The comment sections were full of skeptics, but Thomas was convinced of her authenticity if for no other reason than her birthday was a match for his own. It wasn't much, but it was enough for him.

In three of the four videos, Thomas recognized the same squirrely-looking man just inside the viewing frame. Appearing to be of Spanish descent, the man could be seen smiling broadly at Lillian, arms crossed protectively across his chest. Thomas had spent the last two days searching for the man's identity but was still coming up empty. He thought perhaps this morning his luck would change.

He was thirty minutes into his latest search when a Skype alert appeared at the bottom of his screen. He saw immediately it was a conference call with Lanying and Salomon. Not wanting to wake the rest of the household, he lowered the volume and answered the call.

"We're coming," Lanying told Thomas.

It was strange to see both of their faces side by side on the computer screen - Lanying in Shanghai and Salomon in the Congo. "To Baltimore?" he asked.

"Yes," Salomon nodded, "I was just approved for travel and my paperwork has cleared. I picked up my visa this morning. Now all I need to do is purchase my airline ticket."

Thomas's head was spinning. Two weeks ago they'd been concerned over securing funding, and Lanying had been begging him to help her find a way to get Salomon to the United States. Now it seemed the arrangements were already fully coordinated. "How much money is left in the bank account from your grandfather? Is it enough for your airfare and lodging?"

"There's quite a bit remaining," Lanying replied. "Plenty to get us both there, but if we want to save any for the other light psychics to join us, we're going to need you to help us find a place to stay once we arrive."

"An inexpensive place," Salomon added. "Very inexpensive."

Thomas considered the possibility of having them crash in Mildred's living room, depending on how long they intended to stay. "I'm sure we'll be able to work something out," he told them. "You should probably plan on flying into BWI here in Baltimore. I'm sure you both have things to take care of back home, but how soon do you think you'll head out?"

Lanying welled up then, excusing herself and ducking off-screen. He could hear her blowing her nose and when she reappeared, her eyes were glassy and bloodshot. "I'm sorry," she said. "I keep telling myself I need to stop being so emotional about my grandfather, but every time I think about leaving China, it's like I'm losing him all over again." She blotted at the corners of her eyes with a tissue before squaring her shoulders, taking a deep breath, and lifting her chin. "It just would've been nice to have had someone who really missed me to come back home to, once all of this is said and done."

Thomas had only learned of her grandfather's passing via email the week before, and although she'd mentioned her relationship with her grandfather several times, always speaking of him with great devotion and respect, he'd had no idea about what a valuable asset they lost until she explained about his position as a keeper. "I'm so sorry, Lanying," Thomas told her, thinking of the desperate longing he'd felt when his adopted father Howard died. "I know how hard it is losing someone you love."

She sniffed again and gazed mournfully into the screen. "He was the only one who understood about who I am and about the prophecy. My parents, though…" She shook her head. "They can't be bothered. He was the only real family I had left. And now that he's gone…"

Visibly moved and obviously reflecting on his own loss, Salomon began comforting her. "Lanying, it is true that we have all suffered through great loss, but perhaps it is all part of a grander plan. Perhaps in losing the people we hold most dear, we are being encouraged to rely upon our new family. The members of the prophecy. Me and Thomas and Mia. And even the new one, Jose. And although I know it won't be exactly the same, I for one consider you my sister."

Hearing Salomon's words, Thomas realized that his observation was surprisingly accurate. The intense connection he felt to the others was bizarre, to say the least, and he too felt as if the prophecy had the power to bind them more closely than conventional familial ties.

"I feel the same way, Lanying. And I know Mia does too. We'll help you through this, and you can help us." He could see her face brightening, ever so slightly. "We'll take care of each other. I promise."

"Me too," Salomon added.

She dabbed her eyes one final time and cleared her throat, an indication she was ready to move on from the subject of her grandfather's death.

"There's something else I need to reveal to you both," she said, her voice wavering involuntarily. "I believe I've had a vision of another psychic."

Salomon's eyes widened, mimicking his own. "Light or dark?" Thomas asked at once.

Lanying shook her head. "I couldn't tell. From her surroundings, she appears to be living on an island, somewhere close to the equator, possibly the Caribbean. And I believe she may have the ability to manipulate water. Or perhaps the weather."

"Meaning what?" Salomon asked.

"Meaning I saw her redirect rain from an open fire where she was cooking a meal. Or maybe she just shielded the fire with some type of protection. It was hard to tell exactly what was being manipulated, but she definitely has a gift."

Although for as long as he'd known her, she'd only confessed to having visions of light psychics, Thomas still held out hope that perhaps she'd discovered one of their adversaries. Someone they could stop. "And you didn't get a sense of whether she seemed good or bad?" he asked again.

"I'm sorry, no. Perhaps I'll get a better sense if I have another vision."

He could see Salomon mulling over the implications. "If she is light, that would make six of us all together, correct? There would only be one more of us to find." There was the unmistakable pang of hope in his voice.

Thomas glanced across the screen at Lanying where there was no mistaking the look in her eyes, silently pleading with him to keep quiet about Kate. It was a private issue they'd discussed via email for the better part of two weeks. Lanying felt that Salomon was in a vulnerable place after witnessing the slaughter of his family and that he should be allowed to hope, at least for a little while longer, that they were working to usher in the light. Thomas, on the other hand, thought it would be best to tell Salomon the truth – that one of the seven light psychics was dead and that there would be no fulfillment by the light. That their mission was to prevent the dark from gathering. Nothing more. He believed no good could ever come from keeping the truth hidden away in the dark. It was best that Salomon knew all the facts about the war in which he was now enlisted.

"About that," he began, as Lanying's expectant posture collapsed. "There's something important I need to tell you about the seventh light psychic. Mia and I actually already connected with a woman named Kate before meeting both of you. She shared our birthday and our psychic abilities, but unfortunately, she's no longer with us."

Salomon was confused. "No longer on our side?"

"No longer alive," Thomas corrected.

Salomon stared blankly into the screen as Thomas and Lanying allowed him to reach the only logical conclusion on his own. Lanying shot Thomas a look that could only be construed as anger, and he shrugged slightly at her, hoping to convey his weak apology. After a long moment, Salomon blinked, as if coming out of a daze, but Thomas continued explaining before he could speak.

"Most translations of the prophecy state, 'The first seven to gather all in one place will seal the fate of the world.' Kate may no longer be with us to seal it for the light, but our current mission is just as important. We must prevent the dark psychics from ushering in the age of darkness by keeping them apart."

Salomon grimaced as if he had just taken a two by four to the chest. "No." He shook his head, lips pursed, brow gathered. "This is unacceptable. For my people, my countrymen, it will not be enough just to keep the dark at bay. We must usher in the light. I made a promise I intend to keep. Without the light…" He buried his head in his hands, overcome by hopelessness.

Lanying shot a stern look at Thomas, but as he watched the African shuddering with disbelief, he knew he'd made the right decision in telling him. Better the man know what he was getting into now rather than be blindsided at a later date. It was now Lanying's turn to take on the role of consoler as she directed her attention to Salomon. "We don't know anything for certain. Let's stick with our plan for going to Baltimore and see how it all plays out." He lifted his head and gazed at her, through the screen, across the miles, and it was almost as if Thomas could see the man as Mia saw him, bathed in luminosity. Lanying continued. "It's not the end quite yet. We still have time. And while we still have time, we still have hope."

Salomon nodded, his eyes brightening. "I know a lot about hope," he said.

CHAPTER

6

JOSE

Monday, October 24
Phoenix

Jose made one final pass through the ICU before heading home after what could only be described as the worst shift of his life. When the call came in that a driver, presumably drunk, had taken an off-ramp onto Route 10 in the wrong direction, leaving an eleven-car pile-up in his wake, he knew it was going to be a rough night. Even splitting the accident victims between two hospitals still brought twelve critical patients into the emergency room just after midnight. Needless to say, the remainder of his shift had been both busy and heart-wrenching.

Two of the patients had died on their gurneys right before his eyes.

It was especially difficult when someone passed away on his clock, knowing he had the ability to save them, just not the privacy to administer his gift. If they could survive long enough to make it to the ICU, he stood a chance, but when they didn't make it past the

ER, there was little to no opportunity to get the job done.

Which was why he was slipping through the ICU to where one of the accident victims was now stabilized on life support after a successful four-hour surgery to minimize his internal bleeding. Jose crossed the threshold of the man's room unnoticed and allowed his eyes to adjust to the dim surroundings before fully entering the room. He could hear the whooshing sound of the ventilation machine before he saw it beside the patient's bed. Jose had assisted in the man's preliminary care at his arrival, hoisting him from the ambulance gurney to the evaluation table and monitoring his vital signs. He'd felt an instant connection to the man, a twenty-seven-year-old named Colin Hendron, and it was only after being sprinted away to the operating room that Jose remembered they'd once played on the same little league team.

Now, as he looked at Colin's mangled body, which firefighters had wrestled from the crushed remains of his car with the jaws of life, he knew he needed to heal him. There was no doubt in his mind. Because as nine-year-olds, Colin had chosen compassion over cruelty, kindness over fear. Colin had stood up to a bully on their team on Jose's behalf. And now he couldn't let that type of light be extinguished from the world.

As he kneeled beside him and wriggled his hands beneath the bandages across his midsection, Jose thought about his new friend Mia and how she'd described being able to tell whether someone was good or evil just by looking at them. He considered Colin, his chest rising and falling with the compression of the machine to his left, and knew without a doubt that if

Mia was gazing upon the man now she would see only light. Colin was a man worth saving.

Warmth spread from Jose's fingers into Colin's bruised flesh and he could feel the transformation taking place. He waited, waited, waited until the exact moment when he'd healed the laceration below just enough that Colin would make a full recovery without raising suspicion. *Just another miracle*, the staff and family would remark about his progress in the days to come.

Satisfied that he'd done all he could for the night, Jose left the ICU, taking the back exit out to the staff parking lot. The sun was just cresting the horizon, ensuring his drive home, eight miles east of the hospital, would be a blinding challenge. Behind the wheel, he slipped on his sunglasses and lowered the visor as he backed out of his parking spot. He yawned and yearned for the well-deserved rest that awaited him at home before remembering what today was.

Today was Andrea's first morning working as a line cook at his parent's restaurant.

After their return from Baltimore, Andrea had wasted no time enrolling in the next available culinary class at the local community college and happily accepted an invitation from Jose's parents to study under them at their authentic Mexican restaurant. It was as if her ex-boyfriend Alejandro's arrest had flipped a switch inside of her, igniting a long-suppressed spark of independence.

So instead of turning left on Elm toward home, he turned right, fumbling in the glovebox at a red light for the 'Best of Luck at Your New Job' card he'd picked up for her over the weekend.

There were three cars already parked in the rear lot when he arrived just before 7:30. He let himself in the staff entrance at the back of the building and could hear Andrea's infectious laughter over the tuba baseline of the duranguense music playing on the kitchen radio. Pushing through the swinging door, her back was to him, her long hair woven into a tight braid at her nape and tucked into a chef's net. She was dancing, a ripe avocado in one hand and a paring knife in the other, and it was obvious his mother had placed her on guacamole duty, a job Jose had been tasked with as a child more times than he cared to count.

"Hola, Mamá y Papa," Jose said as he pulled a stool up to the prep counter. To Andrea and the sous chef, Roberto, he said, "Morning, amigos."

"Hola, Jose," his mother said, looking up from the dough she was rolling out for tortillas. "I barely recognize you, stranger."

She was teasing, of course, always ragging him for not spending more of his free time with the family.

"Perhaps now we'll see more of him, eh?" his father said, casting a glance toward Andrea and giving his mother a deliberate smile.

Andrea turned innocently from her prep station, still wielding the knife, now embedded in an avocado nut. "Hey!" she said brightly. "We didn't expect to see you this early. How was your night?"

Jose recounted the events of his evening, glossing over the actual horror of the accidents, focusing instead on Colin Hendron.

"I remember that boy," his father said, grating a large chunk of Asadero cheese. "Nice kid. And not a bad ball player if my memory serves me. You said you think he's gonna be okay?"

Jose caught a knowing look from Andrea. "Yeah. He was pretty messed up, but I heard his surgery was successful and that they think he's gonna pull through."

"The two who didn't survive, though," his mother said, making the sign of the cross with her doughy fingers. "Que Dios proteja a sus almas."

The kitchen was quiet for a moment, save for the music still coming from the radio.

"We can't save them all, Mama," Jose said finally, yawning into his arm.

"You should go home, get some rest," Andrea told him. "Maybe come back for lunch later this afternoon. Your mom said she'd teach me to make enchiladas verdes. You can be my first victim."

He grinned at her, encouraged by the enthusiasm in her voice and glow of her skin. She was radiating joy in a way he'd never seen before, and he couldn't help but feel a sense of pride for his part in her continued rehabilitation. He pulled the card from his back pocket. "Can I steal her away for a minute, Mama?" he asked, rising to his feet and moving in the direction of the main dining room.

"Just for a minute," she smiled, not taking her eyes from the rolling pin she was now pressing against the tortilla. "That guacamole isn't going to make itself."

Jose held out his hand and Andrea took it, blushing slightly as she followed him out of the kitchen. He led her to a far table by the front window where the sun was now cascading across the dining room, catching the glassware and throwing beams of light around the room.

"This is for you," he said, handing her the envelope.

She slid the card out and as she read the inscription, Jose was warmed to see tears pooling at the corners of her eyes.

"Thank you," she said, blotting back the tears with one of the napkins from the table. "That was a really sweet thing to say. You can't imagine how much I appreciate everything you've done for me."

Jose shrugged. "What are friends for?"

He raised an eyebrow. "Friends, huh?"

He remembered their conversation on the flight back from Baltimore. About how they both wanted to take things slow. About how she wanted to get back on her feet and become an 'independent woman' before tethering herself to another man. About how they couldn't fully love other people until they learned to love themselves.

"Friends with serious potential for advancement?" Jose offered.

She nodded, tracing the floral pattern on the front of the card with her finger. "And what about the prophecy and your new psychic friends? Where do I fit into all of that?"

Jose was still trying to decide where *he* fit into all of that. When he'd made the decision to save Mia's partner, Jack, in Baltimore, revealing his abilities to her, he'd halfway expected her to have him detained for questioning or even arrested. But instead, she'd told him about her own abilities, solidifying the strange bond between them. And it had been enough for him to accept that there were others like him, people like Mia and Thomas, who harbored their own secrets and otherworldly abilities, but when she'd shown him the printout of the prophecy and described their place in it, it was almost too much to believe.

Light and dark psychics?

An ancient prediction of the end of the world?

Being chosen as one of the seven to save humanity?

There was no way it could possibly be true.

Except for if it was.

"I don't know," he told her honestly. "I've been doing some research on my own, based on the information Mia and Thomas gave me, and a lot of it makes sense. It's conceivable that it's all true, and if it is…" He considered the implication for his own life as well as everyone else's.

Andrea eyed him skeptically, dust particles glistening around her face in the morning sun. "It seems crazy. Unbelievable in fact," she said, biting her bottom lip. "But then again, what you can do is completely unbelievable, and here you are." She paused, adjusting her hair net to tuck a stray strand beneath. "It's just that, if it is real, and if you have to leave to go save the world or whatever…"

"I'm not a superhero or anything, and I don't think it's gonna go down like that," he interrupted, although he honestly didn't have any inclination about how it was going to play out, one way or the other.

"I'm just saying," she continued, "I'd like to be included, to know you're safe. I'd like to be kept in the loop, one friend to another."

"One friend to another," he smirked, reaching over to take her hand in his. "I'll keep you informed. And I promise to be safe if anything even comes of it."

As he said it, though, he could feel the nagging suspicion that something would indeed come of it and in the not too distant future at that.

CHAPTER

7

PATRICK

Tuesday, October 25
Pakistan

Patrick had a splitting headache. His ears were ringing and his mouth tasted like an old penny. As he became more self-aware and tried to lift his hand to his forehead to investigate the pain, he realized his hands were bound behind his back. He felt his wrists with his fingers, registering the sensation of coarse rope.

I must be dreaming, he thought to himself, trying to remember where he should have been and what he should have been doing. *Am I sleeping on the way to Pakistan?* he thought, searching his memory for something that made sense.

He heard a groan to his right and struggled to open his eyes. The room was too bright and he squinted into the light. He was not on a plane. He was not in the van.

And that's when the memory of screeching tires and being thrown like a ragdoll bubbled to the surface.

There must have been an accident. Perhaps he was in a hospital.

"Nurse," he called weakly, his voice barely above a whisper. He tried clearing his throat as his eyes adjusted, hoping to project more clearly a second time. However, as vision returned he realized he was not at a medical facility. Instead, he was on the ground, his hands tied behind his back. Akantha sat beside him inside what could only be described as a ramshackle building. The floor was compacted dirt, the walls crumbling rock and mortar, and there was no roof to speak of – only a handful of decaying trusses.

He and Akantha were bound at their hands and feet at one end of the narrow room while the driver, the translator and one of the bodyguards were bound at the other. He wondered briefly about the whereabouts of the second bodyguard and assumed he'd either perished in the crash or been so horribly injured he didn't warrant constraints. Patrick was the only one conscious, and he didn't know whether the others were still recovering from the effects of the accident or if they'd been subsequently incapacitated. Either way, he was currently the only member of their captured party who was aware of their circumstances, and he didn't know quite what to do next.

He pulled, unsuccessfully, on the rope around his wrists, twisting for several minutes until his skin began to wear through with abrasions. He didn't like pain. He never had. But it was a small price to pay for the fulfillment of the prophecy. At least that's what he told himself as he considered his other options. He turned toward Akantha and saw her head listing heavily to one side, a thick gash visible across her left thigh. Blood pooled around the open wound but it appeared the bleeding had stopped, at least for now. He shifted over, inching his way across the ground in her direction like a wounded crab. He began whispering her name as he approached, hoping to rouse her. He was rewarded with another weak groan, but even after repeatedly bumping into her shoulder with his own, she did not wake.

His muscles and contusions ached, and he didn't have the strength or willpower to maneuver to the other side of the room to try and rouse the other men. Instead, he resorted to the very last thing at his disposal.

His ability.

Patrick closed his eyes, attempting to block out external stimuli. It didn't take long for him to reach into the astral plane and find his captors in the adjacent building. There were three of them, including the second bodyguard, and their emotions were strangely neutral. Positive even. He could feel how in control they assumed they were. How pleased they were that their bombing had been so effective, causing a spectacular crash that led to his apprehension.

And then Patrick realized they knew who he was. He could feel their excitement of having successfully captured him. He had been their specific target, and they intended on ransoming him for a large sum of money. They would only release him when the ransom was paid.

Or maybe they wouldn't.

This realization burned slow and deep and gave him pause. He reached further toward them, grasping at their emotions, trying to understand how they'd tracked him down after he'd been so careful with regard to his privacy. How they'd known where he was going to be and when he was going to be there. And as he dug around in their thoughts it became clear that his current situation was nothing but pure bad luck.

It was also clear that they had no idea who Akantha was or what power she held.

Patrick shook himself back into conscious reality, unnerved by what he'd discovered but not unhinged. Given the length of time they'd been traveling before the accident and the distance to their actual destination, Patrick surmised they didn't have much further to go. If he could stir Akantha they could get on their way.

Time, regardless of the situation, was always of the essence.

Emboldened by what he now knew of his situation, Patrick made a second attempt to wake Akantha. He nudged her with his body and spoke into her ear. When nothing worked he maneuvered himself up on the balls of his feet and slid backward so he could touch her with his hands. Then he jabbed his fingers into the open wound on her thigh.

She jumped and let out a howl which Patrick knew would alert their captors. She turned to him, wide-eyed, and he returned her surprised expression with his own, hoping to convey a shared disorientation. A combination of fear and rage lit up her face as she yanked at her restraints and gaped frantically around the room.

The men from the adjacent building arrived as Akantha was attempting to get to her feet. They came at her, guns drawn, yelling at her in Pakistani, and she screamed at them in reply, causing one of the bodyguards and the driver to stir. Coming to, the driver began crying out in Pakistani as well, grabbing the attention of the captors. In that brief collection of seconds, Patrick caught Akantha's eye. He motioned to the rafters above and mouthed the word 'fire.'

A moment later sparks ignited over their heads and flames licked along the parched wood, devouring it quickly. In the chaos that ensued, the three captors ran from the room out the only exit into the adjoining building. Patrick waited for the door to slam shut behind them but it didn't. He reasoned they would return, perhaps with buckets of water, unwilling to sacrifice their potential payout for his ransom. He knew there was no time to lose. The beams would fall quickly and once they did the machine guns would be back.

He looked again to Akantha, who eyed him calmly, unlike the other hostages who were carrying on like possessed maniacs. He turned around and held out his hands, trusting she could control her power enough to burn the ropes but not his flesh. A moment later, as the wood crackled and splintered above his head, he felt the heat of the flames around his wrists. He shook them violently, both to extinguish the fire and release the ropes. And then he was free.

In a show of trust, he untied Akantha's hands before removing the rope from his own feet. Once her hands were free it didn't take long for them to slip the bindings from around their ankles. Fully unburdened, she looked to him now for guidance.

Patrick considered his options with regard to the other men. He and Akantha could certainly use as much help as possible evading their captors in the hopes of reaching their ultimate destination and having a translator was an absolute must. But he wasn't sure if the hired help could be trusted. As Akantha looked on, he reached into the astral plane to get a feel for their allegiance and was pleased to discover their anger directed at their abductors, not at him. He motioned for her to join him in untying their ropes, but as he struggled with the driver's ankle restraints, the jailers returned.

This time, however, Akantha didn't wait for instructions. Patrick watched in rapt admiration as she released her fury, long suppressed by her tribe. The kidnappers burst into flames, filling the air with plumes of thick smoke, a putrid stench, and the primitive cries of dying beasts. With Patrick at the lead, the five prisoners clambered past the flailing men, who seemed unable to extinguish themselves despite their best efforts at rolling around in the dirt. The last thing Patrick saw as he fled from the room was one of the largest trusses collapsing to the ground, crushing two of the men beneath it.

Out on the street, Patrick paused briefly to observe his surroundings. There was smoke. There were a handful of Pakistanis milling around. And there was a war-torn dump truck down an alley to his right.

He turned to the remaining bodyguard who was doubled over beside him, retching onto the dirt. "Can you jumpstart a truck?" he asked through the interpreter.

The man lifted his eyes and nodded.

"Then let's go," Patrick said to the group. "We've already wasted too much valuable time."

CHAPTER

8

MIA

Thursday, October 27
Baltimore

If Thomas hadn't been such a gifted musician, Mia might have encouraged him to become a private detective. As she stared at the list of phone numbers printed on the sheet of paper in her hand, she couldn't believe he'd gotten so far in their search for the dark psychics. After Lillian Hall's mother was unable or unwilling to provide them with any sort of leads as to the woman's whereabouts, Thomas hadn't given up. He'd continued to pursue her, watching and rewatching the handful of YouTube videos showcasing Lillian and her abilities, searching for something more. Eventually, he'd found it – the repeated appearance of a specific man in several of the videos. After running facial recognition software, they'd identified the man as Javier Delgado, and they were simultaneously shocked and gratified when they found Javier's name on the known psychics list. Sadly, his birthdate was listed as 'unknown.' Now, however, thanks to the Interpol liaison she'd established through the Kate Malinov Foundation, she had several phone numbers that they'd assured her were linked to him in some way. All she needed to do now was bring herself to pick up the phone.

Her hand trembled as she lifted the landline receiver on her desk. With Jack on paternity leave, she had the office to herself, and she reasoned it was as good a time as any to make the call, especially while her temporary partner was at traffic court on a handful of speeding violations he'd served. She dialed the first foreign area code which Interpol had informed her designated a British exchange. She cleared her throat as the phone rang, calling to mind the handful of questions she needed to remember to ask. She also needed to be careful not to implicate herself lest they discover her ulterior motives.

The call connected on the third ring.

"Meyer Enterprises," came a clipped female British voice.

"Um, yeah," Mia said, trying to come across as young, dumb American, "I'd like to speak with Javier Delgado."

"Connecting you now."

There was a beat of silence before the hold music cut in – the instrumental refrain of *I Swear* by Boyz II Men. Mia chewed nervously at her thumbnail while she waited for the line to connect.

"Javier Delgado's office," another equally terse British woman answered.

"Hi," Mia said. "Can I speak with Mr. Delgado?"

"Mr. Delgado isn't in presently," the woman said, sounding bored and a touch put-off. "To what are you calling in reference?"

Mia took a sharp breath. "I'm a journalist writing an article and was looking for a quote or two from Mr. Delgado."

"In reference to?" Now the woman sounded downright annoyed.

"Global securities?" Mia said, angry at herself that her response came out more as a question than a statement.

"Well, I'm happy to leave your name. Would you like to leave a message?"

Mia considered leaving a message. She considered that Javier, who knew Lillian, a psychic born on their birthdate, was somehow affiliated with Meyer Enterprises, one of the largest conglomerates in the world. And that made her head spin.

"That's not necessary," Mia said finally. "I can just call back again. Is there a good time to catch him?"

The woman sighed audibly. "Mr. Delgado is a very busy man. But you're welcome to call again at another time."

"I'll do that. Thank you." And with that, the line disconnected.

Mia leaned back in her chair, rocking on the rear legs as she contemplated this new information. A quick Google search of Meyer Enterprises confirmed that she'd reached the corporate headquarters in London. A closer look at the company's web page garnered a bit more information. It appeared Javier Delgado not only worked for the company but worked alongside Mr. Meyer himself.

Mr. Patrick Meyer, the website stated, was a self-made billionaire. Paragraph after paragraph described his holdings, corporate acquisitions, and company mergers. It was all Greek to her, talk of strategic management and equity interests. Nothing, of course, to link anyone in his company to the prophecy.

That would have been far too easy, Mia thought.

She was still scrolling through the company's website when her father appeared in the doorway.

"Whatcha working on?" he asked, startling her from her search.

"Uh, just researching some leads for a case," she said, closing her browser. Her father still knew nothing of the prophecy or her presumed part in it. Although he had always been supportive of her abilities, she and Thomas had decided not to tell him anything about it until Lanying and Salomon arrived. They thought it would be best to tell their parents at the same time with all four of them to corroborate one another's stories. Even still, she couldn't help asking for his opinion now. "I was wondering, though, if you know anything about Meyer Enterprises."

He took a step into the room. "They're a big corporate conglomerate, right?"

"Yeah."

He shrugged. "I dunno much beyond that. Why?"

She'd known he would ask. "I was thinking about asking them to sponsor the foundation," she lied. "Just trying to figure out if they're a charitable sort of organization."

"You're on your own there. You're way better at the foundation stuff than I am. In fact, did I see in my newsfeed yesterday that there was another trafficking arrest here on the east coast? Somewhere down south I think?"

Mia felt a flush of pride rise to her cheeks. In the months since its inception, the Yekaterina Malinov Foundation had provided legal counsel and representation to over two dozen freed women and saw to the arrest of six known traffickers. The latest was a small local ring of five former prostitutes being held against their will in an Atlanta motel room for the better part of eight months. "Yeah," she admitted. "Rescued five girls. I think two of them are speaking at a hearing against the accused next week. The rest were taken to rehab facilities."

Captain Rosetti smiled at his daughter. "You're doing a good thing with that. Above and beyond," he said, giving her a wink as he headed back toward the hall. "You working days the rest of the week?"

She nodded.

"Dinner tomorrow night at your house, right?"

"That's the plan," she said.

"Lookin' forward to meeting your new friends."

The rest of the afternoon sailed by, a sea of paperwork and even a few minutes down in her old spot behind the one-way mirror of the lineup room. Several lineups passed through the room, with Mia easily identifying the guilty parties through their dark auras. She had a twinge of nostalgia for a simpler time when her lineup duty seemed like such a pressing matter. Even Thomas's recent foray into the lineup room seemed like a lifetime ago. So much had transpired since then. Their relationship. The basement prison. The prophecy.

She watched now as a lineup of haggard looking women filed into the room. She considered each of them individually and as a whole – their drawn faces, matted hair, cracked lips. A year ago she wouldn't have looked much past their auras. She would have focused in on the darkest to make her evaluation. Now, however, she recognized the spectrum of their auras.

Some darker, some lighter. As the actual lineup continued, she took a step closer toward the glass until she was almost pressing her nose against it, studying the women. Were the dimmest lights about to flicker out? Could the least dark be coaxed back into the light? She'd never spent much time considering the fluidity of the auras she saw, only that they gave her a glimpse into the current state of a person's soul.

Looking at the woman in a torn gray sweatshirt at the far end of the line chewing unconsciously at the worn nubs of her fingernails, Mia tried to look past the darkness which surrounded her. She recalled a conversation she'd had with Thomas early in their relationship regarding whether or not auras changed. Or, more accurately, if people changed. At the time she hadn't given it much thought, explaining that although she'd never seen an infant with a dark aura, she'd also never witnessed an aura changing. She'd always assumed that people were either born to the light or to the dark. Or that in some cases, a light person could become dark if their life circumstances were such that the darkness was allowed to breed and fester.

Now, though, in light of everything that had transpired in the past year, she was beginning to think more about those situations which would cause someone so much pain that their soul would change allegiance to the darkness. Maybe this woman, now twitching as she continued to bite at her cuticle, had been touched by an insurmountable darkness. Maybe she had been abandoned. Rejected. Abused. Maybe she'd been born surrounded by darkness and knew no other way to be.

Behind her, the officer explained the lineup procedures to the witness who'd entered the room. Mia listened, peripherally, as they discussed the crime in question – petty theft from a corner market in the form of a carton of cigarettes.

Mia's shoulder's slumped as the witness easily identified the suspected thief, the woman at the center of the line with hollow eyes and a fading aura. There were a hundred reasons for the woman to have stolen the cigarettes, but probably only one outcome for her arrest. She would be tried, convicted, and would serve a minimum sentence. And faced with a future as a convicted criminal, her light, Mia was certain, would go out.

As the lineup was led away, Mia was struck by the weight of her burden – the responsibility she had to fulfill the prophecy for the light. The world was counting on her. Her friends and family were counting on her. This woman was counting on her.

Hours later, as she lay beside a snoring Thomas in their shared double bed with the worn flannel sheets and squeaky headboard, she was struck by a memory from basement prison. She recalled a conversation between Kate and Lera, a conversation about their shared past of which she was not a part. She'd listened to the sadness in their voices as they spoke in their native tongue and her attention was piqued when she recognized a word of English. A name.

Patrick.

She bolted upright, pulling the covers off of Thomas who stirred.

"What's wrong?" he asked.

"Patrick Meyer is the CEO of Meyer Enterprise."

"Hmmm," he said, rubbing the sleep from his eyes. "And?"

"And I remember Kate and Lera talking about a man named Patrick when we were locked in the warehouse basement together."

He raised an eyebrow.

"I dunno," she admitted. "It's just that Lanying's grandfather says 'There are no coincidences in life.'"

Thomas sighed, rolling over. "Except for when there are."

Light from the street lamp crept between the curtains cutting a line across her face. She held up her hand, letting the beam play between her fingers. It was possible the name Patrick was a coincidence. It was possible that Patrick Meyer was a good, honest man. But there was also the possibility he was not.

CHAPTER

9

PATRICK

Thursday, October 27
Pakistan

Getting the truck's engine to turn over had been easy. Finding their way to Saif Naeem proved to be quite another story. Night fell not long after their escape and they continued on, relying not on maps but on Patrick's gift to lead them over the rugged terrain to their destination. From the passenger's seat, Patrick reached into the astral plane. Once he was able to hone in on Saif's emotions, he used them as a beacon to lead them in what he hoped was the right direction.

Without the rations of food and water which were lost in the accident, they were at the mercy of others along the way. Most were unwilling or unable to assist the derelict travelers. This lack of sustenance paired with a shortage of gas forced the group to eventually stop after eight hours of sleepless travel near a small rural village where a group of children played in the street.

The translator approached the children cautiously, speaking to them in Pakistani.

"Don't be afraid. We aren't going to hurt you. We just need some water and perhaps a bit of food. And also gasoline. Do you know where we can get some?"

Perhaps it was because their party included a white man. Or perhaps their bloodied and beaten bodies seemed less of a threat than they would have if they'd been without the gashes and contusions. But whatever the reason, the children beckoned them to follow, leading them across the street and into what appeared to be some sort of tavern. Patrick instructed the driver to stay behind to protect the truck while he joined the others inside.

As his eyes adjusted to the dimness of the room, Patrick took in the space and its inhabitants. The interior walls appeared to have once been covered in an adobe plaster but much of the smooth surface had long since peeled from the rock beneath. The tables and chairs, scattered haphazardly, suffered from a similar lack of upkeep. The same, he noticed, could be said of the people.

Three men sat at the wooden table closest to the door eating nāshtā, a breakfast comprised of eggs, a chunk bread, and tea. They looked up from their meal as Patrick entered, eyeing the newcomers wryly. Their translator greeted them with a traditional Pakistani greeting.

"As-Salam-u-Alaikumu," he said to them with a note of reverence in his voice.

"As-Salam-u-Alaikum," each of the men repeated in kind. The rest of the conversation was lost on Patrick due to the language barrier, which he despised. There was nothing worse than being kept out of one's own conversation. The only way to combat his exclusion was to slip into the astral plane where he could feel the local men's sympathetic emotions as the translator explained their situation. This was enough to placate Patrick, and before long, tables were rearranged so the two groups could sit together as more bread and tea was brought out.

After a life of excess, Patrick never realized how truly hungry a person could be until he took his first bite of the stale, bland hunk of bread. He was grateful for the tea to wash it down, devouring every crumb as if it might be his last. He zoned out as he consumed his breakfast without pause, unable to concentrate on anything but the much-needed nourishment to his system. One of the Pakistani men handed him a second chunk of bread rousing him from his trance, and as he grabbed for it, he recognized the name 'Saif' in the conversation around him.

"What about Saif?" he asked the translator, interrupting the conversation. "Do they know him?"

The local men in their threadbare salwar kameez and Peshawari sandals glared at him, and Patrick immediately realized they were offended by his outburst. He was accustomed to directing conversations, and he didn't like being relegated to the sidelines. It took everything he had to apologize for his cultural misstep and return to a place of submission.

Still, the conversation progressed, and eventually, the translator turned to him. "They know of this man you are looking for, Saif Naeem. He lives not far from here, on the side of the closest mountain ridge with his family. They are outcasts, shunned from this village because of their criminal associates. And also because most believe he has fallen into the hands of Iblees.

They say that he can do unholy things and that he is not a man of Allah. They are concerned that you too are a criminal, or far worse, have sided with Iblees. I'm sure you can understand why they are hesitant to help if they are questioning whether you are indebted to Satan. They don't want any trouble and will not think twice about sending us on our way without supplies if they feel we cannot be trusted."

Patrick felt their fear and their anxiety and knew there was only one way to proceed. He'd simply tell them what they wanted to hear.

"Tell them we are here on a mission to take Saif away and give him what he has coming to him. That if they help us we will rid them of him and his criminal ways once and for all."

The interpreter relayed the information, and the men's eyes widened. They were coming around. Patrick's breathing quickened knowing he would be with Saif before the end of the day.

Before they responded, another round of tea, bread and, a serving of eggs were procured. As the meal was divided, a larger portion was passed to Patrick as the eldest of the villagers spoke.

"He says he will send his son with you to Saif's house after mid-day prayers. He will take you as far as the ridge top, but you'll be on your own from there."

Patrick thanked the man for his assistance and hospitality, offered to pay for the food but was quickly dismissed.

Two hours later, after refilling the dump truck's gas tank with scavenged petrol, Patrick, his traveling companions, and Bilal, the eldest villager's son, headed off on foot toward Saif's house. They followed what appeared to be an abandoned rail line through the heart of town for about two miles until it came to an abrupt end. Just beyond, where the houses began to thin and the terrain steepened, Bilal made a sharp turn up a rugged hillside. Patrick was happy to have borrowed a head wrap and long sleeve shirt. The sun was brutal and the sand-filled wind tore at his exposed skin. As they trudged up the cliff side, Patrick briefly entertained the possibility that the entire trip would be in vain. That Saif Naeem wouldn't be one of the chosen seven. That he would simply be another self-made deviant without ties to the prophecy at all.

But no. Patrick had come too far for that to be the case. He'd been attacked, tortured, and held for ransom. It would not be for naught.

A lone ramshackle dwelling came into view as they crested the ridge. Bilal pointed in the direction of the building and turned on his heel, scurrying back down the hillside toward town without looking back. Patrick reached out onto the plane and discovered the boy's fear marker. Whoever they were about to encounter elicited unprecedented terror, the likes of which he hadn't felt since they'd discovered Akantha. He stretched his mind further, across the barren landscape to the house itself and discovered his target, Saif. He could feel the man's charisma. His confidence. His power. The only question was if he would be able to convince the man of his birthright before his proclivity for death by electrocution took over.

He turned to Akantha now. She had remained by his side, steadfast through the entire ordeal. Although the situation had been explained to her in her native language before leaving London, so much had transpired in the interim, he couldn't help but wonder if she was still following along with where they were and what was happening. He pointed to himself. Next, he pointed to her. Then he pointed to the house atop the hill. Finally, he brought his hands together, weaving his fingers between one another.

"Family," he told her. "Together."

He stared into her eyes, willing her to understand that they'd found the person they'd been searching for. She'd been instructed not to hurt him but to use whatever force was necessary to help bring him back to London. He hoped they wouldn't need to resort to violence.

"Family," Akantha repeated. "Together."

Patrick smiled. She understood. She knew what she needed to do.

The group split up, with Patrick, Akantha, and the translator finishing the assent to the house and the bodyguard standing post by the footpath. The last thirty feet of dust and rock and soaring temperatures felt prophetic. Like the last mile of a marathon or the last battle in a hard-fought war.

Something great was sure to follow.

He paused at the door, a solid slab of wood hung with iron hinges. He knocked, assuredly. Defiantly.

As he stood waiting for a response he thought of the other doors he'd knocked on over the years. The doors that stood between him and the other members of the prophecy. He thought about the door of Lillian's room in the mental health facility where he found her in a catatonic state, heavily medicated because of her 'condition' – a condition no one seemed to understand. The door that was actually a flap leading into the tent of Wesley's carnival act. The broken sheet of plywood which served as the door to Eshanti's shanty in Dharavi slum outside Mumbai where she was relegated after her husband's untimely demise. So many different situations. So many different doors.

He heard scuffling inside the house before the door opened.

"As-Salam-u-Alaika," Patrick said, greeting the man with the customary Islamic salutation.

"As-Salam-u-Alaika," the man replied hesitantly.

Patrick sensed the man's apprehension and began speaking through the translator.

"My name is Patrick Meyer, and I've come from London. Please know that I mean you no harm and in fact, I bring amazing news. I'm looking for Saif Naeem."

"I am Saif Naeem," the man replied.

Patrick proceeded to ask permission to enter the house three times as was expected of visitors in Pakistan. He was relieved when Saif stepped aside and motioned for his party to enter the house.

It was dark inside the vestibule which also appeared to serve as a greeting space and communal living area. He thought of the floor to ceiling windows of his office which allowed him to look out over his vast empire and felt sorry for Saif, whose three tiny windows were concealed by exterior shutters, blocking any hope of looking out into his own future. Candles were lit around the space illuminating some low seating and a scattering of prayer mats. Saif motioned for everyone to sit down, and Patrick began his appeal.

"Thank you for agreeing to speak with me today. I had hoped you would be willing to listen to what I have to say as I assure you everything you thought you knew about the world is about to change. What's more is that you are one of the proprietors of that change."

Saif listened to the translation and nodded for Patrick to continue.

"I had hoped to show you physical proof of what I am about to share with you but I regret to inform you that my journey to you has not been without setbacks, and I am no longer in possession of the documents. I hope, however, that what I can show you will be proof enough that what I am about to tell you is true."

Saif narrowed his eyes, his face ripe with skepticism.

"I know about your ability. I know that you are able to control the electrical impulses around you and bend them to your will. I know that you resell broken electronics using your ability to make them appear that they are functioning." He paused now, for dramatic effect. "And I know that you have used your ability to take the lives of others."

Patrick tensed as the translation was being spoken. He didn't need the astral plane to recognize the anger welling up inside of Saif and wasn't surprised when the man pulled a handgun from under his seat cushion and pointed it at his head.

Akantha sparked beside him.

Patrick raised his hands in surrender.

"I know these things because a member of our group has seen them with her own eyes. She has been here to your house. By peeking through the windows, she has witnessed your ability, unnoticed by you. And she was able to do this because she has an ability of her own. The ability to be in two places at once."

The gun remained pointed at his head.

"My associate, Akantha, has an ability like yours. She is able to create fire from the air and bend it to her will. She can show you now if you would like."

Saif gave no confirmation but glanced at Akantha with the same furrowed brow. Patrick turned to Akantha and said in a desperately passive voice, "Small fire."

The Amazonian's fingers sparked and a moment later a handful of fire burned in her palms. She bounced it from hand to hand, seemingly unaffected by its scorching heat. The moment Patrick touched her shoulder and asked her to stop, the flame extinguished.

"And what about you?" Saif asked, speaking for the first time since Patrick began.

Patrick smiled as genuinely as he could. "Ah, yes. Well, my ability isn't quite so observable as both of yours. I am able to sense the emotions of other people, often from great distances. I could tell you now that you are suspicious and unnerved, but surely that would count for nothing as your actions are speaking quite resoundingly for your present emotional state."

"What do you want?" Saif asked, finally lowering his weapon onto his lap.

"Nothing more than to offer you your birthright as one of the dark psychics foretold as part of the Sevens Prophecy."

"I have no idea what you're talking about." He was beginning to look more annoyed than angry.

"Of course you don't," Patrick continued. "Although the prophecy is almost as old as man himself, its secrets have remained hidden from most of humanity. But I assure you that every word of it is true, and I am quite certain you, Saif Naeem will be the man to usher in the end of days."

The Pakistani remained silent, unblinking.

"Would you like to hear the actual prophecy? I have it memorized." He couldn't keep the pride from his voice.

Saif nodded.

"There will come a day when seven psychic children of the light and seven psychic children of the dark will be born. From the moment of their birth, strong powers will be in place to bring the seven light together and the seven dark together to form two separate but equally powerful groups. The first seven to gather all in one place will seal the fate of the world - dark for hell, light for heaven. At that point the seven deadly sins will take over the world or cease to exist."

The room was completely silent as the interpreter finished the translation. Patrick noticed someone dressed in a drab-colored burka peering out from behind the doorframe of another room, and it occurred to him, for the first time, that there might be others in the house who would wish to do him harm. Saif, for his part, pulled at his sparse beard which revealed swaths of olive skin between the patchy growth.

"You believe me to be one of the dark psychics?" he said at last.

"Yes. The seventh. All that is left to fulfill the prophecy is to gather in one place."

"Which is where?"

"The rest of the dark psychics are waiting for us in London."

The interpreter's voice grew thinner with each translation, his fear growing as the conversation progressed.

Poor fool, thought Patrick as he waited for Saif to respond.

"And if I go with you to London as you suggest, to gather with these other dark psychics, what's in it for me?"

There it was. What it had come down to for each of them. He'd known the question was coming before it crossed his lips. The trick, he'd discovered, was in crafting a specific reply for each person. Telling them exactly what they wanted to hear.

He responded, knowing what he did about this man from Lillian's observations and his own emotional assessment. "Imagine a world, Saif, where instead of being ostracized for your abilities, you will be celebrated. Instead of hiding in the shadows, forced to live in deplorable conditions, you will live in a palace with those who sought to repress you bowing at your feet. Imagine having the freedom to do as you wish without fear of repercussion. That is what it means to be chosen. That is what it means to be one of the seven."

Saif returned his handgun beneath his cushion and lifted his hands. Tiny sparks of electricity passed from the fingertips of his right hand to the fingertips of his left hand and back again. He juggled the sizzling light from side to side without taking his eyes from Patrick, who recognized the gesture for what it was. An overt warning.

"A palace?"

"One on every continent if you'd like."

"Absolute freedom?"

"Absolute."

Without warning, a shot of electricity buzzed past Patrick's head and blew a small crater out of the plaster wall behind him. "If you are lying to me, I will kill you," Saif said.

Patrick couldn't help but admire the man. "I would expect nothing less."

Saif stood then, turning his back on his guest. "Let me pack a few things and we can be on our way."

CHAPTER

10

SALOMON

Thursday, October 27
Kinshasa - Democratic Republic of Congo

When everything he owned fit in a knapsack, it was easy for Salomon to pack for his trip across the world, leaving him with plenty of time to kill in Kinshasa before his evening flight to the United States. At Marceau's suggestion, he took a taxi to the Musee National de Kinshasa, a museum containing a small collection of the country's historical artifacts dating back to the pre-homo sapien era. Marceau had also encouraged him to inquire at the administration desk about the museum's archives.

"Oh, yes!" the senior curator, Geoffroy Farhani told him when he arrived. "We're happy to take university alumni into the archives. There's not nearly enough space in our small viewing rooms to house everything we've accumulated over the years, but we like for people to enjoy what we have, if we know they can be trusted, of course. When I spoke to Marceau he ensured me that you can be," he added with a wink.

After a brief stroll through the exhibits displaying tribal masks, primitive wood carvings, statues, stone weapons, and pottery, Geoffroy took Salomon to a staircase at the rear of the building which led into the archives in the basement below.

There was a musty odor, the kind of smell Salomon associated with decaying leaves on the jungle floor. The smell of old things. Forgotten things. Three banks of overhead fluorescents sprang to life at the flip of a switch, illuminating rows upon rows of shelving piled high with crates and boxes of every shape and size. Along the perimeter of the room, pushed out of the walkways were larger items, too big for boxes. A few of the observable artifacts were ornate and non-native, clearly from the imperialist era of the late 1800's. There were large upholstered chairs, weapons of the Belgian invasion, and remains of their ostentatious presence. Most of the artifacts, however, were native – wooden totems, intricately carved masks, and primitive tools and farming equipment. Salomon stood at the base of the stairs for a long moment, taking in his heritage, until Geoffroy spoke, rousing him from his thoughts.

"Take as long as you'd like," he said. "Just be sure to put any artifacts you take out back where you found them. Each box is labeled with the item's name, associated number, and a description, so it shouldn't be hard to figure out where everything goes. I'll be right upstairs if you need anything."

"Thank you," Salomon said, inching into the room.

He hadn't anticipated the sudden trepidation he felt which he knew was associated with what he was about to do. During the course of his life he'd had little occasion for using his ability to an end such as this. Now, though, as he was leaving the country, not knowing when or if he was ever going to return, he felt compelled to learn as much as he could about his countrymen. Understand them more deeply than he ever could simply by reading about them in books. Perhaps knowing their stories would help to focus him on the task at hand. All he could think about now was how difficult the path ahead was going to be since one of the light psychics was already gone.

He moved through the space like a cat on the prowl, each move selected with meticulous efficiency. He wanted to be sure the objects he touched would be meaningful, not wanting to become overwhelmed by too much information too fast. After several minutes the label on the side of a small wooden crate caught his attention. It read: Shackles and Hatchets.

It was one thing for Salomon to use psychometry on photographs, experiencing the past through their imagery. It was another thing altogether to witness the memories associated with actual artifacts – the chains that bound his ancestors and the weapons that removed their limbs.

With hesitant, trembling hands he removed the crate from the shelf. It was heavier than he was expecting, and he set it on the floor with a thud. He brushed the dust from his hands onto his pants and sat down beside the crate. It took several seconds for him to work up the courage to remove the lid and even longer to convince himself to touch the objects once he saw the horror of what was inside.

The iron shackles were heavily rusted, especially where the chains had worn thin from overuse. He was almost certain in addition to the rust, century-old blood also stained the hand and foot restraints. Worse than the chains, however, were the hatchets, about five of them, in various sizes and states of deterioration. The only commonality between them was the dullness of their blades as they were each as blunt as stream worn rocks.

Salomon reached for the largest hatchet, with a solid, hardwood handle and a long, narrow blade that was thinner at the head than at the bit. There was a small notch chinked out of the blade where it had been struck against a rock or harder metal. This imperfection in the blade would have been a concern to his people who took pride in precise, effortless cuts, but accuracy didn't seem to be a concern for the Belgians.

The moment his hand connected with the handle he was transported out of the stuffy basement into the searing heat of the jungle. Bugs buzzed at his face and ears, causing him to swat them away with his free hand. The other still held the hatchet.

"Let's go, Gérard," someone called in French from the path ahead. "They're expecting our delivery in less than two hours and we still have collections to make."

Salomon looked down at himself, in the self now connected to the hatchet, and recognized the Force Publique uniform from his history books. The Force Publique had been comprised of imperialist white officers from Belgium and black, indigenous NCOs, recruited from as far away as Zanzibar, Nigeria, and Liberia. The one-time owner of this particular hatchet was obviously one of those native NCOs, tasked with the enforcement of rubber production by any means necessary. Many times this included constraining and beating Congolese citizens who refused to work.

Salomon forced his feet to follow, using the hatchet to help clear a path through the dense foliage.

"We need nine today," another soldier called back as if this should mean something. "And since we haven't come across a single body, we're going to have to get what we need the hard way."

Remembering back to the very first photograph the tribe elders had shown him of his ancestors as a boy – a picture of mutilated Congolese, with severed hands, Salomon now knew what they were searching for. He knew that Force Publique soldiers were expected to provide proof that they had not stolen ammunition or used their military equipment for hunting. To provide evidence that government supplies had not been misused, soldiers routinely hacked the hands off corpses in the aftermath of punitive expeditions to prove each bullet was appropriately used to kill a dissident. However, when soldiers did misuse their equipment, as these men obviously had, they cut hands from living people to cover their activities. Seeing the resulting mutilation in black and white pictures was difficult as a child. Being a part of the brutality now was unfathomable to him.

I could drop the hatchet right now and all of this would go away, Salomon said to himself. But he didn't. He couldn't. He needed to see this through. To experience the pain and the loss so he could carry it with him to America as a reminder of just how high the stakes were for his people.

He followed his fellow soldier into a village. He watched as the Force Publique began rounding up women and stood cemented to the ground as they restrained them and used their hatchets, many of which were identical to the one he held in his own hand. He saw crimson streams pouring from the women's wrists and children hastening to their sides with torn strips of fabric and broad-sided leaves. Everyone was screaming. Many of the victims lost consciousness. He watched the soldiers collect nine right hands off the ground, throwing them into a satchel already stiff with blood.

"Let's go," a soldier called over the villager's cries. "We cannot be late."

Salomon stood transfixed. Unable to help the injured or even compel himself into motion, he knew it was now time for him to leave. He'd suffered through the pain he was seeking, and there were other visions of the past still to experience.

His face hot with tears, he placed the hatchet in the crate, resealing it and returning to the shelf. It took every bit of strength he had to continue, selecting boxes from around the room, forcing himself to experience the histories concealed within. There was war. There was famine. There was joy and hope and dancing. After every box he pushed himself to the next, tears streaming, questioning his obvious masochistic tendencies. He had to know, though. He had to etch these images permanently into his mind to serve as a constant reminder of everything his people stood to gain from the prophecy. And also, everything they had to lose.

After almost an hour in the basement, he was certain he'd been subjected to every emotion of the human experience, from tragedy to triumph and everything in between. He was about to head out, having checked and rechecked the proper location of every item he'd chosen, when he spotted a small cardboard box teetering on the top corner of the closest shelf. He blinked twice in an attempt to refocus his eyes, certain the label couldn't possibly say what he thought it did. Upon closer inspection, he confirmed the inscription – Indigenous Sacred Relics.

Is this a sign? he thought.

Salomon slid a chair from the far side of the room over to the shelf. Very carefully, so as not to damage the upholstery, he stood on the chair and took down the box. The top was covered with a quarter inch of dust; his hands the first in decades to inquire of its contents. He climbed down, taking a seat on the chair and opened the box on his lap.

He didn't know quite what he was expecting to find inside but it certainly wasn't what he discovered. Of course, there were wooden carvings and masks depicting the gods of African mythology, not only human but animal as well. There were strange rocks and bits of parchment with unrecognizable characters. There were snake skins and mummified animal parts. So many pieces of his people's collective faith gathered in one box.

What caught his attention, however, was a carved figurine. At first glance, it appeared no different than hundreds of other carvings archived at the museum. Upon closer inspection, however, Salomon was quick to notice it depicted a set of twin girls, a matched pair, identical in every way, including the necklaces they both wore around their necks, each made of seven stones.

Salomon had grown up hearing the ancient stories from the elders. Fables about how things came to be and legends about the amazing men and women who had come before him. He knew too about the special significance of twins, thought to represent the balance between opposing forces existing in the natural world. Light and dark. Good and evil.

And these twins wore seven stones around their necks.

There were many reasons he'd hesitated to touch some of the other artifacts, but he did not delay with this particular one. He grabbed the carving firmly with both hands and closed his eyes to await the vision.

When he opened them he was shocked to discover there was no jungle. No heat. No animals. No huts. Instead, he was nearly run over by a car.

The driver blew his horn, and Salomon dove headlong from the middle of the gravel street which tore at his knees and elbows. He lay there on the ground, disoriented and frightened as the city opened up before him. Where he expected to find an ancient forest, there was an outdoor market teeming with a kaleidoscope of fruits, vegetables, and textiles. Where he expected a tribal ceremony or elder meeting, there were foreigners perusing the streets and driving past on their bikes and in their cars. Where he expected the past, he found the present.

Everything about it was wholly unexpected.

He rose slowly to his feet, as unsure of himself as of his new surroundings. He took a tentative step forward, toward the market, and noticed the mountain range towering behind the cityscape. It was breathtakingly beautiful, with its jagged ridgelines and snow-covered peaks. Its splendor was enough to compel him further. Another car drove past, slower than the first, and he thought to look at the license plate.

He was in Bolivia.

He called upon the memories of a lone university geography class and remembered that Bolivia was in South America, clear on the other side of the world.

He wondered what it meant, that the carved African relic led him to this strange, seemingly unrelated place. If the artifact was, as he hoped, a symbol of the prophecy, why Bolivia and why now?

He wandered the streets for what seemed like hours, searching for an answer, but nothing materialized. No one stopped to greet him and impart their wisdom. The conversations taking place around him were all in Spanish. Not a single event transpired to provide a clue about the origin of the relic. And so finally, he gave up, releasing the carving from his hands.

It landed in the box, releasing Salomon from the vision. He checked his watch, noting it was time to leave for the airport, and without thinking, replaced the lid. He was returning it to the shelf as he'd been instructed, still confused by the vision, but changed his mind in a moment of rare disobedience. Opening the box once again, he pulled a shirt from his bag and grabbed the carving. He wrapped it hastily in the garment and tucked everything back into his pack. A wave of guilt nearly overtook him as he finally slid the box on the shelf, but it wasn't strong enough to prevent him from walking out of the museum with the artifact in his possession.

CHAPTER
11

LANYING

Thursday, October 27
Shanghai

Lanying checked the contents of her purse for the fifteenth time. She had her ticket, her passport, and her wallet. Everything was accounted for. Everything was in order. Everything, that was, but her relationship with her parents. Her twenty-two-hour flight from Shanghai to Baltimore was set to take off at just after nine o'clock, and she was waiting by the front door for her parents to arrive home from work.

She was waiting to tell them she was leaving.

She was waiting to tell them she wasn't planning on coming back.

She'd arranged for a taxi to pick her up at 6:30, but as the minutes ticked past she worried she would need to leave before her parents arrived. She checked her phone again, fretting over the time and checked through the contents of her purse once again. Moments later, the front door opened.

"Lanying?" her mother said, dropping her briefcase on the floor beside the door and slipping off her shoes. "Why haven't you started dinner?"

She should have expected this sort of response from her mother. Should have expected her to look past the coat and the suitcases and the resigned expression.

"I'm not fixing dinner tonight, Mother," she said. "I'm leaving."

"You're leaving?" she snapped, eyeing the luggage. "Is this a school trip again? And why didn't you tell me before?"

She didn't move from the bench where she was perched. "It's not for school. I'm moving to the United States. For good. Once I'm settled I'll be transferring my credits to a college over there." She paused, watching for some show of emotion from her mother. Something to show she was sad or mad or glad. But there was nothing. Only a blank expression.

"Well, then, I guess you've got my phone number and email address if you should need anything. Will you be waiting for your father to come home to say goodbye or should I just let him know you've left?"

She flinched involuntarily from the sting of her mother's words. While she wasn't expecting a soldier's sendoff, she had anticipated at least a modicum of surprise or even a twinge of disappointment. What she got instead was the same cold indifference she always faced, making it that much easier to walk out the door.

"No," she said, steadying her voice. "I'll wait for him to say goodbye. I have a few minutes before I have to leave."

"Suit yourself," her mother said before hurrying off to the kitchen to start dinner on her own.

Moments later her father arrived, and she was met with the same apathy.

"I assume you have the funding to pay for this excursion?" he asked, standing before her in the foyer, hands on his hips. She knew he was only asking out of concern for his own savings and not because he had any intention of assisting her financially.

"I have an account," was all she said.

He nodded as if money was his only concern. "Well then, don't let me keep you from leaving. Change fees are expensive if you miss your flight."

Another nod in her direction and he disappeared into the kitchen with her mother.

It was all she could do not to cry as she climbed into the taxi bound for the airport. By the time she arrived, she'd composed herself enough to make it through baggage drop off and security without incident. She bought a granola bar and a bottled water at the convenience store beside her gate and contemplated her future in the boarding line while she munched on her snack. There was something utterly surreal about the path she was on, having taken an unexpected turn from her anticipated trajectory over the previous year. Meeting Thomas and Mia and learning of her grandfather's involvement in a prophecy she'd never even heard of was almost too much to fathom. Add moving to the United States to join forces with a group of people who were foretold to save the world and the scales tipped from improbable to full-blown preposterous.

How is this my life? she thought as she slipped past the American businessman who was already seated in her row and took her place by the window.

Lanying had never felt particularly capable. Being bullied as a child had planted a seed of inadequacy from which she had never fully recovered. She stared out the window as the plane taxied to the runway, watching the lights of the ground traffic controllers and jumbo jets positioning themselves like pawns on a chessboard. She couldn't help but feel like something of a pawn herself – her future at the mercy of a reality so much larger than herself.

Sacrificing the path she was on for the path which was thrust upon hr.

It was hard not to be disoriented by the way things had gone. The worst, though, was the incompetence she felt every time she considered the journey ahead. Here she was, on a plane, on her way to the U.S. to join a group of people who were prophesized to save the world. Lanying, with her paltry ability to see into other peoples' lives, couldn't imagine what role she would play in the weeks ahead. What good was an ability she couldn't control? What good was seeing into other people's lives if those people were incapable of helping the cause?

The plane gained momentum, rumbling down the runway at a tremendous speed before lifting almost effortlessly into the air. She was weightless for a moment as the tires left the ground and in that sliver of time, she was whisked back to Donescia's island.

The full-sun of the tropical island was a stark contrast to the dim airline cabin she left behind. She squinted into the brightness while her eyes adjusted, noticing that Donescia was not on the beach as she had been before. This time she was almost fully submerged in the ocean.

Her shoulders and head were visible above the surface, but because the water was smooth and clear Lanying could see the rest of her body below. At first, it appeared as though she might be trying to catch fish with the way her hands were swirling about, but upon closer inspection, she realized there was absolutely no marine life in the vicinity. The woman continued walking through the surf, moving her hands and arms in the water as if she was in a trance. After several minutes, she stopped abruptly, quieting her hands by her sides. She stood there, the water lapping at her chest for a moment more until she reached into a pouch at her side and pulled out a small, metal instrument. She dipped the instrument into the water and waited. After a minute, she removed it from the water, examined it, and repeated the process in another location. She examined the instrument a total of eight times before she placed it back in the pouch and trudged through the water toward the beach.

Back on land, Donescia removed the pouch from around her waist, dropped it to the sand, and stood perfectly still, her eyes closed. Lanying watched as the water droplets covering her skin and her suit evaporated into the air, leaving her completely dry in a matter of seconds. She pulled a purple and orange sarong on to cover herself before heading up the beach toward the palapa.

From outside the building, Lanying could see the woman through an open window and watched as she picked up the receiver of a rotary phone. She dialed the numbers slowly, carefully, turning the dial over and over again. After eleven digits, she paused, leaning against the wall behind her while she supported the handset in the crook of her neck. She proceeded to pick at her nails.

"Hallo!" she said finally once the call connected. "Is me, Donescia!"

Her English was more understandable this time but still held a deep creole-like accent.

"Yeh, yeh," she said to the person on the other end of the line. "Been just out dere. Checked the temperatures gen for yah and even with mah help is still too hot. No. No. Yeh. Ah been doin' di best ah can ta cool it off but ah don know if it gonna be enough ta save da reef off Turneffe Atoll. Yeh. Yeh. Ok, ah try gen tamorrah for yah. Ah, yah welcum mah friend. Ah wanna do what ah can tah help. Yeh. Ok. Buh."

Donescia hung up the phone and sighed, shaking her head. Lanying watched her tidying up the kitchen space as she tried to put the pieces of what she'd just heard together. This woman clearly had a psychic ability – the ability to control water. She'd watched her deflect the rain from her fire. She'd watched her lift the drops of seawater from her skin. And now it sounded as if she was working with someone to cool down the ocean water in order to save a coral reef. There was nothing in her behavior to suggest Mia would see anything but a bright aura surrounding her, which both pleased and discouraged her. Without Kate to complete the group, reaching out to the seventh light psychic served no purpose. What she really needed her visions to show her was one of the dark psychics.

She was still stewing about the injustice of her ridiculous gift, watching Donescia sweeping the hut's concrete floor when she discovered herself back in coach beside a sleeping businessman in an ill-fitting suit.

She felt an urge to pick up the phone to call Salomon to speak to him about what she'd just seen, but cruising at 30,000 feet above the Pacific Ocean meant there would be no communication between them anytime soon. She would have to wait until tomorrow to tell him in person that she was quite positive that she'd found the seventh and final light psychic. She hoped it wouldn't be too much of a disappointment.

CHAPTER

12

Donescia

Friday, October 28
Belize

Once a month there was a built-in break in the tourist schedule, and Donescia returned to the mainland, leaving the sanctuary of the atoll behind. This was a longstanding arrangement established by the Oceanic Society for whom she worked, but today Donescia felt a peculiar sense of loss as she boarded her father's charter boat sent to deliver her home.

Although she had always preferred the peace of the atoll to the bustle of the city, her stomach was especially queasy as the port came into view. A popular cruise destination, Belize City wore a shiny, welcoming smile for the sun-seeking vacationers. The cruise terminal was lined with quaint trinket shops and rental agencies; places visitors could hire transportation to the beach, the Mayan ruins, or the interior rain forest. Places Donescia heard about but had never actually seen. But this pleasantry was only a façade which masked the true face of the city which at its core was little more than a shantytown.

Donescia's sandals clapped against the cracked sidewalk as she trudged with her bag of dirty laundry slung over her shoulder. The walk from the docks to where her family's house was located in the southeast quadrant of the city was a short one but not without the possibility of peril. Two teenage boys approached from the opposite direction, and although they were probably too young to recognize her, she kept her chin tucked and her face hidden from view beneath a wide-brimmed hat. This was the same tactic she always used whenever she traversed the familiar streets of her childhood. Streets where she'd played stickball with her brothers and double-dutch with the neighborhood girls.

Streets where she'd been beaten to within an inch of her life before her father intervened on the night of her eleventh birthday.

As she reached that particular stretch of pavement now, she lifted a reflexive hand to her temple where the scar of that night remained, a thick, dimpled patch of skin in a sea of smoothness. She pushed the memory from her mind, forcing herself past the brick stoop which was still stained with her blood after all these years.

Not long after the attack, she began finding excuses to leave the mainland in order to escape the accusatory eyes of her neighbors. Her father chartered snorkeling tours for tourists, and he allowed her to tag along with him. She loved listening to the foreigners gasp in wonder at the brightly-colored fish and flowing coral just beneath the ocean's surface. Before meeting the tourists, she assumed all the oceans of the world were filled with reefs like the ones just off Turniff Atoll, and it wasn't until she heard them talking about the dangerous, frigid waters of the north and south that she realized how lucky she was to be surrounded by such beauty on a daily basis.

Many days she stayed with her father's groups, listening to their strange accents and teaching them the names of the fish she'd known her whole life, but some days she would ask to be dropped off on the island while he took tour groups to search for dolphins and rays. As much as she enjoyed seeing the larger ocean animals, it was the small, fragile ones like the gobies, damselfish and yellow tangs who held her attention the most. That she was there on the beach the day the first Oceanic researchers arrived had been something of a miracle for her.

She was in waist-deep water off the shoreline the day the researchers anchored their boat beyond the breakers and paddled their raft ashore. There was no dock at that time and so they were forced to row right past where she was playing in a school of triggerfish. After discovering her ability to manipulate water, she'd learned that the small fish liked the shallows and that if she warmed the water slightly their activity levels increased. She wouldn't realize until the fish began to die how delicate the reef's ecosystem truly was.

Luckily, the researchers didn't mind having a Belizean girl around, and they even encouraged her out of the water and onto the beach to socialize with them as construction of the facility began. They shared their lunches with her, listening as she told them about life on the reef. She felt their eyes watching her with amazement, the fish gathered around her in large schools just off shore as they built the dock and palapa. Weeks passed. The rapport between them grew.

Which was probably why when the head of the foundation asked her pointedly about her ability to control water, she told him the truth.

From that day forward, when her father dropped her at the atoll, the Oceanic Society team met her on the beach with textbooks and printouts about the decline of the world's reefs. Under their tutelage, it didn't take long for her to understand their mission and what role she might play in it. She was surprised when, instead of being shunned for her abilities, she quickly became a vital part of their operation, tasked with keeping the waters of the reef at the perfect temperature for both the coral and the fish. They hired her on full-time at just fourteen-years-old, and while her official position on the company website listed her as their cook, the on-sight directors and field researchers knew exactly what purpose she truly served.

From day one, she'd realized the importance of her task. In recent years, however, her job was growing increasingly difficult as climate change threatened the health of the reef and all its inhabitants. This was one of the many reasons she didn't like being away from the atoll for very long and was already counting the minutes until she would return Sunday night, slipping into the shadowy depths to work her magic while the others received the newest group of tourists.

Until then, she would do what she always did during her time in the city – keep quiet and try not to attract attention.

Her mother was sweeping out the front room when Donescia arrived and dropped her thinning broom to greet her oldest child with a squeeze.

"Missin yah morh a morh wen yah be goin'," she said when she finally took up her broom once again. "Too long yah be gun. Need'n yah rund here ah am."

Donescia set down her bags and shook her head. With six children and four grandchildren under one roof, she knew her mother could use her help around the house. But she also knew they needed the financial stability her income provided.

And then there was the matter of everyone's safety. Every minute she stayed on the atoll was time for their neighbors to forget who and what she was. For her to become a memory. A myth. A folktale.

Because although their memories were fickle, her memories were tattooed onto her heart, and she hadn't forgotten the graffiti, the broken windows, and the terror the local boys inflicted upon her family when they discovered her ability to control water.

The word *sòsyè* spray painted across their front door.

But she missed her family and needed to see them. Even the bad memories couldn't keep her away for very long.

"Here til Sunday ah am," she told her mother. "Wat yah be needin mi ta do? Markit fah da beef?"

Her mother wiped the sweat from her brow with the bottom of her apron and leaned against the wall, paint chipping beneath her weight. "Neh. I go tah da markit. Yah stay here an washa di clos." She hesitated then, before making her final request, and Donescia could feel her apprehension. "All di rain ah las week... dirt in di tank it did. Not be drinkin' di wada. Clean up ah be needin from yah."

The neighborhood cistern supplied fresh drinking water for several hundred people in her section of town. Most people had some form of tap water running into their homes from the storage container but not everyone. There were people who tapped in illegally, opening the supply to contaminants, especially when there was heavy rain.

Donecia considered this problem and how easy it would be for her to simply flush out the pollutants in a matter of minutes. To do so during the day, however, would remind people of her abilities. If she was going to do it, it would need to be done under the protective covering of night. She couldn't risk reexposing her family to the judgment of the community.

"Go tanite, ah will. An ah be bringin' Papa."

Her mother smiled, clearly relieved. It felt good to know her gift would be helping her family even though it would also be helping the other families in her neighborhood, whether they deserved it or not.

Just after two in the morning, Donescia and her father crept together along the back alley behind their house, keeping to the edge beneath the overhang which protected them from being seen in the moonlight. They spoke in whispers and hand gestures, not wanting to alert anyone to their presence.

Even without a celestial body to guide them, she had no trouble finding her way to the cistern. Before pipes were run, it had been her job to carry gallon jugs of water in her wagon, from her house to the tank and back again, anytime her mother needed it to cook or wash or bathe. At five years old, she could make the trek with her eyes closed – two lefts, three rights, and another left at the dead end just beyond the corner market where she often stopped to play with the alley cats. She kept a ball of string tucked inside her pocket for that very purpose.

Tonight, though, there were no cats on the prowl and no twine in her pocket. Tonight, there was only a job to do.

With her father keeping watch by her side, she carefully removed the panel on the top of the tank. Its hinges were rusty and the seal was no longer tight, thanks to being repeatedly pried open during unauthorized extractions. It was easy to see how the dirt and debris washed in during the last torrential storm, and she worked to remold the pliable gasket to ensure a proper seal going forward.

"Make quick," her father hissed. "Comin' dey is."

She closed her eyes and took in a sharp breath of air. She knew she should hide but that would mean starting over. Instead she slipped her hands hastily into the tepid water and silently prayed that whoever her father heard was headed in the other direction. Immediately, the sediment which permeated the drinking supply and lined the bottom of the tank separated from the liquid. She left several gallons behind to aid with the cleanup and lifted the remaining fresh water into the air above her head, a giant swirling globe which refracted the moonlight in every direction. If someone rounded the corner now there would be no way to explain her way out of the situation.

"Donescia!" her father murmured. There was no mistaking the fear in his tone. A fifty-year-old and an average-size woman would be no match for any man who wanted to do her harm. She needed to finish and she needed to finish fast.

With the water that remained in the tank, she rinsed the walls and flushed the lines. Then she lifted the dirty water out of the cistern and sent it down the closest sewer drain. She heard the footsteps approaching as she returned the fresh water back to the tank.

It was a Friday night and so it wasn't unusual for people to be out on the street at such a late hour. It also wasn't unusual for them to be inebriated, stumbling home from the nearest bar. What was unexpected was who appeared around the corner as Donescia was replacing the panel.

"Donescia?" the woman called out.

There was no mistaking the voice of her best friend. Or the girl who had once been her best friend.

"Paulita?"

For eleven years she'd shared everything with Paulita Neffers. She'd taught her to skip on the way to kindergarten. Shared bologna sandwiches on the playground swings. Fostered a stray dog they kept hidden from their families and practiced multiplication tables together until they knew them cold.

And then she'd told Paulita about her gift.

She saw her father move out of the shadows, stepping between the women. "Gah now. Yah havin no beznuss here."

Paulita took a step closer, narrowing her eyes at Donescia, straining into the darkness. There was another woman at her side and they were dressed in heels and halters, coming home from a night out. She hoped they would just move on, ignore what they'd stumbled upon, but even in the dim light, Donescia could see her childhood friend putting the pieces together.

Paulita squared her shoulders and tucked her clutch beneath her arm, taking a defensive stance. "Still doin' di black magic? Messin' wit do watta?"

"She fixin' di watta," her father replied, holding his ground. "Cleanin' it fah now all ah us tah drink."

Paulita took a step back, tripping on her heel. "She dah witch!"

Donescia opened her mouth to respond. Her gut reaction was to defend herself as she had done as a child so many years ago. But now to do so would be irresponsible. There was no need to cause a scene trying to explain her abilities. No one would believe her. They never had. They never would.

Not even her best friend.

And so without a word, she fastened the latch on the panel and disappeared behind the cistern into the night.

CHAPTER

13

THOMAS

Friday, October 28
Baltimore

Thomas leaned against the wall, idly scrolling through emails on his phone just beyond the security gate that lead to Terminal D. Lanying and Salomon's flights were scheduled to arrive within minutes of each other and the anticipation of their arrival had him rereading the same sentences multiple times. It was all he could do to concentrate on reading the email from his professor confirming he would be excused from his morning class. She wished him a good weekend with his foreign friends and said she'd look forward to seeing him in class on Monday.

Monday seemed like a lifetime away as the minutes ticked past with deliberate sluggishness. Waiting for this moment, the culmination of weeks of planning to bring the four of them together seemed impossible. And just when he felt as though he couldn't stand to wait another minute, he recognized Salomon rounding the corner on the far side of security.

He was far taller than Thomas anticipated. With skin as rich as coffee, he was unprepared for Salomon's majestic nature, an air of humility and wisdom revealed not by his expression but by his posture. He approached the exit with his shoulders squared and his chin held high. This was not a man to be crossed.

When he recognized Thomas, however, his appearance changed and a warm smile spread across his face. His paces quickened and Thomas found himself hurrying to meet him halfway.

"My friend!" Salomon cried, crushing Thomas in a welcoming embrace. "How wonderful to see your face in person."

Thomas tried not to feel embarrassed by the physical nature of the greeting, although he couldn't help but notice how solid Salomon felt as he wrapped his own arms around his back. He was more rock than man it seemed.

"It's good to see you too," he said. "I'm glad you had a safe flight."

"Indeed," Salomon said, adjusting the bag on his back. "My very first plane ride was a success. May we have much more successes together in the future."

Thomas smiled, knowing how much fulfilling the prophecy meant to Salomon. Although each of them had experienced pain and loss, it seemed Salomon had suffered the most and stood to gain the most from a light fulfillment.

"I do too," he replied, motioning toward a nearby bench. "We have a lot to figure out once Lanying arrives." He checked the monitor above their head and pointed at the center column. "Her flight's on time. She'll be here in the next twenty minutes or so."

The new friends sat beside one another on the bench. They talked about the horrible airline food. They laughed about how difficult it is to use an airplane bathroom. And they shared thoughts about Salomon's in-flight movie choice, *Cloud Atlas*.

"I had a lot of trouble understanding it," Salomon lamented. "Perhaps I need to learn more about the world before I'll be able to follow along properly."

Thomas shook his head. "Um, no. No one in the world was able to follow that movie," he said. "If you're in the mood for a good 'end of the world' flick, *World War Z* is a good one. We can see if it's on Netflix if you want."

"Netflix?"

Already the cultural disparities between them were becoming apparent. He hoped they'd find enough common ground to connect. The world was counting on them being able to work together as a team.

Their ability to reside under one roof required it.

"Uh, yeah. It's this video streaming service for movies and television shows. Instead of needing a DVD or video cassette, you just pay one time and watch whatever you want whenever you want. The videos are just out there on a server waiting to be watched."

Salomon stared at him, unblinking. "That's amazing," he said.

Thomas smiled and considered just how amazing it actually was. "I think you're gonna find there's a lot of amazing stuff to experience outside the Congo," he said.

"The airplane food is not one of them, though, right?"

Thomas laughed. "Definitely not. But Mia's homemade lasagna is another story. She's making it as part of our 'Welcome to the USA' festivities we have planned for tonight."

Salomon's eyes widened. "A party?"

"A small one," he confirmed, glancing up in time to see Lanying exiting the terminal.

Both men jumped from their seats, hurrying to relieve her of the purse and carryon luggage she dragged in her wake. Her eyes were bloodshot and her back rounded as if she was carrying not only her own baggage but the actual weight of the world.

"Hello," she said solemnly before bursting into tears.

Salomon gathered her into his arms, smoothing her hair as she composed herself.

"I'm so sorry," she said a moment later after straightening her jacket and drying her eyes on a sleeve. "I'm not sad. Really, I'm not. I guess I'm just…" She hesitated, searching for just the right word. "Overwhelmed."

"As am I," Salomon admitted, leading her by the arm toward the baggage claim below. "But we're here now, the four of us together, so half the battle is already won."

Lanying nodded, but Thomas was unable to echo his sentiments. Unfortunately, for him, it felt as though the battle was just beginning.

That night, after Lanying put away her belongings in the spare bedroom across from Thomas and Mia, and Salomon commandeered the cot in the unfinished basement beside the washer and dryer, everyone congregated in the dining room. There were six of them gathered around the table where Mia's traditional homemade lasagna took the place of honor in the center. Mildred Pritchett and Carlos Rosetti sat at the heads of the table while Mia and Thomas sat on one side and Lanying and Salomon sat on the other. After wine glasses were filled and the lasagna was divided, Mia's father opened the conversation.

"So, now that everyone's here, what's the big news you all have to share? I assume it has something to do with our guests' arrival."

The four light psychics glanced around at one another, none of them knowing how best to explain. Thomas gave Mia's knee a squeeze under the table and took the lead. "Captain Rosetti," he said. "You know about Mia and her ability to see people's auras. And you know about my ability to sense impending danger. What you don't know is that Salomon and Lanying both have abilities as well."

Carlos set down his fork and made a display of swallowing his bite of garlic bread. "All four of you can do stuff?" he asked.

They all nodded. "Yes," Mia confirmed.

"So, what can you do, Salomon?" he asked.

Salomon cleared his throat, giving Mia's father his attention. "I don't know that it has a name. If it does, I've never known it. When I touch certain objects, I can see their history. I'm able to witness specific times and places in which the object played a significant role."

"So, do you see something when you hold that fork?"

Salomon chuckled. "No. Nothing from the fork, I'm afraid. Most of my experiences have occurred when I've been exposed to an article of historical significance."

"Like what?"

"Like for example, before I left home, I spent some time visiting the archives of a local museum. Most of the artifacts allowed me to see into the past, and I was able to witness a snapshot of history. One of the loveliest encounters I witnessed was when I held a string of ancient tribal beads. They showed me a wedding ceremony between the children of two warring tribes during which the beads were worn by both the bride and groom. It was a magical event with much dancing and joy." Salomon's face brightened at the memory.

"And you always see the past?" Carlos asked, in full police operative mode now, pressing for more information.

Salomon nodded before his lips pressed into a line. "I thought so, yes. But perhaps no. Until yesterday I would have told you I only had the ability to see the past through these objects, but one of the artifacts I held yesterday showed something akin to the present day. If it was the past, it was the very near past."

"You've never seen the present before?" Thomas asked, scooping another bite of lasagna onto his fork.

"No."

"Then why now?" Carlos asked.

Salomon gave him a serious look. "Because change has come for me."

A knowing look passed between the four psychics, but before Salomon could explain himself further, Carlos turned the conversation to Lanying.

"And what about you? Has change come for you as well? Obviously, it must have since you've left China to come here."

A blush spread across Lanying's cheeks, and she blotted the corners of her mouth with her napkin. "A great bit of change, as a matter of fact," she said. "I recently lost my grandfather which was very difficult." A murmur of apologies fluttered through the room. "But coming here to be with you all, my new family, is such a blessing."

"And you're here because of your ability?" asked Carlos.

"Yes. I have visions of other people's lives. Believe it or not, I've known Thomas for many years. I began having visions of him before he came here to live with you, Mrs. Pritchett."

Mildred's eyes widened as she considered Lanying. "You saw Thomas all the way from China?"

"And you too," Lanying smiled.

Mildred leaned forward, gripping the edge of the table with both arthritic hands. "What did you see?"

Lanying sighed and chewed at the inside of her cheek. "Well, let's see. I witnessed his piano concerto during his senior year talent show. There was no mistaking the pride in you or your husband's eyes."

Mildred gasped. "You saw Howard?"

"Tall, gangly looking man with a thinning head of hair and a smile that makes you feel like you're the most important person in the room?"

"That's him," Mildred confirmed. Thomas could see her eyes glassing over and knew how hard it was for her to talk about her husband even after so much time had passed.

"We were lucky to have wonderful men in our lives while we had them," Lanying said, reaching for Mildred's hand.

"Can you still see him, even now?" Mildred asked, the unmistakable twinge of hope in her voice. Hearing it surprised Thomas. His mother wasn't the sort of person who believed in ghosts or spirits.

"No," Lanying said, shaking her head. "I'm not that sort of psychic. I can't see or hear the dead. Only the living I'm afraid."

Mildred nodded thoughtfully, and then her face cleared as if she was remembering herself. "So why do you think you were able to see Thomas?"

Thomas caught Lanying's glance and gave her a slight nod. They'd all agreed it was time to share everything they knew about the prophecy with Mildred and Carlos. It was necessary to secure their trust for the road ahead.

Lanying took a sip of her wine and swirled what remained in her glass. "I believe Thomas and I have a destiny to fulfill. I also believe Mia and Salomon are part of that destiny."

Carlos laughed. "A destiny? What sort of destiny?"

If Lanying was unnerved by the disbelief in Carlos' voice, it didn't cause her to falter. She continued on with a constant, even tone. "My grandfather, the one who recently passed away, was a keeper - a person tasked with protecting an ancient prophecy. The Sevens Prophecy."

The air in the room stilled as Lanying spoke. Everyone stopped eating. Even Carlos settled.

"This prophecy predicts the end of days – a time during which this world will pass and another will come to be. Unlike our world which is controlled by both light and dark forces, when the new world is ushered in it will be controlled by either light or dark forces. One or the other. Not both."

Salomon interrupted, continuing Lanying's explanation. "The prophecy was known to my ancestors in ancient Africa. A prophecy about seven light psychics and seven dark psychics born on the same day, coming together in one place to seal the fate of the world."

"We believe we are four of the light psychics. We all have abilities. We all have the same birthday," Mia explained, turning to her father who looked unconvinced. "We believe we know who two of the other light psychics are as well."

"Perhaps all three," Lanying murmured without looking up from her meal.

Thomas glanced across the table at her. "Are you sure?"

She looked up. "I saw her again on the way here. The island woman, Donescia. If she's part of the prophecy I'm quite certain she's one of us."

Carlos pounded his hands on the table in front of him, causing everyone's flatware to jump. "Well that's it then!" he said, his voice overly enthusiastic, an obvious put on. "Fly the other three in and let's bring on this new, bigger, better, nothin'-but-rainbows-for-as-far-as-the-eye-can-see-world! I've been thinking about retirement anyway!"

Thomas could feel Mia tense beside him. "We can't, Dad," she said flatly.

"But you just said you know who all seven of the light psychics are. What's stopping you from getting on with it?" There was no mistaking his disparaging tone.

Her head was bowed, defeated, but she raised her eyes to glare at him. "Kate was one of us, Dad."

Thomas could hear Mia's shallow breathing. He could hear seconds ticking past on the kitchen clock.

He heard a distance police siren. And he heard his own heartbeat drumming inside his head.

It was Mildred who broke the strained silence.

"There must be someone else."

Out of the corner of his eye, Thomas saw Salomon picking at a noodle with his fork. He knew how desperately his friend needed them to remain optimistic. "We haven't lost hope," he said at last. "That's why Salomon and Lanying are here. We're going to keep searching for other psychics who share our birthdays. And if we don't find another light one, perhaps we'll find a dark. Meanwhile, we're together. Salomon and Lanying lost their families. Now they have us."

At this, Mildred brightened. Thomas knew she was happy to open her home to his friends. She was, and always had been, one of the most charitable women he'd ever known. "Well, as long as Thomas and I have a home, the two of you have a home."

He couldn't keep from smiling, remembering the first night he spent under the Pritchett's roof. "Mildred has a habit of taking in strays," he said winking at her.

"Just keep the bathroom clean, that's all I ask," she said.

The conversation turned then, away from psychic abilities and the prophecy and lost loved ones on to brighter topics like the unseasonably warm weather they were having and which restaurant they should take everyone to first. Much to everyone's delight, Carlos surprised the group with cannolis he brought from his favorite Italian bakery in Little Italy. By the time crumbs and traces of powdered sugar were all that remained on everyone's plates, his cynicism seemed to have been forgotten and things were looking up.

CHAPTER

14

MIA

Saturday, October 29
Baltimore

After being trafficked from the Ukraine and rescued with Mia from the basement prison, Lera opted to stay in the United States instead of returning home. She was invited to live in a communal housing project for single, at-risk women twenty miles outside Baltimore in rural Carroll County. The home was partially funded by the Yekaterina Melanov Foundation, partially funded by a handful of local churches, and partially funded by the women themselves through their own earnings.

Lera worked full-time as part of the janitorial staff at McDaniel College, a private liberal arts school atop a grassy knoll in the heart of Westminster. Along with her paid position, she was attending school part-time and taking classes free of charge as part of a rehabilitative endowment program. Mia was constantly humbled by the kindness of strangers who gave generously to the program.

She pulled up to the college now, where she and Lera planned to meet for lunch at The Pub, a campus sandwich shop. Although they texted and spoke on the phone with great frequency, their busy schedules had prevented them from seeing one another since Dalton's sentencing several months before. As she climbed the steps to the second floor of Decker Center, a rush of nostalgia overcame her when she saw Lera through the window at a café table engrossed in a textbook. She called to her friend as she entered the restaurant and Lera sprung from her seat, sidelining her with a hug and kisses before she got past the front counter.

"It is so very good to see you," she said, taking Mia by the arm. "I was so happy you called me yesterday."

"Me too," Mia said, noticing how the flush of color on Lera's cheeks confirmed what she already knew. He friend was thriving in her new environment. "Did you order?"

Lera shook her head. "I was waiting for you."

The women ordered at the counter – a tuna salad sandwich and chips for Mia and a garden salad for Lera – and sat together back at Lera's table.

"So," Lera said, closing her text and setting it aside, "how are things for you?"

"Good," Mia said and began filling her with news of her move into Thomas and Mildred's, Jack's baby, and the recent work of the foundation.

Lera reached out, taking Mia by the hands. "I'm so glad to know more women are being saved because of Kate. Ten months ago, I never would have thought I would be able to say that things were going to be okay ever again. But thanks to you, I have found my happiness. I have an honest, good-paying job, a nice place to live, a wonderful circle of friends, and a bright future ahead. Without you, I would have been dead by now."

Although it was always nice to hear that her involvement was appreciated, any joy she felt was always tainted by Kate's loss. A void she would never be able to completely fill. An empty seat at their table. She couldn't allow herself to dwell on it, though, or it would mire her in the past. She'd saved Lera, and that was more than enough.

Their food arrived, and Mia took a bite of her sandwich and a sip of soda. "I'm glad you're doing so well," she said simply, before turning the conversation in another direction. "I have a confession. My visit today isn't purely social. I actually have something I wanted to ask you about our time together in the basement. About a conversation I overheard between you and Kate about the trafficking."

A glint of trepidation passed over Lera before she composed herself, jaw muscles clenched. "Yes. Anything."

Mia cleared her throat, knowing she might sound crazy and knowing she was probably going to have to explain her line of questioning once she began. "Do you remember talking to Kate about a man named Patrick?"

Lera pursed her lips, her fork stopping halfway to her mouth. "Yes."

"Can you tell me about him? Tell me who he was?"

She blotted the corners of her mouth with her napkin and returned it to her lap. "Who he still is, I presume," she said. "Patrick was one of the men I met back in the Ukraine when I signed up for what I thought was a job corps experience." She lowered her chin which Mia read as embarrassment. "He introduced himself as an investor, said all the right things to lure us in. He was quite charming if I'm being honest."

"Do you think he knew about the trafficking or do you think he was just a pawn? Someone to fund the operation without really knowing what was going on."

She shrugged. "I never considered that he didn't know. I always assumed he did. Why are you asking? Has something happened involving him?"

"I don't know. I think so. Maybe." Mia fumbled over herself, having no desire to explain to Lera about the prophecy, her part in it, or the search for the dark psychics. "Do you remember what he looked like? I mean, if I showed you a photo?"

"Yes, of course," Lera said leaning forward. "Do you have one?"

Mia pulled out her phone and did a Google image search for Patrick Meyer. Dozens of pictures emerged. Patrick at an awards reception. Patrick at a London movie premiere. Patrick at one of a number of galas. Patrick looking incredibly dashing with perfectly coifed hair and killer cheekbones. The man oozed sex appeal.

She pulled up one of the photos that had the best full angle of his face and handed her phone to Lera. In the second it took to pass it across the table, Mia waffled between being certain Lera wouldn't recognize him and petrified that she would.

Lera let out an audible gasp. "Oh, yes," she said. "That's the man. The man from the meeting." She didn't take her eyes from the screen.

"You're certain?"

Lera nodded. "Yes."

Mia took back her phone and finished her last bite of sandwich, licking a chunk of stray tuna from her finger. Her mind was racing. Lillian, a known psychic who shared their birthday, was somehow associated with another psychic Javier Delgado, who worked for Patrick Meyer, who was somehow involved in the trafficking ring. The question now was how deeply involved he was. Did he know what he was an accomplice to or was he somehow an unwitting pawn?

She and Lera visited for almost two hours, talking about Lera's classes and her plans for the future and how she'd spoken recently to Kate's family in the Ukraine. After splitting an ice cream sundae, they said goodbye, exchanged hugs, and made plans to get together again soon.

On the drive back to Baltimore, Mia mentally constructed a plan for moving forward with the new information from Lera. Now that she knew Patrick Meyer was involved with the trafficking ring, she needed a way to determine in what capacity he was linked to the kidnappings. Given his association with Lillian Hall and Javier Delgado, there was a possibility he might be a dark psychic. If that was the case, Lera's kidnapping might give her probable cause to have him arrested and possibly imprisoned, thereby preventing him from fulfilling the prophecy. What she needed more than anything, though, was confirmation of his involvement, and by the time she pulled into Mildred's driveway, she'd come up with only one solution.

She was going to need to speak with Roger Dalton.

CHAPTER
15

PATRICK

Saturday, October 29
London

Patrick was surprised but not disheartened when he felt a cosmic shift in the middle of the night while in the airspace over central Europe. Another psychic joining the light ranks was of little concern to him at this point. That they now numbered six was of no consequence when the dark psychics officially numbered seven and would soon be gathered in London to fulfill the prophecy. It was no wonder that despite being physically exhausted he found himself unable to sleep. He was far too excited about the promise of the upcoming day to miss a moment of the glorious anticipation, which is why instead of sleeping, he found himself staring out the window of his Gulfstream G6 at the lights of some sleepy French town.

He tried to imagine how his life would change as he moved through the coming day, now that the age of darkness was about to be unleashed. Would the effect be immediate as he expected? Would those who embraced the darkness feel a call to rise up against the submissive establishment, finally taking a stand against the weak who foolishly chose to commit their lives to the greater good? Would the dark rise into immediate power? Would the light ultimately see the ignorance of their compassion?

Patrick wondered all of this as he cast his gaze on his sleeping companions. Beside him was Akantha, her head resting precariously against the aircraft's sloped ceiling, too tall to sit completely upright. Across from her, Saif snored softly into his chest thanks in part to the mild sedative Patrick had slipped into his dinner before taking off. Although he'd been compliant throughout their introduction and subsequent departure from the country, Patrick was still wary of the Pakistani. He couldn't risk having someone with the ability to control electricity alert during the flight, especially given the general feeling of unease still radiating from the man. The only other passenger who was still awake was Saif's translator, who Patrick knew, despite the novel in his hands, was far too nervous about his job's unforeseen outcome to concentrate. Patrick considered the man's fate as the translator pretended to read the same page for several minutes. In the past, untrustworthy employees were simply eliminated once their services were no longer needed. Now that prophecy was going to be fulfilled, however, there would simply be no need. It wouldn't matter whether the man went to the authorities with his knowledge of their plans. Patrick would be the *only* authority, and so perhaps he would allow the man to live.

Or, he thought, imagining how powerful he'd feel to skin the man alive, *perhaps not.*

He checked his watch, confirming they were scheduled to land in less than an hour and were indeed approaching the English Channel. It was finally happening. The prophecy was about to be fulfilled.

Two hours later, Patrick led the others through the sliding glass doors of the Heron Tower, past security who waved the group through with a smile and a nod, and up the private elevator to the 32nd floor where the remaining four dark psychics had been ordered to wait. He was surprised by the relative calm he felt as the elevator ascended. He'd expected to experience a fluttering of anxiety just below his perpetually cool exterior and had even prepared to compose himself by counting slowly backward from one hundred if necessary, but as the bellman stepped aside and the doors slid open, what he felt more than anything was pride. He had done what he set out to do, even when everyone else doubted his methods. He was the one responsible - more than Javier or Wesley or even Lilian, for seeing to the assembly of the group.

And he alone would take the position of complete power before the day was through.

He strode across the vestibule, the others clipping at his heels, and barked at his assistant. "Is the entire group gathered in my office as I requested?"

"Yes, Sir."

"No one else?"

"No, Sir."

He stopped short of the hallway and turned to her. "Please see that we aren't disturbed."

"Yes, Sir," she said obediently, focusing on her cherry red heels so as not to accidentally look him in the eye. Her submission wasn't lost on Patrick, who had always appreciated her subservience. He paused to consider how best to repay her loyalty once he had ushered in the darkness but realized immediately he was getting ahead of himself. First things first.

As he stood at the entrance to his office, a room in which he'd spent countless hours in mindful preparation for the moment which was about to transpire, he hesitated slightly for the first time in his twenty-six years, his hand resting on the knob. *This is what it feels like to fulfill one's destiny,* he thought before throwing open the door open and calling out to his fellow psychics.

"We have returned triumphant to fulfill the prophecy! Come! Let us gather all in one place!"

There was a rush as those who had been waiting stood from their positions around the room and converged upon him, crying out with adulation.

"Oh, Patrick," Lilian crooned, nesting herself into his chest the moment she reached him. "We've been sooooo worried about you."

She drew out the word 'so' in her thick southern accent, and Patrick couldn't help but swell with pride. "Certainly there was no reason to have worried when I assured you I've always had everything under control." He gave her a brusque squeeze before quickly shaking her off as Javier approached.

"As promised," he said to the Spaniard, nodding toward Saif who remained dumbfounded by the door.

"I never doubted you for a second," Javier replied, reaching out to shake Patrick's hand. "You're one persistent SOB, I'll give you that."

Persistence was one of the qualities Patrick liked most about himself and that Javier recognized him for this virtue assured his continued survival. Patrick glanced around the room wondering how many of the other dark psychics would be as lucky.

Wesley would definitely not make it through the night.

As if on cue the Australian came strolling across the room, past the mahogany desk with a tumbler of Patrick's best scotch in hand.

"Enjoying my Macallan?" he asked dryly.

Wesley shrugged and offered his hand in greeting. "Figured if you didn't come back I couldn't let it go to waste."

"I told you I was coming back."

"Accidents happen." Wesley gulped back the last of the scotch and set the empty glass on Patrick's desk. "Now, how's this all gonna work, eh? We gotta sit in some sorta circle and sing Kumbaya?"

Patrick glared at his accomplice, annoyed by the mockery he continued to make of the process.

"There won't be any singing, no, but there are some references to being joined, so I believe we may all need to take one another's hands."

Wesley smirked. "Dibs on Lillian."

Several minutes later, after Lillian, Wesley, Eshanti, and Javier had been formally introduced to Saif, Patrick instructed everyone to form a circle in the center of the room by relocating various chairs from around the space. Everyone did as they were told, lugging wingbacks and dragging club chairs across the hardwoods while he made an extravagant display of sidestepping their labor, crossing to one of his larger bookshelves where he kept several volumes of prophetic text. He selected the second volume, a leather-bound behemoth with gold inlay, containing a number of passages he knew better than the contours of his own face. But this presentation wasn't about him. It was about the others. It was about making sure they fully understood the importance of this moment and his place at its helm.

After joining the group in the circle, seated in his favorite Eames, he opened the book on his lap, or rather, the book opened itself along its spine to the only pages Patrick had shown any interest in since he was a boy. He cleared his throat and rolled his neck, enjoying the delicious cracking of his vertebrae, before he began to read.

"There is much circumspection as to the events which will transpire immediately following the gathering. Scholars agree that ancient translations of the prophecy use the terms 'gather' and 'join' interchangeably, leading to speculation about whether physical contact between the psychics will be required."

"So we are joining hands and singing Kumbaya after all?" Wesley interrupted.

Lillian was unable to suppress a giggle from where she sat between the two men but grew silent with one disapproving glare from Patrick.

"It sounds as though, yes, we are going to need to be physically joined in some way."

Wesley held out both of his hands, his left to Lillian and his right to Eshanti. "Well, let's get on with it then."

"No!" Patrick roared, slapping the book on his lap with the palms of his hands. Eyes widened around the circle, and he was glad to have returned their attention to him. He would not allow Wesley to usurp his destiny. "We will usher in the age of darkness when the time is right. And I decide when the time is right.

There is still more you need to know of what is to happen."

Wesley rolled his eyes disrespectfully, but Patrick ignored his insolence and continued reading from the text. "Once the gathering of dark psychics is complete, chaos will immediately ensue. The gloom of nightfall will settle over the space, spreading like a winter's fog to obscure the surrounding geography before expanding throughout the world. Within a matter of days, there will no longer be a distinction between right and wrong, good and evil, acceptable and unacceptable. There will be only personal choices and consequences, otherwise known as anarchy."

Patrick closed the book without looking at his fellow psychics. Instead, he methodically traced the book's inlaid border with the tip of his finger, inhaling and exhaling with intent. He let the anticipation permeate through them, the weight of it pressing upon their psyches with the force of a thousand judgments. And when he could no longer stand the pressure, he stood.

"Rise, dark psychics of the Sevens Prophecy, and claim your destiny."

He held out his hands to Lillian on his right and Javier on his left. Lillian took Wesley's hand. Wesley took Eshanti's hand. Eshanti took Saif's hand. Saif took Akantha's hand. And finally, with every eye in the room focusing on the last connection, Akantha took Javier's hand.

His breath caught in his throat and for many long seconds he was unable to look away from their hands. The room was still. No one moved. No one spoke. He took a tentative glance upward, expecting to see the darkness settling in, but there was nothing but the unobscured view of the vaulted ceiling.

To his right, Wesley released a curt cough and whatever spell had been cast was broken.

Obviously, the book's description of what should have come to pass was mistaken.

Either that or something was terribly, devastatingly wrong.

CHAPTER

16

MIA

Wednesday, November 2
Baltimore

The North Branch Correctional Institution was a maximum-security prison operated by the Maryland Department of Public Safety and Correctional Services in Allegany County near Cumberland. Although the facility housed roughly 1,500 inmates, Mia was only interested in speaking with one.

She surrendered her badge and her sidearm as she went through the security check at the front of the building. She'd been given special permission to meet with Dalton outside of normal visiting hours after work. The evening drive had been uneventful, even with the rush hour traffic, but now, as she followed the correctional officer into the building's depths, her palms began to sweat.

She hadn't spoken to Dalton since the morning she confronted him in the foyer of his Federal Hill rowhouse. She'd avoided making eye contact with him during her time on the stand during his trial, and as she stood now at the doorway into their private visitation room, she couldn't help but remember how he'd mouthed the words 'see you soon' after his sentencing. She was convinced the man was no mild-mannered felon.

He was already waiting for her, shackled at his hands and his feet, sitting at a stainless steel table in the center of the windowless room. She felt him watching her as she crossed the space between them, lowering herself into the folding chair across from him. She set down the dossier folder she'd brought with her, opening it and rustling through a few papers before giving Dalton the satisfaction of her attention. Truthfully, the folder only held one necessary document. Other than that, it merely made her look official and gave her something to do with her nervous hands. Something other than punch Dalton in the face, which was, more than anything else, what she desperately wanted to do.

"Officer Rosetti," he offered when she didn't immediately speak. "How very nice to see you."

Despite the shackles, the closely cropped hair, and dark circles under his eyes, Dalton was still an intimidating man. He conveyed the same air of superiority he had the very first time she'd met him on the morning of his commissioning.

And his aura, of course, was still heavy with darkness.

"I wish I could say the same," she said, straightening her shoulders. "Although I guess I could rightly say that I'm glad to see you're *in here*."

Dalton smirked, unable to hide his hatred. "Well, then, we'll skip the pleasantries and move straight on to the business at hand. But, you'll have to excuse me, what exactly is the business at hand? No one's told me anything, and I'm only here because frankly, curiosity got the better of me."

Mia steadied her breathing, balling her hands into fists to keep them from shaking. It wasn't lost on her that she was face to face with the man who nearly killed her. The man who had a hand in destroying the lives of so many young women.

"Tell me about Patrick Meyer." It wasn't a request.

She noticed the corner of his left eye twitch almost imperceptibly. The name had registered. He knew something.

"Isn't he some billionaire mogul?"

"He is."

Dalton shrugged. "That's about all I know."

"No. It's not," Mia said. "How long have you known each other?"

Dalton pursed his lips, but Mia held his gaze, defying him to look away.

"You left me locked in the basement with the other girls. You had to know they would talk to me. You had to know they would tell me what they knew. And who they knew. But I guess that didn't matter to you because you never intended on letting me out. It didn't matter what they told me because I wasn't supposed to survive." She was being purposely evasive, hoping to give Dalton just enough rope to hang himself with. "But I did survive. And I know about Patrick."

He blinked but gave away nothing. "If you already know so much about Patrick Meyer, what do you need from me?"

Now it was her turn to feign disinterest. Because she had a secret weapon. "It's not what I need from you, Mr. Dalton. It's what you need from me."

He laughed, like a bark from a caged dog, his chains clanking as he shook. "I certainly don't need anything from you."

"I think maybe you might."

He stilled and leaned forward across the table. Mia could see a vein pulsing at his temple. "What could I possibly want from you, Ms. Rosetti?"

Mia ignored the snub of her title. "When was the last time you saw your daughter, Trina, Mr. Dalton?"

The mention of Trina's name elicited a visceral reaction. Dalton drew a sharp breath, and Mia wouldn't have been surprised to hear a growl escape his lips. "Tell me why you're here or get the hell out of my face."

She pulled a signed affidavit from her folder and slid it across the table to him. "As you know, I have a few connections within the department. This would allow for two supervised visits a year with your daughter, and perhaps at some point your grandchildren, for the remainder of your stay here at North Branch, as long as you remain in good standing and you provide me with the information I'm looking for today."

He eyed the paper skeptically, keeping his hands at his sides. "The DA signed off on this? And the Warden?"

"Yes. But only if you tell me everything I need to know." Mia was grateful for her connection in the District Attorney's office. Jack's wife, Stella, had proved once again to be an indispensable ally. That she had gotten the Warden to sign off as well, with little push back, had been something of a miracle. Perhaps he'd agreed more for Trina's sake than Dalton's.

"Twice a year?"

"That's what the paper says."

"Patrick Meyer?"

Glaring across the table, she saw resignation behind his calculated veneer. He sighed.

"What do you want to know?"

Mia's heart quickened involuntarily. She'd broken him. "I need to know about his connection to the trafficking ring. Anything you tell me will be off the record. Inadmissible. You won't ever be linked back to this conversation."

Dalton shook his head. "He'll know. But I'm locked safely away in here so what's he gonna do? Send another con after me?" He sneered. "Unlikely. I run this place."

It was no wonder that Dalton's intimidating presence proceeded him. Even behind bars, people would bend to his will.

"How will he know? Does he have people here, on the inside?"

Dalton glanced around the room at the security cameras recording his every move. "I only met the guy twice, but I've heard rumors about him from people who are part of his inner circle. Rumors that he doesn't need people to get information. He just knows things. He can sense them."

The hairs on Mia's arms stood on end. Was this confirmation that Patrick Meyer had a psychic ability?

Was this evidence that he was part of the prophecy?

Mia fought to suppress the woozy feeling that was threatening to overtake her. She needed to focus on getting as much information out of Dalton as she could.

"So you've met Meyer, and I assume this was with regard to the trafficking ring?"

He nodded. "Meyer ran his own operation and was looking to expand. About two years ago he contacted me about an acquisition. I made the deal but stayed on to run logistics here on the east coast."

"And people say he has some sort of psychic ability?"

He shrugged, but there was something less than dismissive about his coy expression. "There are people who say he'll lead a new world order with his abilities. And when he does, I'm outta here."

See you soon…

"And yet, you still took my deal."

If Patrick Meyer was a part of the prophecy, he certainly wasn't one of the light. Which meant that if Patrick and Javier and Lillian were all connected and they all had psychic abilities, there was a chance she'd just discovered the dark psychics.

Questions peppered her thoughts, causing her to lose focus. Was it just the three of them together so far? Were there more? Were they convening in London and if so, how hard would it be to keep them apart, especially if someone as powerful and well-connected as Patrick Meyer was at the helm? Would she be able to find enough admissible evidence connecting him to the trafficking for an arrest warrant?

"Ms. Rosetti?" Dalton said, pulling her from her thoughts. "Are we done here?"

She hadn't expected to get so much from him in such little time. She was expecting to have to pry information from him piece by piece. But the conversation had taken an interesting turn, not only confirming that Patrick was very much involved with the trafficking ring but also a potential prophetic psychic.

"One last question, as long as I'm here and I'm paying full price for this conversation."

He pushed back his chair, preparing to stand. "What?"

"How does it feel knowing you're a failure, in every possible sense of the word?"

He called for the guard as Mia gathered her papers and started for the door. He was swearing at her as she reached the threshold and turned to speak to him one final time. "You know, that affidavit that says Trina can come visit you twice a year? Just because she can doesn't mean that she wants to. Have a great night."

CHAPTER

17

PATRICK

Wednesday, November 2
London

Patrick hadn't left his house in five days. After none of the predicted immediate outcomes followed the gathering, Patrick holed himself up at his estate, poring over his ancient documents and scrolls looking for a viable explanation. His initial reaction was one of disbelief. Certainly, it was the scholars who were mistaken about how the prophecy's fulfillment would come to pass. A descending fog was a ridiculous notion anyway; the work of poets and swindlers, not actual soothsayers.

Certain that the prophecy had indeed been fulfilled without the theatrics described in the literature, Patrick sent the others out to test the situation. He encouraged Akantha to set several of his competitor's warehouses ablaze to see if authorities would intervene. He sent Javier and Lillian to hold up the Barclays Bank near London Bridge to see how far they could get before the authorities were called. He instructed Wesley and Saif to interrupt electrical service to the BBC in an attempt to overtake their broadcasting. And, of course, he locked Eshanti away in a makeshift studio on the third floor of his estate, hoping she would paint something to prove the prophecy had indeed been fulfilled.

The results of the group's efforts proved the antithesis of what Patrick was hoping to verify. Instead of confirming the fulfillment, all signs indicated absolutely nothing had changed. Fires were extinguished. Heists were thwarted. And the media never fell under their control.

Patrick sat in the meditation room just off his bed chamber. This meditation room was similar to the one he had at his office, although it was about twice the size with additional seating options to include an ergonomically designed chair he'd commissioned solely for the purpose of accessing the astral plane. Today, however, even the perfectly molded contours of the chair couldn't ease him into the existential realm.

His thoughts were tied far too tightly to the problematic prophecy.

It was apparent, after days of testing, that the prophecy had certainly not been fulfilled. Now, the question tearing him apart from the inside was why not. And although he was reticent to admit it, he already knew the answer.

One of the seven was not part of the prophecy.

Moving forward, he would need to figure out not only which one of them was the imposter but also who the genuine seventh psychic was. It wasn't going to be easy, but at long last after hours of self-imposed sequestration, Patrick finally felt as though he had a plan.

An hour later, the group was assembled in his front parlor; a sitting room decorated with priceless antiques from fifteenth and sixteenth century France, gold gilded fleur de lis accents, and heavy, plum-colored draperies at the windows which gave the room a majestic, opulent feel. The throne-like armchair where he presently sat was the reason he'd chosen the room for his discussion. He was the king and demanded to be treated as such.

"One of you isn't a dark psychic of the prophecy. When I discover which of you is the imposter you will be removed from the premises and dealt with accordingly."

Eshanti glared at him from her tufted seat across the room. "Is that absolutely necessary, Patrick? Does it even matter which of us isn't chosen?"

"Exactly," Wesley chimed in. "Don't you think it's more important for us to be looking for the real seventh dark psychic instead of worrying about which of us doesn't belong?"

Patrick wasn't surprised by their opposition. Of course, some of them would contest his authority. Especially those who didn't want to risk being exposed for what they were – subservient. But he would not go forward without knowing absolutely who deserved to stand beside him in the new world and who did not.

"My decision is final. I will begin the interrogation process immediately following this discussion. I'll begin with Javier and will continue to question each of you in the order in which you were discovered. I've devised a series of questions which I will ask while reading your emotions on the astral plane. You will not be able to lie to me there. Meanwhile, once you have been cleared you will go to the office to join my investigative team which is already scouring the globe for a possible replacement. You must understand the urgency of this. The light numbers have grown to six and there is no time to lose."

His declaration was met with silence. Their faces seemed almost bored. Apathetic. Anger rose inside of Patrick, threatening to spill over.

"Go then!" he cried. "All of you but Javier. But do not leave the premises, and I will call when I'm ready for you."

As he had suspected, Javier proved indisputably to be one of the dark psychics of the prophecy. There had truly never been any doubt in his mind, but it was necessary to assess everyone equally so that once the imposter was discovered no one could accuse him of being unfair. He was quite certain, given their notable lack of dedication to the cause, that either Wesley or Eshanti was the fraud. It was under the guise of impartiality, however, that he called Lillian into the room.

"Patrick, darling," she said as she glided across the antique parquet floors, "I do hope this is just a formality. You don't actually think I'm not one of the seven, do you?"

"Take a seat, Lillian," he said, nodding toward the velvet Chesterfield across from him. She slid past but he couldn't feel her presence in the room. He knew immediately something was amiss. "Please tell me you're actually here."

Her chin dropped. Instead of meeting his gaze she stared at a balled-up tissue she was shredding in her hands. "I left three days ago."

"Lillian!" he roared.

"I know," she said, still focusing on her hands. "But it's hard being here in person. I figured it would be okay if I just biolocated here when you needed me. I didn't know we were going to be doing all of this." She finally looked up from her tissue. "I can catch the next flight out and be here by morning."

Patrick sighed heavily. Lillian drove him crazy, and not in a good way. She was so selfish. "Fine," he told her.

"Thank you," she said. "But while I'm here, there's actually something else I needed to discuss with you."

He raised an eyebrow.

"Somethin' happened right before you discovered Saif."

Patrick suppressed a groan. "What kind of something?"

Lillian tucked the tissue under her leg and lifted her chin. "Someone's lookin' for me."

"Who? And for what reason?"

"Some man named Thomas Pritchett. I don't know exactly what he wants, only that he called my parents' house looking for me. Said he knew I had psychic abilities and that he needed to speak with me. Apparently, he drove my mother crazy trying to get a hold of me. I discovered a message from her about him at the same time you found Saif, and I guess the whole thing just slipped my mind, what with you leavin' the country and all."

Patrick wasn't sure where she was going with all of this. He had other people to interview, and now she was officially wasting his time. "And?"

"And all this time we've been looking for other psychics without stopping to consider that maybe the other psychics might be looking for us too. Maybe this

Thomas guy is actually number seven. The prophecy itself says 'strong powers will be in place to bring the seven dark together.' What if he's our guy?"

Patrick remembered the day he met Lillian. How he and Javier had traveled to the United States in search of a young woman who, from what they were able to discover, was the last person they needed among their ranks. He remembered reaching out to her family himself in much the way this Thomas had, only to discover they'd institutionalized their daughter for a borderline personality disorder after she attempted to commit suicide. It hadn't bothered Patrick that they were dealing with a potentially sick individual and in fact, it had been easy enough to convince her to leave the hospital, especially when they agreed to give her what she wanted – a home in St. Tropez and the hope of ending her abusive father's life. In the end, even slipping her out of the facility unnoticed hadn't proven difficult. In the months that followed, he'd felt certain Lillian's main contributions to the cause would be her stunning beauty and ability to biolocate. Never once did he imagine her intellect would ever play any role.

But here they were.

He leaned forward and briefly acknowledged to himself that he missed the fragrance of her perfume. "Can I trust you to take the lead on this?"

Her eyes widened. "You believe there's something to this Thomas fellow?"

"We don't have the luxury of leaving any stone unturned," he said. "Reach out to your mother. See if she has any contact information for him. Work with the team to see if he shows up in the database. And when you find him, let me know right away so I can reach out to him and get a feel for what we might be up against."

"Okay." Her voice was hopeful.

Patrick was glad to have another lead. Grateful to have another outlet for his energies. "Thank you for sharing this information with me, Lillian. Now if we're finished here, I need you to send in Wesley and get right on your assignment."

She nodded wordlessly and started for the door. Patrick waited for the waft of her perfume, but of course, the air remained still and odorless.

"And Lillian," he called before she slipped through the door. "Get on that plane. I need you here by morning."

CHAPTER

18

SALOMON

Thursday, November 3
Baltimore

Sleeping in a basement by himself was far different than sleeping in a hut with his family. Salomon missed the sounds of the jungle. The insects incessant chirping. The howl of the monkeys. The steady rhythm of his wife's gentle snores. While he was grateful for the accommodations, there wasn't much to be said for the metal cot, squeezed between a washing machine and an aging furnace which woke him every time it sprang to life in the middle of the night. A single hanging bulb was the only light source, casting dark shadows across a pile of cardboard boxes and a stack of spare paper towels stored in the corner of the room. Having the light on reminded him how closed in he was and so he preferred to sit in the dark. It was comforting to imagine that instead of the basement ceiling, the vastness of the night sky lay above him, full of possibilities.

To say that Salomon was homesick did not begin to describe the longing of his heart. He turned his head to see if he could tell whether the brightness seeping in the lone window was from the street lamp or the rising sun but the difference was indiscernible. He lay on the cot, flat on his back, worrying what the day would bring. Over the course of his days in Baltimore, he and Lanying had worked out something of a schedule. While Thomas attended class and Mia went to work, they spent most of their days at the Enoch Pratt Free Library downtown researching the prophecy, searching for leads on possible dark psychics, and, at Lanying's suggestion, reaching out to other known keepers for help. It was tedious work and at this point, fruitless as well.

He startled at the sound of someone at the top of the basement stairs. Despite the noise of creaking door hinges, the visitor tiptoed down the stairs, barely audible even to Salomon's sensitive ears. He sat up to let whoever it was know they didn't need to continue slinking around.

"Oh, Salomon," Mia gasped. "I'm so sorry I woke you."

He shook his head and propped himself on his elbows. "I was already awake."

She headed toward the dryer and began gathering its contents into her arms. "Outta socks," she said by way of explanation.

"Off to work then this morning?"

"In a little while," she said. "I woke up before the alarm. Again. Stuff on my mind." She gave him a soulful look. "You know."

He did know. His own mind was swimming. In fact, there was one particular topic he couldn't stop

126

thinking about. Mia turned, her arms full of clean laundry, and headed for the stairs, but something compelled him to stop her.

"If you have just a minute to spare, could I speak with you?"

Of the four of them, he and Mia were the least familiar. He'd gotten to know Lanying quite well over the past months and Thomas too, through their many phone conversations. But Mia worked long hours and most of his communications with her had been short and casual. Much of what he knew of her he'd learned second-hand from Thomas.

"Sure. Of course. I've got plenty of time. What's up?"

He sat up straight, making room for her to sit down at the foot of the cot. She returned her laundry to the top of the dryer and sat beside him.

"I was thinking about what you told us last night, about this man Patrick Meyer and his connection to the known psychics Lillian and Javier. You said Patrick was involved in your friend Kate's kidnapping?"

Mia nodded thoughtfully. "Yes. Roger Dalton confirmed he had a part in the trafficking ring that brought Kate to the U.S."

"And you believe he may have a psychic power of his own?"

"Perhaps," she said, picking a piece of lint off her pajama bottoms. "Dalton mentioned that he has some sort of sixth sense."

He remembered Lanying's mantra. "And there are no coincidences."

Mia nodded. "There certainly haven't been as far as this prophecy is concerned. Which is why I can't keep from rushing to the easiest conclusion, even if it's the most ludicrous one. We have a saying here that goes 'when you hear hoofbeats, think of horses, not zebras.' I don't know whether I'm hearing horses or zebras at this point."

Salomon laughed. "In the Congo, we would have to say 'think zebras not horses' but I know what you mean. I think we have to move forward assuming these three individuals are not only part of the prophecy, but obviously on the opposing side. The question now is what to do about it?"

She curled her feet underneath her legs, fully settling in. "Well, the easiest solution to our problem is for me to find evidence of Meyer's involvement in the trafficking ring on my own. The information from Dalton was off the record, but if I can find another lead we might be able to have him arrested and maybe even convicted. The dark psychics can't gather in one place if one of them is in a maximum-security prison."

They sat in silence for several moments while he contemplated not only the difficulty of the path ahead but also how to tell Mia about his own secret.

He cleared his throat, shifting his weight on the cot. "There's something more I think you need to know, especially if we are working under the theory that there are no coincidences."

She looked at him expectantly in the dim light of morning.

"My ability to gain information from objects has never been particularly useful. It didn't help feed my tribe. It certainly didn't save them from the rebels. But I think perhaps, finally, it may prove to be of some use."

She leaned toward him, and he could see where dark circles had taken up residence in the hollows of her eyes. "Go on."

He explained to her about his time in the archives at the museum in Kinshasa. He told her about the historical events he experienced through many of the artifacts. And then he told her about the carving of the twins.

"It was stored in a box labeled 'Indigenous Sacred Relics,' and when I held it I was transported to Bolivia."

"Bolivia the country?"

"Yes. La Paz, I believe."

"Why would an indigenous sacred relic from Africa show you something from South America?"

He shook his head. "I don't know. And the strangest part wasn't the place. It was the time. All the other artifacts showed me the past. This one showed me the present. Or at least the very recent past. Unfortunately, I didn't see anything specific. Nothing stuck out as being particularly important."

Mia pulled more lint from her pajamas, flicking it onto the floor. "So now you're thinking like I am. There are no coincidences. There's something or someone for us in Bolivia."

He swallowed hard, glad to have shared his secret. "Yes."

She shifted on the cot, turning to face him. "Have you done any research into the area or how it might connect to what we already know since you've been here?"

The thought hadn't occurred to him. "No," he said.

"Well, you should," she told him. "At this point that one vision is all we have to go on so you're going to need to try to remember as many details as you can, regardless of how small or insignificant the might have seemed." She paused to chew at her thumbnail. "If only you could go back and take another look, especially having this new information about Meyer. Maybe he has an office there or something you might have noticed if you'd known."

Salomon's pulse quickened. "I can do that," he said, slipping off the cot onto the floor.

"You don't need to start researching this very minute," she laughed. "Have some breakfast first, at least."

He was on his hands and knees now, shuffling through the contents of the duffle he stored under the cot. A moment later he felt the wrapped bundle he was searching for and returned to his seat beside Mia. He held out his hand, offering her the wad of fabric.

"What is it?" she asked.

"Open it."

He watched as she unrolled the torn piece of cloth to reveal the carving of the twins. "Is this what I think it is?" she asked, eyes wide.

He couldn't keep from grinning even though he knew how wrong it was to have taken it from the museum. He vowed to return it once the prophecy was fulfilled.

"So then, not a complete Boy Scout after all," Mia mused, turning the artifact in her hands. He didn't know what she meant, but from the tone of her voice it sounded as though she thought taking the relic was a good thing. "Have you held it a second time?"

He hadn't, and he didn't know why not. Perhaps it was because there was a part of him who was afraid he wouldn't be able to glean anything useful with his ability. And perhaps it was because there was a part of him who was afraid that he *would* see something but that it would confirm all hope was lost.

"Well, then," she said, handing him the carving. "No time like the present."

What he knew of Mia was this – she was direct, she didn't waste time, and she wasn't afraid to take chances. There was no denying why Thomas loved her.

"Now?"

She shrugged. "Maybe you'll see something different. Maybe there'll be a clue about whether or not Bolivia is of any importance to us."

Carefully, gingerly, he took the relic still wrapped in the material. He gave her one last glance which was met with a grin, and without any further hesitation, he grabbed the carving with the palm of his hand.

The streets of La Paz were somehow familiar to him inside this second vision. The cobblestone streets. The colorful, weathered flags flapping overhead. The locals wrapped in woolen blankets woven from vivid reds and greens and yellows like the petals of a daylily. The bustle of the crowd spilled over from the storefronts onto sidewalks and from the sidewalks into the streets where an occasional car lumbered past. Almost immediately he was swept into the throng, surging forward toward what appeared to be a central marketplace.

For as long as he could remember, whenever he had a vision, he'd always taken the form of someone associated with the object in the past. However, in both visions of Bolivia, he was shocked to discover when he looked down that his body remained his own. He was contemplating this phenomenon, staring in disbelief at his hands when a surly-looking woman approaching from the opposite direction knocked into him with her shoulder. He turned to apologize but when their eyes connected she looked straight at him, not with annoyance, but with recognition.

Salomon slowed his pace as the awareness of what had just transpired settled over him. He turned just in time to see the back of the woman's head disappearing into the crowd. He hesitated for a fraction of a second before making the impulsive decision to turn on his heel and follow her. The sidewalk was thick with patrons, now all moving in the opposite direction. The woman was shorter than Salomon by over a foot, but because most of the men and women in La Paz were similarly small in stature, seeing above the crowd was relatively easy. Without much difficulty, he maneuvered through them and caught up with his target. She was wrapped in a tan shawl which covered several layers of cardigan sweaters, full-bodied skirts and aprons. She also wore a thinly rimmed black hat which appeared to be several sizes too small for her head. He was almost directly behind her when she ducked into a storefront on her right.

Although the moniker above his head read 'ADIVINO,' Salomon had no idea what type of store lay beyond the door since there was nothing displayed for sale on the sidewalk and it was too dark inside to distinguish anything at all. He hesitated just outside the opening wondering whether it was advisable to follow her inside, but Mia's earlier words of encouragement compelled him forward. He took a tentative step through the opening.

As his eyes adjusted to the darkness, he realized the room was empty. Nothing hung from the walls. No merchandise was displayed on shelves or racks. The floor was earthen. The only light came from a doorway in the back corner of the narrow space, and he heard voices coming from that direction. One cautious step after another led him to the rear of the building where he could now distinguish two separate voices, one male, one female, coming from above. Fearful of being seen by the woman again, he hung in the shadows and slipped up the narrow staircase. When he reached the top, he stood quietly at the entrance peering into the room beyond.

As if she could sense his presence, the woman looked up at him from the contents of her bag which she had spilled across a rustic wooden table. "Has llegado por fin," she said in Spanish, grinning widely at him. And then in English, continued, "As I knew you would."

The moment Salomon released the carving he was back on the cot in Thomas's basement. Mia greeted him, wide-eyed. She reached for the artifact on his lap, wrapping it carefully in the fabric before it fell on the floor. "Did you see something about Meyer or any of the others?"

Salomon shook his head, still trying to comprehend what he had just witnessed. An empty store. A purse full of runes and parchment. And a Bolivian woman who could not only see him inside of his own vision but was expecting him to be there.

"I'm not sure what just happened," he managed. "But I'm pretty sure I need to go back."

CHAPTER
19

PATRICK

Monday, November 7
London

Patrick hated failing. He never failed. Failure in any form was completely unacceptable, and he was loath to accept the truth.

The truth was, however, that he had failed. After interrogating each of the dark psychics in turn he was unable to deduce which of them was the fraud. Each was able to answer his litany of questions succinctly and directly without any indication of betrayal. All of their emotional markers indicated they were in fact devoted to the cause and that they believed themselves to be part of the prophecy. Nothing was lost in translation. There was no reason to believe any of them weren't exactly who he thought them to be.

And yet, here they were. Seven dark psychics, each born on the same date, gathered together in one place as foretold by the ancients, but the prophecy remained unfulfilled. The world remained exactly as it was.

With nothing but one dead end after another in the quest to bring the dark psychics together, what remained was an opportunity to buy himself more time. The chance to prevent the light psychics from gathering before a solution could be found for his own problems.

He sat at his office desk, gazing out at the London skyline, and pondered the many ways he would like to kill the light psychics when his secretary knocked at the door. He beckoned her to enter.

"Mr. Meyer, Lillian just emailed over the information about Thomas Pritchett she's been researching."

He waved her into the room. "Bring it here."

She glided across the room in her stilettos and form-fitting pencil skirt. Patrick loved having her on staff, both in and out of the office. She bent down slightly to hand him the printout, her ample bosom just inches from his face, and for a moment he forgot about the prophecy altogether.

"Would you like me to contact him for you, Sir?" she asked.

He scanned the email, noting the address printed at the bottom of the sheet. Baltimore, Maryland. He was glad she'd finally found him. There was no one by the name Thomas Pritchett in any of their birth record databases which was probably why he hadn't already popped up on their radar.

"Was she able to find any record of the man's birthdate?"

She nodded. "Yes, Sir. It took some digging. There's no record of him having a driver's license, but she did discover his adoption certificate."

"And?"

"And the birthdate listed on the certificate is February 7th."

Patrick swallowed, willing himself to remain calm. He wondered why he hadn't considered the possibility that a fellow dark psychic might be looking for him. He also didn't know why he hadn't specifically attempted to track down the light psychics long before this. He supposed his own pride was to blame on both counts. He just never thought it would come to this. Now, however, he was left with no other choice.

"Thank you, Phoebe."

He didn't need to ask her to leave. She knew her place and disappeared back into the atrium without another word. He considered retreating into his meditation room to do what needed to be done, but he couldn't wait the thirty seconds it would take him to get there. He closed his eyes and reached out into the astral plane. Now that he had a name and a location, finding Thomas Pritchett wouldn't be difficult. All he needed to do was scan his markers to determine whether he was dark or light. His instinct told him the man was light. He didn't know why. Maybe because it depressed him to think with all of his resources that Thomas Pritchett was searching for him and not the other way around. And so even though it would be far easier to hope Pritchett was dark so they could gather together and try again, a part of Patrick yearned for him to be light, just so he would have a target for his suppressed aggression.

He slipped onto the plane, searching for Pritchett. He quickly found Dalton, who was coincidentally in the same general vicinity. His former project manager was dejected. Patrick could sense his disappointment with the way things had worked out for him. He felt no pity for the former police commissioner. He'd allowed his emotions to interfere with the trafficking ring's operations. At least in prison, he couldn't make any more mistakes.

Patrick continued to search for Pritchett, finally pinpointing his location just outside of Baltimore. Unfortunately, his location was all he could sense. There were no emotional markers. No indications of whether or not the man was light or dark.

It was the first time in his life he'd been unable to read someone across the plane.

"Damn it," he said to himself, breaking out of the trance.

He pressed the intercom button on his desk. "Phoebe, find Lillian. I want her in the office in two minutes."

Ninety seconds later, Lillian materialized in one of the leather armchairs on the other side of his desk. "You need me?" she crooned, her voice hopeful.

"Yes. I need you to biolocate to the U.S. To Baltimore. I want you to look into Thomas Pritchett for me. We need to know if he's light or dark so we can make a decision about what to do with him."

She raised a manicured eyebrow. "You can't get a read on him yourself?"

He would not admit the truth. "Yes," he lied. "But I'd like you to confirm my findings before moving forward. We can't afford to make any mistakes this late in the game." He reminded her of Pritchett's location from her email.

"Be back in two jiffs," she said with a wave of her fingers.

Two jiffs turned out to be more like twenty minutes, and Patrick had succumbed to pacing the length of his office and was on his second glass of scotch by the time she returned.

"Well?"

She beckoned him to the seating area beside the windows, crossing her legs neatly as she slid into the wingback. "Oh, honey," she said. "You are gonna owe me big time for this one."

He refused to sit, standing above her, ice clinking in his glass. "Tell me."

She shook her head, gazing up at him with a coy smile. He took the gesture as insolence but was powerless to admonish her for it until he had what he needed. "You need to give me something first."

Heat rose to his face. "I'm not playing games with you, Lillian. You're a part of the group and you do what you're told because it's your birthright, not because you're owed anything in return."

She uncrossed her legs and motioned as if to stand.

If he didn't need her to fulfill the prophecy he would have killed her outright, there in his office. "What do you want?"

She lowered herself into the chair. "I want access to your research team."

"They're busy searching for psychics, Lillian. You know that. We can't afford to spare them." He was annoyed by her request. She was always so needy. "What use do you have for a research team, anyway?"

"I'm looking for rapists."

He didn't even pretend not to roll his eyes. "Oh my god, again with this? I get it. You think your father took advantage of you. But don't you think it's a little close-minded to punish all men for something they can't control? Especially when so many women practically beg for that sort of attention with the way they act and dress?"

He saw her knuckles whiten with her grip on the armrests. "Do you want to know what I saw in Baltimore or don't you?" Her voice was calm and measured, slow even for her usual Southern drawl.

His shoulders sagged under the weight of her demands. "Fine. I'll give you access to one small team, but not another soul until after the fulfillment. Now tell me what you saw."

She composed herself, recrossing her legs and smoothing her skirt. "I found Pritchett. He was with a woman. They were discussing another person and his psychometric abilities."

"Another psychic?" he interrupted.

"Yes. This man uses objects to learn about the past. They were discussing a hair comb that belonged to some girl named Kate. Apparently, this psychic guy touched it and was able to confirm the girl is one of the prophetic psychics. Perhaps these are the ones you've felt gathering together all this time."

"And were you able to discern…"

"They are light. I have no doubt."

Patrick finally fell into the chair beside Lillian, his empty glass still firm in his grasp. His mind was racing. There was really only one thing to do. "We need to kill them," he said with clear resolution.

Lillian looked at him impassively. "It certainly would buy us more time knowing we weren't racing them to the finish line."

He considered this good fortune, that Thomas Pritchett had reached out to them without knowing it would seal his own fate. He checked his watch, noting how long it would take his flight crew to prepare for the trip to Baltimore. "Give me twelve hours and everything will be taken care of," he said.

"And my research team?"

"I'll reassign them before I go."

CHAPTER

20

LANYING

Monday, November 7
Baltimore

Lanying and Salomon were at their usual computer terminal in the reference section of the Enoch Pratt Library on Cathedral Street. There were dozens of library branches around the city, but the largest selection of sacred resources was at the central location, making it their obvious choice.

"Looking for another keeper is a fabulous idea," Lanying said, thumbing through her grandfather's leather-bound journal. "I wish I'd known the right questions to ask Grandfather while he was still alive, but perhaps it will be possible to track down another keeper to help us along the path to fulfillment. Or at least help us figure out what all your visions of La Paz are all about."

Salomon nodded in agreement. "I learned in my time at University that the dissemination of ideas cultivates the best plans. This is the reason it was important for us all to be together here in Baltimore.

We are shrewder together than we would have been in isolation."

Lanying smiled. It was nice to have Salomon by her side, day in and day out, to share ideas with, even if they had yet to solve a single one of their puzzles. It felt as though she'd been through her grandfather's journal a thousand times, and although she didn't specifically remember seeing mention of another keeper, it was never something she'd looked for specifically. Now, as Salomon continued his online search for incriminating information about Patrick Meyer which might positively link him to the trafficking ring, Lillian Hall, and Javier Delgado, she scanned lines of Chinese characters hoping for a clue.

"Listen to this," she said, reading aloud from her grandfather's journal. "Not all who feel called to the prophecy are worthy. It takes more than an impressive ability or a willing heart to seal the fate of the world." She tapped her pencil against the desk. "What do you think that means? Could it be talking about us?"

Salomon didn't look away from his monitor. "I don't know. Maybe. But I'm happy working under the assumption that my impressive ability and willing heart will be enough."

She saw his smile reflected in his computer screen and nudged him with her shoulder. "Me too," she said, returning to the journal. It didn't take long before she happened upon an unfamiliar name.

"Hey," she said, "can you run a quick Google search for the name Bartholomew Elsner? B-A-R-T-H-O-L-O-M-E-W E-L-S-N-E-R."

He nodded. "Give me a second." His fingers hovered over the keyboard, hunting and pecking for each letter. Finally, he began reading from the screen.

"It says here there's a Bartholomew Elsner who teaches religious studies at the University of Poitiers in France."

Her breath caught. How coincidental. "Religious studies?"

"That's what it says here."

"Any contact information for him?"

He scrolled down the screen and clicked through several different pages. "Yes. I have an extension for his university office and also an email address."

They glanced at one another and she could already sense what he thought they should do. What she knew of Salomon was that he was a doer. He didn't waste time considering what to do next, he just made a decision and went with it.

"You think we should call?"

He glanced at the digital clock in the lower right-hand corner of the screen. "It's probably six, maybe seven hours later there." He shrugged. "He might still be in the office, if we're lucky."

"I don't speak French."

Salomon smiled. "You're pawning this conversation off on me, then?"

"Think of it as an opportunity to practice using your native language," she said, passing him her phone.

He held it in his hand, rubbing his finger over the smooth surface of the screen. "Just because I'm fluent in French doesn't mean I know what to say."

She considered this, and he was right. There was nothing normal about the conversation they were about to have with a stranger they knew nothing about. It was quite possible he'd be completely ignorant of the prophecy. It was possible he wasn't a keeper at all.

"I think you should just introduce yourself and let him know that you're researching the Sevens Prophecy and wanted to know, with his background in religious studies, if it's something he's familiar with. You might mention that you've been studying under my grandfather, Manchu. Maybe ask if he knew him."

"And if he doesn't have any idea what I'm talking about?"

She shrugged. "Thank him for his time and apologize for bothering him."

He eyed her skeptically. "And if he does know what I'm talking about?"

"Ask if he's a keeper. Tell him who we are."

He dialed the extension as Lanying read the numbers aloud. He held the phone to his ear and they listened, heads together, as it rang. She startled when a voice cut through the silence.

"Bonjour."

Salomon began speaking to the man in fluid French which poured poetically off his tongue. Although she couldn't understand what he was saying, she could tell by the tone of his voice he was having some success.

"Oui," he said into the phone. "La prophétie des sept. Vous le sais bien?" He was nodding emphatically now as if the speaker on the other end could see him. "Oui. Oui. Nous recherchons des protecteurs."

Lanying listened to the easy back and forth between the man in a language she didn't comprehend. At one point she heard him recite his email address, but other than that she was completely in the dark. Finally, after several minutes, Salomon said goodbye and disconnected the call. She looked at him expectantly.

"Your grandfather's notes haven't proven valuable once again. Bartholomew, or Bart as he asked to be called, knew about him and his work. They met in person twice, in fact. He is one of the keepers, as we suspected. And he's sending me a list of the other six." His excitement curbed when he realized what he'd said. "Or rather, I guess the other five, now that your grandfather's gone."

Lanying pushed the sadness aside and rearranged her face to express a more suitable emotion, that of enthusiasm over what they'd just discovered. "Is he willing to help us? Did he have any suggestions about why you keep being transported to Bolivia?"

Salomon returned to the computer screen and logged into his email. "Yes, he's willing to help us, and he actually had a few good suggestions of ways to combat the dark psychics. More than that, though, he also had some valuable information about a specific woman, another keeper, who might be of considerable assistance to us."

She was confused. "Where can we find this woman?"

He glanced up at her from his email. "La Paz."

"You're kidding."

"No," he said, pointing at the screen. "Look. Here are the names he just sent me. Third one down, Kamila Cabrera Mendez. What are the chances this is the old woman I've seen in my visions? What if the woman I keep seeing is a keeper? What if she can help us?"

"That's a lot of 'what ifs.'"

He hit control P to print the list of names and regarded her seriously. "That's really all life is. A series of 'what ifs.' So far the 'what ifs' have lead us here, and we have to believe we're on the right track. At least I need to believe."

She knew ushering in the light had to mean more to Salomon than it did to the rest of them. Although not without pain, their lives were more fortunate than tragic. Salomon's life, however, was fraught with unimaginable adversity. For him, the prophecy was the only guarantee his countrymen would ever have a better life.

"So what are you going to do? Are you going to use the carving to go back to Bolivia? Try and find the woman again?"

"I think I have to," he said. "And I think we also need to move ahead with trying to find something on the all dark psychics we've found, not just Patrick Meyer. I know it seems impossible, but maybe we'll discover something criminal and maybe we'll be lucky enough to get one of them arrested."

His eyes were wide. Hopeful. But they also bore a sadness no level of positivity could mask. And so as much as she knew it was a longshot, she booted up the desktop in the cubicle beside him and emailed Mia about her access to Interpol files. She never wanted to have to say she didn't turn every stone at their disposal.

CHAPTER
21

THOMAS

Monday, November 7
Baltimore

Thomas was on the bus. Usually, Mia was able to pick him up from his Monday afternoon classes, but today she was working overtime following up on an old assignment. She could never walk away from a rape case, especially when a child was involved, which is why she'd taken the call when social services rang just before her shift ended about a thirteen-year-old named Janelle.

About two years before, Mia had been assigned to the girl's case, successfully arresting and convicting her rapist while she moved through the foster care process. Mia visited her at the Girl's Rescue Alliance several times a month ever since, checking in and catching up. From what she told Thomas, Janelle was a smart, friendly child with a beautiful singing voice and a sharp sense of humor which is why Mia was surprised when after all this time, she still hadn't been placed with a family. She was even more surprised when the call came in that she'd run away from the facility.

So now, Mia was off searching for Janelle and Thomas was on the 55 bus bound for Parkville. Since moving in together, he hadn't ridden the bus quite as much, but he didn't mind the trip. He never had. There was something comforting about everyone bustled together, each with their own agenda, making their way across town. He sat beside a teenage boy, rank with kitchen grease, probably on the way home from his shift at a fast food restaurant. The guy kept glancing at Thomas's textbook, Fundamentals of Musical Theory.

"You a musician or somethin'?" he said finally.

Thomas glanced at him out of the corner of his eye. "Classical pianist."

The guy nodded in approval. "Nice. I play bass in a band. You may have heard of us – The Fish Sticks."

Thomas had definitely not heard of The Fish Sticks but had no intention of bursting his traveling companion's bubble. 'Great name," he said.

"It's an homage to our high school cafeteria's best dish. Our drummer was pushing for Tater Tots, but Fish Sticks won out."

Thomas couldn't believe he was having this bizarre conversation. "Maybe you can use Tater Tots as one of your song names. Or maybe an album."

The guy nodded again. "That's not a bad idea. I'll keep it in mind."

"Glad to help," Thomas told him, although he wondered if it might have been more helpful to have just kept his mouth shut instead of encouraging the rebranding of foodstuffs. He needn't have worried though because a moment later the bus stopped and the guy got off.

"Later," he said, throwing Thomas a wave.

"Later."

With the seat to himself again, he tried returning to his reading assignment on the analysis of music styles. He chuckled as he read a marginal notation listing some of the most popular genres, noting 'garage band' was not among them. The bus plodded steadily along and he was engrossed in a chapter about linear and global models of formalized analysis when, out of nowhere, a sensation of panic overtook him. He looked around, certain he would see someone dangerous in a neighboring seat, but nothing appeared out of the ordinary. People read newspapers, listened to music, played on their phones. No one looked the least bit threatening. But trusting in his ability to sense danger, he decided to get off the bus, pressing the call tab along the edge of the window.

"Next stop please," he called out to the driver.

Less than a minute later he was on the sidewalk, the thick black of the bus's exhaust permeating the air around him, but it brought no relief from the danger. Instead, the anxiety remained. Worse still was that it seemed to be growing in intensity as the seconds ticked by. He began walking the three blocks to the next closest stop where he could catch an express line to Parkville but with every step the instinct to run increased. He remained steadfast, glancing over his shoulder at regular intervals to check for muggers or a rogue vehicle careening out of control, but there was nothing. Cars passed. Pigeons pecked at the cracks in the sidewalk. A homeless man dug through a bag of trash outside of a convenience store. Everything appeared as it should.

And yet, Thomas knew undeniably he was in mortal danger.

He was less than a block from the bus stop, the signpost in sight when a migraine set in. Black orbs played at the periphery of his vision and within seconds threatened to block out his sight altogether. He stumbled away from the curb toward a storefront just as the pain in his temples threatened to take him down. He fell to his knees and lowered his head, hoping the rush of blood would bring his vision back, but instead he was met with only darkness. And that's when the auditory hallucinations began.

"They're in Baltimore. I can sense at least four of them in the area, but I've felt them connect to two more so they might be close as well. Akantha and I are leaving tonight and plan on being back in twenty-four hours. It shouldn't take long to root them out and eliminate them. Realistically, we only really need to find one and this Thomas Pritchett's location is confirmed."

"This is great news, Patrick, but are you sure you wouldn't like for me to come along as well?"

"It's not necessary. Akantha proved her worth in Pakistan. She'll be perfect for this assignment as well."

The two men's voices began to fade as Thomas's vision returned. He felt someone standing over him.

"Sir, are you okay?" a woman asked.

He lifted his head and her face came into focus. She was middle-aged with a bleach-blond pixie haircut. Her arms were laden with reusable grocery bags with sayings like 'Whirled Peas' and 'Reduce, Reuse, Recycle. He scrambled to his feet.

"Yeah. I think so." He grabbed his backpack off the sidewalk. "Must be low blood sugar or something, but I'm feeling better now."

She looked unconvinced. "Are you sure? Can I get you a water or something?"

He needed to get to the bus stop. He needed to get home. He needed to talk to Mia and Salomon and Lanying. "No. No thank you. I appreciate it, though," he said, making his way toward the stop.

The woman turned away, continuing down the sidewalk. He concentrated on remaining upright and on suppressing his urge to run. At least now he knew what he was supposed to be running from, he just didn't know how to go about getting away.

By the time he staggered through the front door, he'd already left two voicemail messages for Mia and replayed the conversation between Patrick and one of his associates in his head fifty times. There was no denying what he heard. The dark psychics were coming for them, and they were coming soon.

He found Lanying and Salomon in the kitchen – Lanying at Mia's work computer and Salomon at the stove preparing dinner. The smell of curry wafted through the air, and Salomon looked up from his pan when he heard Thomas come through the door.

"Welcome home," he called. "Curry chicken for supper tonight."

It was obvious that Salomon had been a leader in his tribe, undaunted by domestic chores and manual labor alike. Where there was a need, Salomon filled it, and Thomas was grateful to count him as a friend.

"We need to leave," Thomas said breathlessly as he tossed his backpack onto the table.

"Can we eat first?" Salomon asked. "I'm just waiting for the sauce to thicken.

Thomas shook his head. "No. You don't understand. I mean, we can't stay here in Baltimore any longer. We need to leave town, preferably tonight.

Lanying, how much money is left in the bank accounts? Enough for plane tickets for the four of us?"

She closed the lid on Mia's computer and gave him a serious look. "What's this about, Thomas? Why do we need to leave?"

He sat at the kitchen table beside her and explained to them about the anxiety and the migraine and the auditory hallucination.

"You're certain it was Patrick Meyer you heard?" Salomon asked.

"Which other Patrick could it be?"

Lanying chewed at her cheek. "And you're certain this wasn't just some sort of panic attack? A response to the stress we've been under?"

Thomas didn't like her questioning his abilities. "I know what I heard as certain as you know what you see."

She nodded once, solidifying a nonverbal agreement between them. There was a mutual respect there, and it was clear she would honor it. "You're certain they're coming here?"

"He said specifically that my location was confirmed. He said Baltimore. He and someone named Akantha are on their way. I can only assume they're coming from London which gives us about seven hours to get outta dodge."

Salomon looked confused as he set the lid on his pan. "Where is Dodge?"

Although the mood in the kitchen could not have been more serious, he couldn't help but smile at his friend's misinterpretation. "There is no Dodge. It's just an old expression. It means we need to leave, I just don't know where else to go."

The three were silent with only the sound of Salomon's dish bubbling on the stove. After a moment Lanying spoke up. "There's plenty of money in the accounts. Enough to get all of us wherever we need to go as long as we have somewhere to stay once we get there."

Thomas wracked his brain, calling to mind names and faces of family and friends who might offer to take them in. The problem was getting far enough away without having to explain their situation. And then it hit him. "We need to call Jose."

Salomon's head snapped up. "The other light psychic. The one who lives in Phoenix."

"Yes. Yes. He's perfect," Lanying said. "Do you think he has room to take all of us in?"

He considered this, the idea of all four of them descending on Jose virtually unannounced. And then he recalled the malice in Patrick Meyer's voice as he discussed eliminating them. There was something more to consider.

"I'm not sure how he found us. Probably tracked me through my call to Lillian. But it's not his researching abilities that has me worried. It's something he said about 'sensing' us here. His ability, whatever it is, must allow him to feel our connection. He knows six of us know about each other. I wonder if Donescia is one of the six?"

The timer on the oven rang signaling that Salomon's rolls were finished baking just as Mia threw open the kitchen door.

"Dinner smells delicious," she said brightly as she took off her belt and sidearm and tossed them on the table beside Thomas's backpack. "We found Janelle, and I'm starving." When no one mustered a reply, she scanned the room, meeting Thomas's gaze, before continuing. "Oh, God. What happened?"

"They're coming after us. The dark psychics. They know where we are, and they're on their way to stop us."

Thomas watched the light leave her eyes and the terror take over.

"You're certain?"

He nodded.

"How much time do we have?"

"Six hours. Maybe seven?"

"Do we stay here and confront them?"

He hadn't considered this option. In times of conflict, his gut reaction had always been to run. To put as much space between himself and the threat as physically possible. It was emasculating to know that when it came to fight or flight, he inevitably chose flight while Mia chose to fight, but both strategies had worked for them individually over the years, and in this particular situation they had more than just themselves to consider.

"Do you think we should?" Salomon interjected. "Do you think we could overtake them?"

Mia lowered herself onto the dinette chair between Thomas and Lanying. "I don't know. This is what we've been working toward, isn't it? Rooting them out so we can keep them apart? It was silly to think they weren't going to be doing the same thing, but now that they've found us it might be the perfect opportunity to challenge them. On our own turf no less."

It worried Thomas that Mia wasn't taking the risk serious enough. She was treating the situation like a turf dispute between rival gangs, not the deadly threat it actually was. "The difference is they don't just want to keep us apart," Thomas said. "They won't hesitate to murder. Patrick used the word eliminate. And we have absolutely no idea what abilities they might have to kill us off. That Lillian woman can be in two places at one. He's bringing along someone named Akantha, and there's no telling what they're capable of together."

Mia chewed on her thumbnail, mulling over their unique set of circumstances. When she didn't speak, Thomas continued.

"Our strategy against them was never to kill anyone, and I just don't think we're ready for a confrontation. Seven hours isn't enough time to plan, and we don't have enough information. I say we leave. Go somewhere safe. Make preparations there."

Mia cocked her head to the side, and he could tell what she was thinking. She knew he was right, but she didn't like the idea of backing down. She never did. "They'll keep coming for us now that they know who we are."

He'd already considered this. "I felt them coming this time. I'll feel them coming next time. I'll keep us safe."

Resignation spread across her face. "Where do we go?"

"We were just discussing that," Salomon said, passing plates of chicken around the table. "Phoenix seems the most logical choice because of Jose, but just before you got here we were talking about Donescia. We have no idea if Patrick knows about her or not."

"You're thinking if he does he might go after her too, especially if we're not here."

A murmur of agreement spread through the kitchen.

Thomas pushed a chunk of chicken around his plate, covering it with curry sauce, considering their options. If the dark psychics were coming after them, they obviously didn't know about Kate's death. This meant that they would still see Donescia as a threat with regard to the fulfillment, assuring if they found her, they wouldn't hesitate to kill her. Thomas couldn't have her death on his conscious. "What if we split up? What if Salomon and I go to Phoenix to make preparations with Jose while Mia and Lanying go find Donescia?"

Mia scoffed. "We don't even know where she is."

Lanying looked up from her plate. "I think I might, actually," she said, suddenly commanding everyone's full attention. "I didn't say anything because knowing more about her didn't seem that important given the direction of our strategy, but the last time I saw her in a vision she mentioned something about a place called Turneffe Atoll. I looked it up, and it's a group of islands just off the coast of Belize. Given her creole accent and what I've seen of the landscape, Turneffe Atoll would be a perfect match for her location."

Everyone was silent for several minutes, picking at their food, lost in their own thoughts.

"Lanying and I would have to fly so there would be searchable records of our travel," Mia said.

"The only name I heard Patrick use was mine," Thomas said. "That doesn't mean he doesn't know about you guys, but because he used my name specifically and no one else's there's reason to hope the rest of you might just be nameless entities to him. Either way, Salomon and I should drive to Arizona so there's no record of where we're heading."

"And we'll just take our chances with the flight to Belize and back," Mia said confidently without a hint of sarcasm in her voice. She turned to Thomas, taking his hand and giving it a firm squeeze. "I have faith you'll be able to keep us safe. You can give us the heads up if they're coming after us."

He nodded but found that he lacked Mia's confidence. Channeling his abilities for the sake of other people was a skill he was still honing. He hoped this very real threat to Mia's life would serve as a successful trial by fire. He closed his eyes in an attempt to project his abilities onto her when he had another thought.

"What about Mildred?"

The four psychics glanced around the table at one another, forks in midair.

"We have to tell her. We have to keep her safe."

Mia picked up her phone and began dialing. "Dad? Hey, yeah. No, I'm at Thomas's. At home. Yeah, we found her, but that's not why I'm calling. I'll explain everything in detail later, but right now I need you to assign 'round the clock surveillance here at Mildred's house. I know it's outside of city limits, but I need you to make an exception or work something out with the county." There was a long pause. "Yes, of course, there's a credible threat, I just don't have specifics right now. Just promise me you're on this. Yes. Two officers would be better than one but one will be better than none. Okay. Thanks, Dad. Love you too."

She turned to Thomas, wary smile at her lips. "Okay?"

It wasn't much but it was something. "Okay," he said. He checked his watch. Everything was planned. Now it was time to move.

CHAPTER

22

MIA

Monday, November 7
Baltimore

An hour later, Mia was back at the precinct in her office filling out a leave of absence form. She hated leaving her interim partner and father in the lurch, but her life was in danger and she had no other choice. She left the others at home making hasty preparations. Before she left for the station, Thomas was already on the phone with Jose, and it sounded as though he and Salomon would be welcome in Phoenix. They would take Mia's car on the thirty-four-hour drive, stopping only long enough to sleep and eat along the way. Lanying was online securing two seats on the ten o'clock flight from Baltimore to Belize, and Salomon was responsible for packing everyone's belongings for their various destinations.

All that was left now was to tell her father what was going on. She put a tentative return date on her sheet and headed into the hallway in search of the chief. She found him, as she suspected she would, pacing the length of his office.

"I thought you were at home," he said when he noticed her in the doorway.

"I came back," she said, inching into the room. "I need you to sign off on this form."

"Is it about Janelle? I'm glad you were able to find her."

She hung back, clutching the paper to her chest. She didn't know why she was so hesitant to tell him her plans. "We found her at a friend's house. A girl she knows from school. Apparently, the girl invited her home for dinner, and Janelle didn't feel the need to tell anyone where she was going. Typical teenage stuff, I guess, but the head of the facility was definitely freaking out. I'm glad they called me, though. It didn't take long to find her."

Carlos eyed her suspiciously. "Me too. But that's not why you're here. You're here about the officers you want me to post at Mildred's, aren't you?"

Mia relented, crossing the office to stand beside him. It didn't matter how old she got or how self-sufficient she was, she always felt meek by his side. Like a child with a bad report card, she thrust the paperwork into his hands. "I'm here because I'm going away for a bit. I'm flying out of the country with Lanying tonight. I don't want to tell you where I'm going because it'll be safer if you don't know."

"Mia, you're scaring me," he interrupted without looking at the form. "What are you involved in?"

She took a deep breath and considered the question. What was she involved in? She attempted to explain her situation as succinctly as she could. "It's the prophecy. The dark psychics. The bad guys," she explained when her father looked confused. "Somehow they discovered where the four of us are staying, and they're coming to split us up." She purposely avoided using stronger language, not wanting to alarm him any more than he already was. "Thomas and Salomon are going to stay with Jose in Phoenix for a bit, and Lanying and I are going to check in with another woman we believe may also be in danger."

"Are *you* in danger?" His voice was strangely composed.

Always, she thought but didn't say aloud.

"Thomas can sense if something bad is about to happen, remember? He'll keep us safe. He always does."

"But you all are leaving and you want me to protect Mildred?"

"Yes."

Finally, he looked down at the leave form in his hands. As he scanned it, his face distorted into a grimace. "You didn't fill out a 'return to service' date."

She let out a sigh. "I know."

"It says here you have three weeks of leave accrued?"

"Twenty-two days, actually."

He lifted his eyes from the paper. "And you're planning on using all of it?"

"I don't know. I hope not. I hope what needs to be done won't take that long."

"What is it exactly that needs to be done? I'm not signing off on the leave until you tell me the truth, Mia. I'm your father. I have a right to know."

Everything inside told her to not to share the details of their plan with him. All of her police training warned her against giving him too much information –

information he could inadvertently share with the wrong person or that could be used against him if things didn't work out. And yet, something in the way he was looking at her now demanded truthfulness.

"Without Kate, our only hope of saving the world is to keep the bad psychics from ushering in the darkness. Our plan was to find them and figure out a way to keep them from gathering together all in one place, but now that they've found us, our immediate focus has changed. I wanted to stay here and lay in wait for them, but I was outvoted, and rightfully so. I'm not prepared to kill any of them, and short of murder I don't know what else I could do to keep them apart here in Baltimore. So that's why we're splitting up, hoping to keep the six of us safe until we have a better plan."

Carlos was thoughtful for a moment, propping himself on the corner of his desk. "So they don't know about Kate."

She shook her head. "If they did I don't think they'd waste time dealing with the rest of us now."

He surprised her then by handing her a folder off the top of his file cabinet. "What's this?" she asked.

"Look inside."

She opened the cover and was greeted by a copy of the prophecy, printed from the website where she first discovered it years before. She'd memorized the words, reciting them so often inside her own head they were as familiar to her as the Miranda warning or her favorite Beatles song. Seeing them printed here, in her father's office, felt strangely comforting. Was it possible this aging curmudgeon was interested in becoming an ally?

"What is this?" she asked again, flipping through the small stack of printouts which amounted to just about everything available online about the prophecy.

"After dinner the other night, I got to thinking. I was pretty critical of you all, and it was unfounded. I reacted poorly because I didn't understand."

"It's a strange thing," Mia reassured him, encouraging him to go on. "I've been studying it for quite a while now, and there's a lot about it I still don't understand."

"Yes, well, I decided to do a little investigating myself, and if all of it is true and you are one of the light psychics, you can't give up."

"We're not."

He shook his head. "No. I mean, even without Kate. I know you think she was one of the seven."

"It's not just speculation anymore, Dad. Salomon experienced a vision when he held Kate's hair pins and was able to confirm not only who she was but bore witness to the strength of her abilities." She lowered her head. "We were careless with her life and now there will be no fulfillment of the light."

Carlos shrugged, picked up his pen, and signed her form. "Everyone has both," he said, handing them to her.

She took the paperwork and checked her watch. She needed to hurry if she and Lanying were going to make it to the airport in time to catch their flight, but she couldn't leave when her father was obviously trying to make a point. "What does that even mean?"

"I don't know," he said, rocking back in his chair. "Something you said to me a long time ago, when you were a little girl."

She considered him for a moment, not remembering what she'd meant. "Light is light. Dark is dark," she told him now. "And I've got to get going. Thanks for signing this, and I promise to call to let you know what's going on."

He stood up to give her a hug, and it felt as though he was holding on a little longer and a little tighter than he usually did. "Just don't give up, huh?" he said, giving her a gentle nudge.

"I won't. Love you, Dad."

And with that, she was out the door.

Back at home, chaos reigned. Mia set right to packing and was pulling a suitcase from the hall closet when Mildred arrived home from Monday night bingo at the senior center.

"What in heaven's name is going on here?" she wondered aloud as Thomas flew through the kitchen, gathering up computer cords and phone chargers.

"We gotta talk, Mom," he said, planting a kiss on her cheek. "But you gotta give me ten minutes to finish what I'm doing, or I'm gonna lose my train of thought."

She approached Mia at the closet door, her coat in her hands. "Has something happened?" she asked tentatively.

They'd decided to give Mildred the least threatening version of their current situation; enough to appease her curiosity but not enough to worry her outright. "Something's come up with the prophecy. Thomas and Salomon are going to Jose's, and Lanying and I are going to visit with the woman we believe is the seventh light psychic."

Mildred handed Mia her coat to hang up. "But why now? This all seems very sudden."

She recalled what she was supposed to say. And what she wasn't supposed to say. "We discovered today that the dark psychics are looking for us. We thought it would be best if we split up until we have a plan to address them properly."

"You're not going with Thomas." It was a statement that came out as more of a question laced with concern.

Everything had been decided so quickly and with such finality that she hadn't given their separation a second thought. Now, though, that it had been brought to her attention, she didn't like the way it made her feel. The last time they had gone more than twenty-four hours without seeing each other had been when she was locked in the basement prison. Since then, they'd become inseparable. He was her constant. The person she relied on to always be there, no matter what.

"It just made sense for one of us to go with Salomon and the other with Lanying. Neither of them can drive which means Thomas and I will be responsible for transportation here in the States." Mildred was giving her a look which led her to believe she wasn't buying her explanation. Maybe it was because she was having trouble convincing herself. "It's all gonna work out. Everything will be fine. We'll be back together in no time."

"You two are a team," she said, following Mia into the living room where Lanying was printing out boarding passes.

"We are. The best team. But our team has gotten a little bigger recently, and it's not just about what we want anymore. We need to do what's best for everyone."

This seemed to placate her, at least for the moment.

"We need to leave here in about fifteen minutes to have enough time to make it through security," Lanying called over her shoulder to Mia from the couch. "Thomas laid some clothes out for you upstairs. Oh, and make sure you have your passport."

Mia lugged her suitcase up the stairs where she found Thomas sitting on their bed. He looked as haggard as she'd ever seen him.

"You okay?" she asked, sitting down beside him.

"Hmm," he said. No?"

She took his hand, lacing his long, lean fingers between her own. They were the fingers of a pianist. A musician. Not a fighter. "Me neither."

"I miss you already," he said. "And I'm scared I'm not going to be able to protect you from so far away."

"I don't need you to protect me," she said. "I'm a police officer, remember? I'm the one who does the protecting. I know what you mean, though, but you shouldn't worry. You're good at what you do."

He sighed. "Am I? I mean, like right now, it's all I can do to concentrate on something other than this compulsion I have to leave. I know with every fiber of my being that they're coming after me, but what will I feel when we're apart? Will I be able to distinguish a threat against me from a threat against you?"

"I guess we're about to find out." She knew he needed her to express her confidence in him. He'd proven repeatedly in their time together that he was up for the challenge. She just wished he believed in his abilities as much as she did. She leaned in, taking his face in both of her hands, and kissed him gently on the lips. "I believe in you, Thomas Pritchett."

He returned her kiss with a quiet desperation she recognized immediately as longing. And perhaps fear as well. The abused foster child of his youth never hid himself very far beneath the surface. It left him wary of losing loved ones. Kept him guarded against the unknown.

"Now who's being the cautiously optimistic one?" he said, at last, brushing her cheek with his fingertips.

"Mia! We need to leave!" Lanying called up the stairs.

"I love you," she told him. "I'll call you the minute we land. And we'll meet you in Phoenix as soon as we're able."

He nodded. "I love you, too. We're going to finish this. One way or another."

She kissed him one last time and headed for the door. "One way or another," she repeated.

CHAPTER

23

PATRICK

Tuesday, November 8
Baltimore

The flight from Heathrow to Baltimore-Washington International Airport was smooth, as Patrick had known it would be. There was a certain satisfaction being able to climb aboard your own personal jet whenever you desired with the assurance that accommodations would be made for you at every turn. On this particular trip, they were flying into the country under an assumed status. He didn't want to risk anyone knowing he'd left London, particularly the authorities or the media. Better to keep his presence in Baltimore confidential for everyone's sake.

It was under this guise of anonymity that he and Akantha crept through the chartered passenger terminal just before four o'clock on Tuesday morning wearing sunglasses and hooded coats. An executive town car was waiting for them curbside, and he felt a rush of excitement as he slid across the leather seat behind the driver.

If he couldn't yet secure the prophecy for the dark, at least he could prevent the light psychics from gathering first. A small step in the right direction.

Akantha was wide-eyed as they made their way past the brightly lit Baltimore skyline en route to the address Lillian had procured for Thomas Pritchett. It still bothered him that he was unable to trace the light psychic along the astral plane. Once he had names and locations for people, he was always able to track their whereabouts from that point forward. That he wasn't able to pinpoint this man's exact location at the present time seemed of little consequence, however. Lillian had already confirmed he was at the home with at least one other member of the prophecy. There was no reason to believe he wouldn't still be there this morning.

The crowded city gave way to a suburban landscape with fast food restaurants, strips malls, and apartment complexes lining the road. It was all quite garish, and Patrick couldn't keep from chuckling to himself as the driver stopped in front of a small, nondescript two-story house with a listing stoop and smattering of overgrown shrubbery. Of course, this would be the type of place the light psychics would choose to gather. He felt a swell of self-satisfaction knowing his dark psychics were gathered in the refined luxury of his London estate.

The house was dark save for the dim glow of the two exterior porch lamps. No one stirred within. Patrick smiled to himself knowing their timing was perfect; it was far too early for anyone to be awake, preparing for the day. The inhabitants, Thomas Pritchett and his associates, would still be sleeping, unaware of their untimely fate.

He turned to Akantha who's excitement was almost palpable. In much the same way as they prepared for their trip to Pakistan, he'd explained to her back in London exactly what her assignment entailed. Now, as they craned their necks to take in the house, she spoke.

"Burn. It. Down?" she asked in her static, broken English.

"Yes," he confirmed. "You may burn it down."

She opened the door and stepped into the morning, the streetlight from overhead illuminating the obvious joy she felt with regard to what she was about to do. Patrick watched from the back seat as she squared her shoulders and lifted her hands. A moment later, the front porch was engulfed in flames. Warmth flooded the interior of the car as fire lapped the sides of the building and erupted into a deadly inferno. Between the smoke, the searing heat, and the flames themselves, which multiplied as if fueled by Akantha's own desire, he was certain nothing inside the house would survive. Akantha was a lethal assassin. It was a thing of beauty, watching her at work, and he didn't realize how engrossed he was in her display until he heard the rapping of knuckles on the window beside his head. He turned to see a police officer standing just outside the door and the town car's driver crouching behind him on the curb on the other side of the street. Patrick hadn't even realized the coward had gotten out of the car.

"BCPD. I need you to open the door slowly and get out," the officer said. The name on his uniform read Hudson, and his gun was drawn at Akantha. "Keep your hands where I can see them, and don't make any sudden moves."

Akantha must have heard the officer because, for the first time since her initial spark ignited, she turned from the firestorm to meet Patrick's gaze. Their eyes locked, and he was grateful in that moment for all the hours he'd spent building their rapport back in London's warehouse district. He gave a slight nod of his head before throwing himself onto the floor of the car. Outside, he heard Officer Hudson screaming as Akantha set him on fire. Even silhouetted by the burning house behind her, he could make out the white of her teeth, smiling at a job well done.

Once he was certain he wouldn't be caught in the crossfire, he emerged from the backseat of the car and stood beside the Amazonian. She watched intently as what remained of the officer sizzled and smoked on the ground until Patrick brought her attention to the driver who'd begun running down the street.

"Burn him?" she asked.

"Yes, please," he said.

A moment later the driver added to the artificial glow of morning, the sun still hours away from cresting the horizon. Patrick scanned the street for bystanders – nosy neighbors peering from their windows or early risers, out for their papers with steaming mugs of coffee, but the area was deserted.

"Well," Patrick said, turning to Akantha. "Not exactly how I imagined this was going to play out, but good enough. Bravo."

She grinned broadly at him, giddy from the praise. "More?" she asked.

He laughed. Her thirst for destruction was insatiable. "Not right now," he said, motioning for her to get into the car. "Maybe later."

Unaccustomed to driving himself, especially on the wrong side of the road, Patrick carefully pulled the town car away from the curb, past the smoking remains of the police officer, the driver, and the unmarked police cruiser parked several houses away from the Pritchett residence. He slowed as he drove beside the Dodge Charger, confirming there were no other officers inside, before reaching the end of the street.

He was hungry. Starving in fact. It was time to find some breakfast. He needed nourishment if he was going to think properly.

"Food?" he said to Akantha. "Are you hungry?"

She nodded.

"Okay. Let's find something."

He made an illegal U-turn back in the direction from which they'd just come. He remembered seeing a diner with cars in the parking lot and lights on inside not far from where they were. Akantha laughed as they drove past the engulfed house one last time. The roof was almost completely caved in and fire now threatened the surrounding homes. As they turned onto the main road, Patrick could hear fire sirens wailing in the distance.

Fifteen minutes later, he and Akantha were seated at a two-top in the back corner of the Bel-Loc Diner. A young waitress stood over them, snapping her gum as she fumbled in her apron pocket for her pen.

"Two coffees?" she asked brightly once she found it.

"I'll take a hot tea, sugar, no milk, and my friend here will have the same."

Her pen paused in mid-air. "Oh my god! You're British! I love your accent! Say something else."

Patrick stifled the urge to strangle her. "Now. Please," he said.

"Okay, hon. Coming right up. Don't look for any bangers and mash on the menu, though. Think the closest thing we've got is sausage and hash browns."

Patrick didn't dignify her comment with a response. He also didn't correct her about his accent being South African and not British. It wasn't worth his time. Akantha busied herself stacking the packets of jams and jellies. Six strawberry. Four grape. Seven marmalade. She was a simple creature, and he liked that she didn't require constant attention the way Lillian and Wesley did.

He also liked that while she occupied herself he was free to let his mind wander, which is what he was doing now. The waitress returned. They ordered. The food arrived. They ate. And all the while there was something nagging at Patrick. Something that would not let him bask in the satisfaction of their morning's accomplishment.

And then it hit him.

Fire sirens were just beginning to wail as they fled the scene, and yet, the police were already there.

He let this sink in as he took a bite of his buttered toast.

The police were already there.

They arrived far too quickly to have been called by a neighbor, which could only mean they were laying in wait.

Somehow Thomas Pritchett had been tipped off.

Somehow Thomas Pritchett had known he was coming.

"Bloody hell," he said to himself.

Out of habit, he released his mind to the astral plane, searching for the light psychic's whereabouts hoping to put his mind at ease. For a moment, he was relieved when he wasn't able to find him. Perhaps they'd killed him after all. But then he remembered his frustrating inability to track the man, dead or alive.

He was torn now, between returning immediately to London in the hopes of uncovering the traitor in his midst or staying in Baltimore to discover whether investigators would unearth any human remains buried in the smoldering ashes of the Pritchett household in the coming hours. His gut told him where he was more likely to find what he was looking for.

The only question now was who would be the next person to die at Akantha's hand? One of the light or one of the seven supposed dark psychics?

CHAPTER
24

LANYING

Tuesday, November 8
Belize

The six-hour flight to Belize was uneventful. Lanying and Mia landed early Tuesday morning and were met on the tarmac by warm, tropical breezes and a cloudless blue sky, prompting them to shed their winter fleeces in favor of the t-shirts they wore underneath.

"Too bad it's the end of the world," Mia quipped as they grabbed their suitcases from the luggage carousel. "A girl could get used to this kind of weather in November."

Lanying slung her duffle back over her shoulder and pulled out the handle of her wheeled bag. "I definitely agree with you," she said. "But there's no time for sunbathing. Not when we have a light psychic to protect."

As they walked through the terminal, side-stepping honeymooners and families on vacation, Mia pulled out her phone to call Thomas. Lanying was surprised to hear her leaving a message instead of having a conversation.

"Hey. It's me. I just wanted to let you know we made it safely to Belize. We're on our way to the boat now, and I'll call you as soon as we find Donescia if I have reception. Hope the drive is going well and that you and Salomon are safely out of Maryland." She hesitated for a breath, and Lanying could hear the concern in her voice. "I love you," she said finally before ending the call.

"No answer?" Lanying ventured as they headed back outside to ground transportation.

Mia shook her head. "Probably in an area without service. Half of West Virginia's a dead zone. I'm sure they're fine."

Lanying wasn't sure which one of them Mia was trying harder to convince, but she decided to change the topic. "This will be my first time on a boat," she said.

Mia raised an eyebrow. "Really?"

"Yes. Being a part of the prophecy is leading to all kinds of new experiences. Let's just hope I don't discover I'm susceptible to motion sickness."

Before leaving Baltimore, she'd secured transportation from the mainland to Turneffe Atoll through a boat charter service about twenty minutes from the airport. Now, even with the slight language barrier, she had no trouble explaining to their taxi driver where they wanted to go and by eight o'clock they were speeding across the ocean waves on their way to Donescia.

They both stood on the bow of the boat, their hair whipping around their faces, soaking up the Caribbean sun. It was warm on her cheeks, and if she closed her eyes, she could almost imagine that she was living someone else's life.

"You think she's gonna believe us?" Mia asked, interrupting her daydreams as a group of islands came into view at the horizon.

"I wish I could say for sure," she said. "All I know is how I felt when you and Thomas approached me about the prophecy. It was such a feeling of relief, almost as if I'd known somehow I was a part of it all along but had just been waiting to acknowledge the truth. Salomon said he felt similarly, that it was like a homecoming. And it sounded as though Jose didn't resist either. I can only assume it will be the same for her."

Mia pulled her hair out of her face, securing it in a ponytail with a band. Her eyes were hidden behind her sunglasses but she could sense the depth of her friend's concern.

"I've been thinking about something my dad said to me yesterday about not giving up."

This surprised her, not only because of how her father had reacted to their involvement in the prophecy, but because she didn't think Mia had ever considered giving up. She let her continue, though, without interrupting.

"I know the whole reason we're coming here is to keep Donescia safe. To let her know she's part of the prophecy so she can take precautions to protect herself should the dark psychics come looking for her. But we might want to rethink that approach. Maybe we should bring her back to Phoenix with us if she's willing to come along."

Lanying's initial reaction was to balk, especially considering the logistics of international travel for someone from a third-world country. A person who was presumably without any travel documentation. It wouldn't just be tough. It would be close to impossible, especially given their timeline.

"Why?" she asked finally.

Mia lifted her sunglasses onto the top of her head and turned to face her. There was something more than just the sun's reflection off the water making her eyes sparkle. "You're gonna think I'm crazy, but I think I might know a way we can fulfill the prophecy for the light. I haven't worked it all out in my head, and it might just be exhaustion taking over, but I think it might still be possible."

The boat began to slow as they neared a large island. Lanying immediately recognized the outcropping of white and green-trimmed buildings from her visions. There was no doubt now. They were in the right place. Donescia had to be here.

"How? Kate's gone. Six is not seven."

"I know. Like I said, I'm still working on it. Just think about how we might be able to take her back to the States with us, okay? You've done it before with Salomon. Prepare yourself to do it again."

There was a finality to Mia's voice that told her their conversation was over, at least for the moment. The boat lurched as it pulled up to the dock, nearly knocking the women off the bow into the water. They grabbed onto each other, laughing as they steadied their legs and clambered onto the pier.

They were immediately welcomed to the island by two local women who showed them their accommodations at the small but comfortable resort and helped them into their room with their belongings.

"What brings yah two tah di island?" asked a squat, older woman with graying cornrows and a wide-toothed smile.

"We're actually looking for someone," Laying told her, throwing her jacket across the bed. "A woman named Donescia. Maybe you know her?"

The second of the two women shot a knowing look at the first. She was younger, built thin and tall, tendons and sinew peeking out from beneath her white blouse and floral skirt. At the mention of Donescia's name her pleasant demeanor shifted. She eyed the visitors warily. "Small island it is," she said. "E'body knows Donescia. Works down di beach fah di Oceanic Society. She di cook. At least dats what she be tellin' us."

A flutter of excitement released inside Lanying, and judging by the eager expression on Mia's face, she felt the same.

"The Oceanic Society. Is that the place with the white outbuildings and large palapa we passed in the boat on the way in?"

"Is di same," the older woman answered, making her way toward the door.

"And can we walk there from here?" Mia asked, unable to mask the anticipation in her voice.

"Yeh. No problem." Both women saw themselves out, but before closing the door behind her the younger one leaned her head back into the room. "I be careful tho ah dat one iffin I was you. People say she practice obeah. Black magic." She shrugged. "Been warned yah have." And with that, she was gone.

After a quick change of clothes from jeans and t-shirts into shorts and flip flops, Lanying and Mia set off down the beach in the direction of the Oceanic Society

Research Station. Lanying slipped off her shoes and let the warm sand seep between her toes. She'd never been to the beach before. She'd never swam in the ocean before. She wondered what sea life waited just beyond the breakers.

"Do you think we'll have a chance to take a dip while we're here?" she asked Mia.

Mia was strolling along the edge of the surf, the froth leaving lines of demarcation between the sand and the sea. She kicked at a wave. "Sure. Why not? The prophecy first, though, huh?"

She smiled. "Yes. Of course. Prophecy first."

They walked in contemplative silence. A flock of pelicans fed just offshore as the waves lapped at their feet. After half an hour, the thatched roof of the Oceanic Society's palapa came into view, and after a full night of preparation, Lanying silently rehearsed what she wanted to say to Donescia one last time.

The research station appeared deserted as they approached. The boat which had been docked along the pier earlier in the morning was gone now, presumably out on an excursion. As they made their way closer to the palapa, however, Lanying heard the distinct sound of music.

Mia cocked her head to the side, listening. "Sounds like singing," she said.

"Coming from the hut," Lanying finished for her.

Their eyes locked for a second before they quickened their pace, past a group of mangroves into the encampment. They stood together at the doorway to the palapa and Lanying composed herself.

"You ready?" Mia whispered.

She nodded. "Let's go."

Inside was cooler than she'd expected. The breeze off the ocean filtered through the open windows and doorways providing refreshing cross ventilation throughout the space. The source of the melody was obvious now, and Lanying immediately recognized Donescia as the woman singing and slicing peppers at a wooden table. She looked up from her prep work as they entered the room and set down her paring knife.

"Gud maanin," she said with a smile.

"Morning," the women replied in unison, inching further into the gathering place.

The Belizean woman rose to her feet, an act of service, drying her hands on her skirt. "Wut mi do for yah?"

"Please, don't get up," Mia said, hurrying in her direction. "My name is Mia, and this is Lanying. We don't mean to keep you from your work, but we were wondering if we could have a few minutes to speak with you?"

Lanying enjoyed watching Mia morph into police mode. Her small stature didn't stop her from being remarkably persuasive when she needed to be.

"Yeh yeh," Donescia replied, returning to her seat. "Tell yah bit bout di island?"

Lanying pulled out a chair across the table from where Donescia had resumed her slicing. "Actually, no. We're not here to visit the island. We're here to visit with you."

The woman's hands froze mid-chop, silencing the room. Her smile was gone, and she stared at the table, no longer meeting their gaze. "Who be sendin' yah here?"

Beside her, Mia reached across the table toward Donescia, palms open in surrender. "No one sent us.

We're here of our own accord. We're here because Lanying has been here before. Watching you. Inside the visions of her own mind."

They let this admission sit with Donescia for a moment, watching her face for some hint of understanding. When the woman didn't move, Lanying explained. "I have a gift. A psychic ability I was born with. It allows me to see into other people's lives. For the past several years I've been visiting special kinds of people. My visions led me to Mia through a man named Thomas and another named Salomon. And now they've brought me to you." She paused, waiting for a response. "I know about your abilities, Donescia. I know about the water. And I know it's not black magic like some people say."

At the mention of her abilities, she finally lifted her eyes. They were hard. Skeptical. "I not be tellin' yah mi name."

Lanying nodded. "I know. I heard a man here on the island call you by your name during one of my visions. A big man. A mean man." She hoped this blunt characterization of Donescia's adversary would let her know they were on her side.

She lifted her chin, considering the women. "Wut yah know 'bout di watta?"

Lanying leaned forward, closing the space between them. "I know you can control it. I saw you protect your cooking fire from the rain. I watched you cooling the ocean with your hands."

"And yah was here?"

"No," she explained again. "I saw you in my mind, inside of my visions while I was in China and the United States. I just came here to the island for the first time this morning."

Something flickered across the woman's face. The fear was ebbing now, morphing into something less guarded. "Wut yah here fer?"

Mia took over the conversation. "We're here because all three of us have abilities. I see auras — brightness or darkness surrounding all people which let me know if they are good or bad. As I look at you now, I can see that you are good. There is so much light around you."

"The other people from my visions, Thomas and Salomon, have abilities too," Lanying continued. "Thomas can sense danger, and Salomon has visions when he touches certain objects."

"The five of us, plus two others, were foretold of in an ancient prophecy. We have a destiny to fulfill. And we're here to share the truth with you."

Donescia shook her head, using both hands to steady herself against the table. "Dun no nuthin' 'bout no prophecy."

"I understand," Lanying said, touching her arm cautiously. "I didn't know anything about it either. Not until Mia and Thomas taught me about its history and my place in it." She glanced beside her at Mia. They were losing her. They needed to get her back.

In a voice that commanded both attention and respect, Mia recited the prophecy. "There will come a day when seven psychic children of the light and seven psychic children of the dark will be born. From the moment of their birth, strong powers will be in place to bring the seven light together and the seven dark together to form two separate but equally powerful groups. The first seven to gather all in one place will seal the fate of the world - dark for hell, light for heaven. At that point, the seven deadly sins will take over the world or cease to exist."

"Your birthday is February 7th. You're twenty-six years old. Am I right?" Lanying asked.

"Yeh. How yah be knowin' dat?"

"Because it's my birthday too. And I'm twenty-six."

"Me too," Mia said.

"And it's the same for Thomas and Salomon."

"And Jose and Kate, the final members of our group."

Donescia was fully engaged now, looking back and forth between Lanying and Mia as they spoke.

"We're here because we need you. And you might be in danger. And if you're willing to hear us out, there's so much to teach you about the mission we're on." Lanying took a deep breath and took Donescia's hand in hers. She was pleading now. If they didn't reach her there was no telling what Patrick and the dark psychics might do to her. "Is there any chance you'd like to hear more of what we have to say?"

She looked between them again, scrutinizing their faces for signs that she could trust them. Although it felt hyperbolic to think that the fate of the world rested on her response, Lanying knew it was certainly the case. If she walked away now they would be unable to help her.

"Yeh," she said, at last, rising from the table. "Lemme git more knives an yah can tell mi all 'bout it while we chop di fud."

CHAPTER

25

THOMAS

Tuesday, November 8
Mid-West

Thomas and Salomon left Baltimore the night before, hoping not only to get out of town before Patrick's arrival but to encounter less traffic traveling late at night then they would have if they'd waited until morning. Thomas was so keyed up with adrenaline from the excitement of the day, he knew there was no way he was going to get any sleep even if they did try to sneak in a few hours of rest before heading out, which is how they came to find themselves speeding past the horse farms of eastern Kentucky in the pre-dawn hours of Tuesday morning.

Their drive had been completely uneventful through all of Maryland and West Virginia, but as they neared Lexington, Thomas could no longer ignore the familiar sensation pricking his spine. He tried to split his focus between his growing sense of danger and the scores of eighteen wheelers jockeying for position on the road around him, both demanding his full attention.

He pulled off the interstate and exited onto a gas station parking lot. Salomon got out to use the restroom and grab a snack, but Thomas stayed behind and attempted to focus on not only the origin of the gnawing premonition but more specifically, which of them were in harm's way. After several minutes of self-reflection, he determined he and Salomon were not in danger. The threat was to someone else.

He shifted his focus to Mia and Lanying, concentrating solely on the two women, imagining them where he believed them to be at this exact moment in time. He stole a glance at the clock on the dash. It was just before five o'clock in the morning. They should have landed safely in Belize by now, but she hadn't called to let him know they'd arrived. Panic gripped him, his gut seized. He checked his phone for a missed text or message only to discover he had no service. He tried to think logically. He had no idea how long he'd been out of range. Perhaps there'd been no signal when she called. Perhaps she was safe after all. He thought of her again, trying to determine if the danger he felt was somehow attached to her, but he felt nothing out of the ordinary. Only calm.

He saw Salomon through the window of the convenience store at the register. He'd be back in the passenger seat in no time, and Thomas needed to concentrate. He emptied his mind, allowing his thoughts to drift to Mildred. She was the last one he needed to protect.

Immediately he was overtaken by the inclination to flee. Someone was coming. Someone was already there.

He picked up his phone for a second time, held it in the air trying to increase the signal strength. When the indicator still read 'no service,' he got out of the car and began wandering around the parking lot in search of better reception.

He was high atop a grassy knoll beyond the gas pumps pressing SEND repeatedly when Salomon found him. "What are you doing?" he asked.

"Trying to call Mildred. She's in danger, and I need to let her know, but the call won't go through."

Salomon turned, pointing back in the direction of the service station. "I think I saw a payphone on the other side of the building as we drove up. It might be worth a shot."

The men ran across the lot, past Mia's car, to the other side of the store where there was most certainly a payphone attached to the wall. Unfortunately, it had no receiver.

"Dammit," Thomas swore, holding the useless wire in his hands. The urgency of his anxiety had increased tremendously since he felt the initial pang of concern. Every cell of his body was screaming for relief. He had to contact his mom. There had to be another way.

"I'm going inside. Maybe there's a phone I can use in there."

Salomon followed him to the register where a middle-aged man with two-day stubble and a Marvel comic book greeted them with a nod. His nametag read 'Tony.'

"I was wondering if you have a phone I can use. My cell has no reception and the pay phone outside is out of order. I wouldn't be asking if it wasn't an emergency, but my mom's in danger."

The cashier narrowed his eyes and cocked his head to the side. "Maybe you should call the cops."

He remembered Mia's call to her father and felt a twinge of hope. "The cops are already there. Please, Tony." He was begging now. "Just let me use the phone to call my mom. Consider it your good deed for the day."

Tony rolled his eyes but grabbed the phone from under the counter and slid it in Thomas's direction. "Two minutes, dude. Seriously. I can get in trouble for this."

His fingers shook uncontrollably, causing him to misdial. He dialed again. And again. After his third attempt, the call connected.

Mildred's sleepy voice cut across the line. "Hello?"

Thomas released a shudder which had been building up inside of him. "Ma. It's me. I need you to get out of the house. I need you to leave right now."

"Thomas, I'm still in bed. In my pajamas. What time is it? It's still dark outside."

"I dunno, Ma. Early. We don't have time to talk, though. Just throw on your robe and slippers and go to Edna's down the street. Wake her if you have to, just get outta the house. Promise me." He knew his voice sounded frantic and was probably frightening her, but he didn't care. He needed her to understand she was in danger.

"Yes. Okay. I promise." He could hear her rustling around, getting out of bed. "Did you have one of your feelings? About me?"

"Yeah. Yeah, Ma. I did. Now I'm gonna hang up, and I want you to get outta there. I'm calling from a gas station because I don't have cell service out here so you can't call me back, but I'll call you later to check in, okay?"

"Yes. Okay." He heard her voice hitch. "I love you, Thomas," she said.

"Love you too, Ma. Talk to you soon."

He held the receiver to his ear until the call disconnected. When he slid the phone across the counter to Tony, his was met with a look of utter disbelief. "What're you, some kinda psychic?"

"Something like that," Thomas told him before thanking him for the use of the phone.

"Yeah. Anytime," he said.

Back in the car, Thomas attempted to compose himself before turning over the engine. He was still shaking, and the anxiety had not yet subsided. Salomon sat stoically by his side, groceries in his lap, staring out the front window. He concentrated on his breathing. Oxygen in. Carbon dioxide out.

And then, all at once, the urgency was gone. His muscles immediately relaxed. His breathing steadied.

"I think she's okay," he whispered to Salomon who placed a comforting hand on his shoulder.

"That's some gift," Salomon said. "I could have used you back in the Congo when the rebels came for my family."

He knew Salomon's comment was meant as a compliment and harbored no malicious intent, but it still felt like a kick in the gut knowing he'd been able to save his family while Salomon had not.

"I wish I could have been there to warn you," he said at last.

Back on the road, a voicemail alert from Mia popped up on his phone as they neared Louisville. He didn't realize until he saw her name on the screen how worried he'd been, but now his relief was palpable as the muscles in his jaw relaxed. He smiled with the assurance that wherever she was, she was still alive and well. He listened to the message on speaker so Salomon could hear as well, and when they called back discovered the women had already found Donescia and that the newest light psychic was keenly receptive to being part of their group. It was nice to celebrate a small victory, even if it was long distance.

With cell phone reception restored, his second call was to Mildred. He tried her cell phone first, but it went straight to voicemail. After a moment of alarm, he concluded she'd probably left her phone at home in the haste of her early morning departure and hadn't found time to go back for it. Just to be sure, though, he tried the house number, which resulted in a fast busy signal. This was strange, of course, but after a moment of dread, he convinced himself it was nothing to freak out about. He considered tracking down Edna's number but decided not to bother her, especially since he didn't know where Mildred had ultimately fled.

The rest of the day's drive was uneventful. After lunch, they pulled into a rest stop and grabbed a few hours of sleep before taking off again just before nightfall. Cell reception had been particularly spotty across Missouri, so he was surprised when a call came in as they were making their way across the southern part of the state late Tuesday night. Thomas placed the call on speaker as they sped along Interstate 44.

"Thomas, this is Carlos. Where are you, boys?"

"Dunno," he said. "Somewhere in Middle of Nowhere Missouri. Why? What's up?"

Carlos cleared his throat. His voice was ragged. Emotional. "Are you somewhere you can pull over to the side of the road and park? I have something to discuss with you, but it will be best if you aren't driving while I talk."

Even in the faintness of twilight, Thomas saw the color drain from Salomon's face as his chest seized.

"Uh, yeah. I'll pull over on the side of the road right here. There's a full shoulder." He eased the car off the interstate onto the gravel beyond. "Okay. We're parked. Now, what is it? It can't be Mia. I just spoke with her a little while ago."

The sound of Carlos' heavy breathing cut across the line. "No. It's not Mia. But something happened here in Baltimore. At your house."

Thomas began to shake. "Oh, God. Where's my mom? I called her this morning and told her to get out of the house and go to a neighbor's. I felt the danger. Please tell me she's alright, though. I haven't been able to reach her all day. I just assumed…"

There was a heavy pause. Thomas could feel Salomon staring at him. "I'm sorry, Thomas. There was a fire. An inferno really."

Thomas cut him off. His eyes wild, his gestures frantic. "But you had an officer stationed there, and she got out. Tell me the cop got her out."

"I'm so sorry, Thomas. The officer was found dead at the scene along with another unidentified man."

"And my mom?" He was yelling now, composure forgotten.

Another cough. More heavy breathing. "The fire department sent their arson investigators to the site this afternoon. I was waiting to call you until I had something from them to report." Another pause. Another deep breath. Thomas knew what was coming. "They found human bone fragments. I'm so sorry."

The air around him stilled, and it was as if he was no longer confined by the constraints of his own body. Cell by cell he was pulling apart, imploding and exploding at the same time. His head spun. His vision blurred. He no longer wanted to be who he was. He wanted to disappear.

He'd called her. He'd warned her. He'd felt the threat withdraw.

"Thomas?" Carlos's voice brought him back to the car, but he didn't respond. He couldn't. "Thomas, do you think this act of violence is somehow associated with your prophecy?"

He heard the words. Tried to make sense of what Carlos was saying. But their conversation was impossible. A figment of his own mind.

"Yes," Salomon answered for him. "We knew they were coming and they came. Now, we must remain vigilant."

"Forget vigilance," Thomas said, finally pulling himself together. "We've gotta stop these bastards, no matter what."

CHAPTER
26

PATRICK

Wednesday, November 9
London

The seven dark psychics were gathered around Patrick's dining room table for the third time in as many weeks.

"This is getting to be something of a dreadful habit," Eshanti said from the far end of the room. Patrick was glad she was far enough out of reach that there was no risk of him physically assaulting her. He couldn't let his anger jeopardize the fulfillment.

"We wouldn't have to keep meeting all together like this if you all could be trusted. Clearly, however, one of you can't be. And I intend to find out who the untrustworthy member of our group is tonight."

"Haven't we already been through this, Patrick?" Wesley said as the kitchen staff placed dinner on the table before them. "First you were positive one of us wasn't actually part of the prophecy, and now what? Someone's selling you out?"

He still wasn't convinced that one of them wasn't an imposter since there was no denying the fulfillment hadn't taken place. But now he was also confident that someone from inside their operation was working against them, feeding information to the light psychics. There was no other explanation for why police would have already been stationed at Thomas Pritchett's residence prior to their arrival. He had to have known they were coming. He had to have been tipped off.

"Yes. Someone is selling *us* out. The true dark psychics." He went on to explain what had transpired in Baltimore the day before. "They knew we were coming and had police staking out the house from down the street. We were just lucky Akantha has such a powerful gift. At least she was able to get the job done."

"So you were able to confirm the light psychic, Thomas Pritchett, perished in the fire?" Eshanti asked.

Patrick called to mind the news report broadcast on every local channel the night before. "The media confirmed human remains were found in the debris."

"But you don't know for sure that they were Pritchett's," Wesley said, taking a bite of his prime rib.

Patrick resisted the urge to lash out. "Who else could it be? Lillian confirmed that it was his residence."

"Remember, Patrick, there were two other names listed in the public records," Lillian interjected. "It's possible the remains belonged to someone outside the prophecy."

Heat rose to his face, threatening to erupt, but he forced himself to remain calm. "I can't feel his presence," he said matter-of-factly.

Javier set down his fork and turned to Patrick at the head of the table. "But didn't you say you were never able to connect with him?"

It was all he could do to keep his temper in check. He'd never known such disrespect. But the point of their meeting wasn't to discuss whether or not Thomas Pritchett's death was confirmed. It was to discuss the mole. He needed to get the conversation back on track.

"Regardless of whether or not Pritchett is still alive, which I'm certain we will be able to confirm in the coming days, the point of our gathering here tonight is to determine who tipped him off to our arrival. I'm determined to find out which of you gave us up."

"Why would one of us do that?" Lillian asked. "We all want what you want, Patrick. I think you've lost sight of that."

He'd considered this question himself and had come up with a number of reasons, each one more plausible than the next. "Surely you're not so dim-witted, Lillian," he said. "Control is a powerful motivator. As are lust, envy, wrath, and greed. I just need to determine who is being encouraged by which stimulus."

Silverware clinked against china. Mouths chewed. Someone cleared his throat.

"This feels a bit like a witch hunt," Javier said cautiously. "And I'm certain that's not your intent."

"Isn't it? Because to me being accosted by the authorities whilst on a prophetic mission for the rest of you feels a bit like betrayal, and I will not apologize for this interrogation. Frankly, I'm perplexed that more of you aren't as outraged as I am about this."

"You truly believe one of us would sabotage all these years of hard work?" Lillian asked.

Patrick pushed his plate away and removed the napkin from his lap, smacking it heavily against the table. "Not only do I believe it, but I intend on proving it. Right here. Right now." He saw Eshanti roll her eyes but chose to ignore her.

She set down her fork. "Did it ever occur to you that perhaps we're being thwarted by the light psychics? They have abilities too, you know. Maybe they saw you coming and called the police themselves. In fact, maybe the reason we weren't able to usher in the darkness has nothing to do with us and everything to do with them. Maybe they're blocking the fulfillment."

For the briefest of moments, Patrick considered this. Were the light psychics capable of such a thing? He tried to recall if he'd ever encountered such a notion in the ancient texts but had no memory describing anything of the sort – no mention of a psychic having the ability to prevent the fulfillment. And as for the strength of the light psychic's abilities, he'd seen where they were gathered. If their powers were as pathetic as their accommodations, there was nothing to worry about. Clearly Eshanti's suggestions were nothing more than a calculated diversion by a guilty party. He decided to ignore her and moved on with his interrogation, hardly missing a beat.

"Wesley, I spent last night looking into your finances and noticed you've been receiving wire transfers at regular intervals for the past six months to the off-shore account I established for you. My team has assured me they will have the name of your benefactor by close of business tomorrow, but you can come clean now and tell me if one of the light psychics is paying you off. I know how powerful the allure of money can be."

Everyone froze. The only sound was the ticking of the grandfather clock in the hall.

Wesley wiped at his mouth with a linen napkin and turned to face his accuser. Their eyes locked and Patrick suppressed the pang of intimidation he felt. "First of all, Patrick, you're a wanker. You have no right to subject me to this sort of unwarranted scrutiny. However, since you've already weaseled your way into my personal affairs, I'm happy to save you the anxiety of waiting to hear from your researchers tomorrow. The money in the account is being deposited by a French diplomat. I've been blackmailing him since the spring. I've seen things about him using my abilities which would destroy his entire way of life. He pays me to keep what I know out of the tabloids." He sucked on his teeth, picking a bit of food from between them with his nail. "I don't know any light psychics. I've never met any light psychics. And I sure as hell haven't gotten paid by any of them for giving up information about our group. So you can focus your angst somewhere else."

Patrick swallowed hard, bearing down on his teeth to keep from saying something he would ultimately regret. Instead of gratifying Wesley with a response, he turned his attention to Javier. "Last week, when I was speaking with the security officer over at headquarters, he mentioned to me that he's seen you there late at night meeting with an unknown associate. Has it come to this? Has it finally gotten to you, all the years of living in my shadow? Are you striking out on your own, helping the light psychics with the intention of smiting me? Coveting the spotlight for yourself at the prophecy's expense, after everything I've done for you?"

The look that crossed Javier's face wavered between utter disbelief and embarrassment. Javier lowered his chin and folded his hands in his lap. A sense of accomplishment rushed through Patrick's veins. At last, the truth was about to be revealed.

"I'm preparing to take my A-levels," he said quietly into his chest.

Patrick was certain he'd misunderstood and leaned in to hear more clearly. "You're doing what now?"

Javier lifted his head and glared at Patrick with a most unprecedented expression of resentment. "I've been meeting with a tutor, preparing to take my A-level examinations. I never graduated from secondary school, and I'd like to apply for some classes at the university level, but I can't without first earning my General Certificate of Secondary Education." He pursed his lips as if he needed to force himself to continue. "I hired a tutor over the summer to help me prepare. We meet at the office because there is adequate space and a sound internet connection. And if you must know, to my knowledge, the tutor is without any psychic ability."

Javier's admission came as a swift kick to the gut, causing Patrick's shoulders to hunch and his smile to fade. "Well then," he said. "All the best with that, I suppose." He wrung his napkin nervously in his hands. Coming into the dinner party, he'd been certain of himself. Certain that he would have no trouble rooting out the mole. Now, however, with only one lead left, his confidence wavered. He cast his gaze to the far end of the table. "I've been to your studio, Eshanti. I've seen the paintings. I know about the American man whose likeness graces your walls; the one you've been in almost constant communication with over the past year. The team is researching to see if he has connections to any of the light psychics, but I have a feeling I already know the answer."

The chain of rhinestones Eshanti wore on her diadem jangled slightly against her forehead as she lifted her face, giving Patrick her attention. "You have no right to go into my personal space."

Patrick couldn't restrain himself, releasing a laugh so maniacal it caused Javier to startle at his side. "*Your* personal space? You mean *my* personal space. You have no space of your own. No belongings which are rightfully yours. Even the silk you wear on your back belongs to me. I found you in the gutter, an untouchable. Pulled you out of the garbage. I gave you your personal space, and I can't rightfully invade that which is already mine." He pulled back then, settling into his seat as he composed himself. He didn't want to appear out of control. "Tell me who the man is, Eshanti, and I may just let you live. If I find out he's in any way connected to a light psychic at a later date, I can't guarantee you'll receive the same offer."

"You have no right," she began.

"I have every right. Now tell me who he is."

She returned his steely gaze with her own. "No."

He rose from his seat. "Pardon me? Did you say no?"

"You can go to hell," she said.

Patrick considered her for a moment sitting smugly in his dining room, eating his food, and wearing the clothes he purchased. His initial reaction was to look to Akantha for assistance, but then he had a better idea.

He turned now to Saif who was fitted with a translation device so he could understand the conversation around him. After making his request,

Patrick would be unable to understand the man's response, but this detail was of no consequence. It was only important that Saif did as he was told.

"Saif," he said, ignoring Eshanti's insubordination, "please demonstrate your ability by passing a ball of electrical current between your hands."

The Pakistani, who'd resumed his meal as the interrogation of the others continued, set down his fork. Immediately, sparks rose to his fingers and gathered between his palms. A moment later, he held a ball of glowing white electricity roughly the size of an orange.

"Thank you," he said to Saif before turning his attention back to Eshanti. "I'm not sure how many volts he's holding in his hands right now," he began. "But I'd venture to say it would be enough to make you piss your pants if not kill you outright. Now, we certainly don't want that, but I'm willing to let Saif give you a little taste of his power if you decide you still don't want to tell me about the man in the paintings."

"Patrick." Lillian broke in with her sweetest southern drawl. "Is this entirely necessary? We're having dinner, for heaven's sake."

Patrick ignored Lillian and fixed his gaze on Eshanti. "Tell me about the man," he repeated, "or I'll instruct Saif to light you up."

For the first time in many months, Eshanti flinched, revealing a crack in her poised persona. She took a deep breath and looked Patrick straight in the eye. "If you must know, the man is an American businessman named Paul Kauffman. We met for the first time as children when his parents brought him on holiday to my village. He was nine. I was eight. We exchanged addresses. Became pen pals. We wrote to one another several times a month for seven years."

Patrick ignored the way her eyes glistened. He wouldn't be swayed by manufactured emotion.

"After my marriage to Aarush was arranged, all contact with Paul was forbidden. But that didn't stop me from drawing his likeness. And although I created the paintings unconsciously, that didn't stop my husband from beating me each time a new one appeared." She glared at him with the intensity of a laser beam, a lone tear trickling down her cheek as she continued on. "I draw him now because the recollections of my time with him are the only good memories I have left. And don't think for a second I will ever allow you to tarnish them or take them away."

She stood, scraping the feet of her chair against the hardwood floors in what Patrick saw as a show of passive aggressive defiance. She didn't look back as she floated out of the room, her half-eaten meal cooling on her plate.

What remained in her absence was a feeling of mistrust. An air of cynicism lingered in the room. And Patrick, for the first time in many months, was at a loss for words.

Lillian leaned close and took him by the arm. "There isn't a mole. No one is sabotaging us. Things just happen sometimes. You have to start believing the rest of us are on your side because you know what they say about a house divided."

He knew what they said about its inability to stand, but he'd been so certain he was finally going to root out the imposter that his interrogation felt like an opportunity to shore up the footings, not destroy the foundation. Was it possible she was right? Was is possible he'd gone too far?

Wordlessly and without meeting their eyes, Patrick left the dining room through the butler's pantry, grabbed his coat and scarf from the front hall, and headed out the front door into the night.

CHAPTER
27

SALOMON

Thursday, November 10
Phoenix

After the phone call from Carlos, it had taken almost an hour for Thomas to collect himself to the point where he was able to drive safely again. Salomon remained by his side in the passenger's seat watching him alternate between fits of debilitating anguish and unmitigated rage.

He wasn't sure how they made the rest of the way across the country over the next day and a half, but as the world flattened around them and the cloudless sky opened above them into the great beyond, Thomas settled into a contemplative silence that carried them to Jose's house.

They were met in Phoenix with the joyful embraces of reunion and, after sharing about Thomas's mother, the tragic tears of loss. They were shown their accommodations – two air mattresses on the floor of Jose's cramped one-bedroom apartment. They unpacked. They showered. And now, as the desert bats took to the evening sky, they gathered together with Jose and Andrea around a small picnic table on the outdoor cobblestone patio of Jose's parent's restaurant.

"This is delicious," Salomon said, taking another tortilla chip from the bowl. "What do you call it again?"

"Guacamole," Andrea told him, helping herself to a scoop. "I made this batch this morning from fresh Hass avocados. The secret to making it taste so good, though, is Jose's mom's special seasoning." She held her hand over her heart. "I can't tell you what's in it, though. Sworn to secrecy."

Salomon took another bite, savoring the cool creaminess of the fruit with the spicy heat of the seasoning. He followed it with a sip of his *cerveza*. Thomas had been especially quiet all afternoon. He watched his friend now as he mindlessly swirled the dregs of his own beer in the bottom of the bottle, his mind clearly elsewhere. He knew what it was to be paralyzed by loss. His job as Thomas's friend was to focus his attention elsewhere, on something less painful.

"You're enjoying culinary school, then?" Salomon asked Andrea from across the table.

She nodded enthusiastically. "So much. It's like when I'm cooking, everything else seems to fall away. It's just me and the ingredients and the freedom to create. I stop thinking about all the other stuff, you know what I mean?"

He did know what she meant. He felt the same way when he was out in the fields, tending to the crops in their straight, orderly lines. There was solace to be found in a job well done.

"So, what's the plan?" Jose asked, awkwardly changing the subject. "Last I heard was you guys were looking for the dark psychics in the hopes of keeping them apart. But now that they've obviously found us, where do we go from here?"

Thomas's chin dropped to his chest, and he sighed heavily. "The last I heard from Mia and Lanying was that they'd convinced Donescia to travel here with them. After what happened to my mom, Mia's convinced all six of us need to be together. She also mentioned something about having an idea of how to fulfill the prophecy for the light, but I have no idea what she's talking about." He looked up at the others. "Still, if there's anyone in the world who might be capable of the impossible, it's Mia. I'm not counting her out just yet."

"Donescia has travel documentation?" Jose asked.

Thomas nodded. "The company she works for on the island is called the Oceanic Society. The headquarters are in San Francisco and several of their employees have spoken before the U.S. Congress about environmental concerns, specifically climate change and its effects on tropical ecosystems. As it turns out, Donescia traveled to Washington D.C. three years ago to speak to Congress on their behalf using a government issued passport." He shrugged. "She's free to travel."

"That's good news," Jose said. "I guess now we just need to figure out what to do once they get here."

Salomon loaded another chip with guacamole. "I might actually have some insight into that." He told Jose and Andrea about the carving of the twins, explaining how he and Lanying thought the woman from his vision was a seeker named Kamila Cabrera-Mendez.

"Have you tried going back to talk to her?" Andrea asked.

"Actually, no," he said. "Things got crazy, and I still haven't gotten a chance to see if I can find her again."

He watched a look pass between Jose and Thomas before he asked, "D'you bring it with you?"

"The carving? Of course. It's at your apartment."

As soon as everyone finished eating, they carpooled back to Jose's place where Salomon immediately dug the ancient carving out of his bag. The others passed it around, fingering the smoothness of the worn wood, commenting on the obvious visual ties to the prophecy.

Andrea eyed Salomon skeptically from where she sat beside Jose on the faded chenille sofa, holding the relic protectively. "So when you touch it with your bare skin, you see the object's past?"

"Typically," he explained from the recliner by the door. "But this object's been different. I haven't seen who carved it or where it's been. All I've seen is La Paz, and I'm quite certain the artifact has never been there before. The listing at the museum said it was discovered at a dig site near Uganda in the early twentieth century. That's all I know beyond what I've seen in the visions."

Jose gave an impish grin. "Well?" he asked. "What are you waiting for?"

Andrea held out the carving balanced on her palms. Salomon took it from her using the cloth he kept it wrapped in to prevent it from touching his skin.

"There's no guarantee I'm going to see her again. I didn't the first time."

"Trust the process," Thomas said wisely. "You see what you see. We'll wait here." Then he gave a gentle nod.

He let the cloth fall to the side and inched his fingers toward the wood. The moment they connected he was no longer in the apartment but 4,500 miles south on the market street in La Paz. The colorful flags and open storefronts of the marketplace helped him established his bearings quickly, and he wasted no time heading south in the direction of the old woman's shop on the quiet end of the street. As he approached, he was relieved to see that nothing had changed. The overhead sign was askew just as it had been the time before. The door was propped open. He made his way inside.

"Welcome back, Salomon," a voice greeted him from deep within the gloomy interior. Her English was thick with Spanish inflection. "I've been waiting for you."

"Kamila Mendez?" His voice reverberated through the space, far louder than he'd expected it to be.

A throaty laugh gave way to a coughing fit. Finally, she spoke again, her cronish figure appearing in the thin shaft of light spilling from the door. "You've done some homework, my friend." He could hear the pride in her voice. "Tell me, how did you discover my name?"

Although he was relatively certain Kamila did not wish to do him harm, he was wary of giving her too much information, especially without the promise of gaining some knowledge in return. "I'll tell you," he said, "but first I need to know how it is that you can see me as I am? It should be quite impossible as I am not actually here."

She laughed again and stepped back into the darkness. "Come upstairs with me. I'll tell you what I know."

He followed her through the narrow store and up the back stairway to the living space above. The table stood in the center of the room as it had before and now, fully illuminated by the daylight through the far window, he took in Kamila Mendez.

Closer to her now than he had ever been, he was able to see each line and wrinkle of her face. Deep creases spread across her cheeks and forehead, around her mouth, and under her chin. It was her eyes, though, more than anything else that drew his attention. There was an unspoken wisdom there. She'd seen things. She knew.

She motioned for him to take a seat across from her at the table. There was a small leather satchel bound by a length of twine to her right. She took the bag and dumped the contents across the space between them.

"Do you know what these are?"

He'd seen stones like these before, as a child. One of the tribal elders carried a few in his pocket at all times, for luck. "They're runes," he told her.

"Smart man." She smiled, turning over one of the smooth stones between her fingers. "Do you know what the symbols on these runes tell the story of?"

He returned her smile, feeling the warmth of it. "I'm hoping it tells something of the Sevens Prophecy. Because that's why I am here. But first, you were going to tell me how it is that you are speaking to me now inside of this vision."

She held up both hands, palms forward. A gesture of surrender. "You learned my name so I can only assume you discovered what I am."

He nodded once. "You are a keeper."

She chose a stone from her pile and pushed it toward him. "A keeper. Yes. Represented by this stone here. But also, I am something more."

He thought about what he knew of the woman. About the sign on the shop which, when translated, read 'fortune teller.' He thought of what she'd said to him the last time they met.

You have arrived at last, as I knew you would.

"You're clairvoyant. A seer."

She chose another rune from the pile and slid it to him. "Yes. Very good. And you gain insight through objects. I suspect a very special carving brought you here to me." She handed him the stone. "This rune represents your part in the story."

He was surprised to discover the object carried weight, that inside this vision, he could hold it, feel it, experience it with all of his senses, not just his sight. It was smooth and cool against his skin, and he felt the engraving that somehow symbolized him. He glanced up at the remaining stones.

"What about the other psychics? Are they here too?"

She picked out six runes and lined them up across the table. She named each one as she pointed them out. "Mia. Thomas. Kate. Jose. Lanying. Donescia."

His eyes widened at the sight of them. She knew them all.

How much more did she know about the prophecy and everyone involved?

At least a dozen runes remained unidentified on the table. "Who are they?"

"These represent the rest of the story."

The weight of her response floated in the air around them like a balloon waiting to be popped. He thought of the other light psychics and the important knowledge this woman possessed. "Do you know the rest of the story?" he asked. "Do you know how it all ends?"

She smiled across the table, showing a mouthful of crooked, chipped teeth. "Even if I did, I couldn't tell you. It's part of the code. I'm not supposed to interfere."

He considered her and felt a sudden pang of comradery. "That's what I've been told. And yet, here we are."

Her eyes danced. "Yes. Here we are." There was measured silence while she gathered the runes together on the table, lining them up in what appeared to be some sort of order. Once she was satisfied with their arrangement she regarded him again. "I've been watching all of you over the past several years. Watching and waiting. I've been in a unique position, you see. As both psychic and keeper, my loyalties are somewhat divided, but fortunately for you, I tend to err on the side of the psychics.

"The end is coming," she continued, shifting the runes again. "I've known for some time the final gathering would happen here in the city of La Paz. When I learned of his location, I followed one of the prophetic psychics here about a decade ago and have been waiting for the fulfillment ever since."

Although he wanted desperately for her to continue on, he couldn't keep from interrupting. "There's a psychic who is part of the prophecy here in La Paz?"

She nodded, sliding a stone in his direction. "A man, yes, by the name of Rolando."

"And you've met him?"

"Only once. And he didn't know who I was. He had no knowledge of the prophecy. By all accounts, he has no knowledge still."

Salomon mulled over this new information, coming quickly to the only sensible conclusion. "And this psychic, Rolando, he is dark?"

She blinked once before steeling him firmly with her gaze. "I have no means of confirming his allegiance one way or the other."

There was something unnerving about the tone of her voice. Something like the hint of a memory teasing unremembered at the edge of consciousness. He tried to force himself to understand. "But he must be dark. We have already identified all seven of the light. We are all together, except for Kate, of course, who is no longer alive."

The corners of her lips turned down, and she made the sign of the cross against her chest invoking Santa María's name. She took one of the runes and turned it over so the engraving faced down. He felt an aching in his own chest for the fellow psychic he'd never met. From what he knew of her there was no doubt they would have been fast friends.

"All is not lost, Salomon," Kamila said at last. "Be sure to tell the others, there is still a way."

He was confused. What exactly was she saying? "A way to stop the dark psychics or a way for the light to fulfill the prophecy?"

She shook her head and collected her runes into a pile before sliding them back into the leather pouch. "I've said too much already. Just come to La Paz. Bring your friends. I'll wait for you here."

It was obvious their conversation was finished. She motioned with her hands for him to scoot in the same way she might shoo a vagrant dog. "You must go now. Be on your way. But hurry back with the others."

She stood from the table and rushed out of the room. He listened as the sound of her footsteps grew distant on the stairs and a moment later he released the twin carving from his grasp.

He opened his eyes having returned to Jose's apartment. Although it seemed to him that at least an hour had passed, only seconds had passed for the others

He glanced around the room at their expectant faces, taking them in. "Have Mia and Lanying bought their tickets for their flights to Phoenix?"

"I don't think so, why?" Thomas asked.

"Because we're not going to be here. We're going to La Paz. All of us are going to La Paz."

CHAPTER

28

PATRICK

Friday, November 11
London

The fog was still lifting from the Thames in tendrils of milky vapor. Patrick looked across the river to the opposite bank where his view of Shakespeare's Globe was still partially obscured by the haze. He pulled his collar around his neck and tightened his scarf against the morning air as he thought about the man, Shakespeare, and how four-hundred years after his death, he was still revered by most of the world. As it was for Shakespeare, so too it would be for him once the prophecy was fulfilled. People on every continent would know of Patrick Meyer.

After his horrific dinner party with the other psychics earlier in the week, Patrick had decided to keep a low profile, avoiding any further possible confrontations between them. He took his meals in his office. Found respite in the courtyard garden. Took several walks with Akantha when he knew the others would be otherwise occupied.

On his way out the door for his morning walk, his assistant informed him that Eshanti had scheduled for a driver to pick her up at noon. She was flying back to Mumbai that afternoon. Thinking about this now, Patrick stopped dead in his tracks.

When she left she would certainly take her paintings. Paintings he now struggled to remember. He'd been so focused on the portraits of Paul Kauffman, he'd nearly forgotten about the other canvases. Now, however, he called to mind the image of a mountain landscape, quite different from her previous rendering of the highlands of Pakistan. Perhaps there was something important about the location after all.

He had to get back home. He had to know for sure.

With an uncharacteristic swiftness to his step, he raced past the early morning dog-walkers and bike couriers starting their days. By the time he reached his estate, he'd devised a plan to distract her long enough for him to enter her room undetected.

"Phoebe!" he called into the servants' quarters at his arrival. "Order a full breakfast spread from the Indian restaurant off Fleet Street and have it delivered straight away. Then ask Eshanti to meet me in the dining room at eight. Offer her my apologies, and explain that the breakfast is a token of my esteem. Let her know I will be joining her there as soon as I am able."

"And if she refuses?" his assistant asked.

"Then you'll be kind enough to inform her that her presence is not only requested but required if she hopes to depart from London today."

Phoebe nodded and hurried from the room. Patrick reached into the astral plane to feel for the exchange from the privacy of his office. He quickly detected Eshanti's rage but was relieved when she eventually acquiesced, noting a hint of satisfaction in her demeanor. She thought she'd broken him. That she now held the upper hand. But Patrick was no fool. He was still convinced her allegiance lay elsewhere, and he wouldn't stop until he had proof.

Minutes later, Phoebe appeared at his doorway to inform him that Eshanti was on her way to the dining room. "Tell her I'll be there in just a moment. I'd like to freshen up a bit from my walk."

He wasted no time getting to Eshanti's studio in the east wing of his estate where he was dismayed to discover that the paintings were already gone. He cursed under his breath before taking a second glance around the room, this time taking note of the two large steamer trunks set beside the door. Their hinges were locked, but he picked them easily with the tip of his pocket knife; a valuable trick Javier taught him in his youth. The lids popped open to reveal over a dozen canvases and scrolls, each one more confusing to him than the last. As he lifted one after another out of the trunks, he was confounded by the seemingly arbitrary nature of the works. A portrait of an old woman. A mountainous landscape. Eshanti's American lover. A barren storefront in a colorful marketplace. Indian children with haunted, hollowed eyes. Nothing about them seemed cohesive.

In his confusion, he nearly forgot his tight schedule. In order to move things along, he began snapping photos of each piece of artwork with his phone. He didn't have time to waste taking multiple angles - a single shot of each would suffice. It was better than nothing at all, he decided as he returned the last canvas to its trunk and relocked the latches. He fired off a quick email to his research team with copies of the photos. Hopefully, he would have some answers by later in the afternoon.

Breakfast with Eshanti went smoothly. He forced himself to bite his tongue, and when she departed he waved after her with the gusto of a dear friend. It was all he could do to keep up the charade of civility, but it was all worth it when he received the call from his research team just before dinner.

Fifteen minutes later, he let himself into the secured service elevator which descended into the basement of the Heron Tower. The doors opened to reveal the heart of his research facility, teeming with seventeen of the best freelance investigators money could buy. Banks of computers with large scale monitors lined the walls, providing an unobstructed view of Eshanti's paintings from every vantage point in the room. The air was ripe with anticipation.

"Well?" Patrick asked as he entered, tossing his woolen blazer across the back of the closest chair as he rolled up his sleeves. "What do you have for me?"

Raul, his lead researcher, stood up from his computer and greeted Patrick with a handshake. Raul was a founding member of his team, someone he could trust with his deepest secrets. But it wasn't just a hefty paycheck that secured his discretion. Raul truly believed in the cause and looked forward to the world to come.

"We've run facial recognition software on the portraits, of course. Unfortunately, there were no matches for the elderly woman. We've been searching for additional information about Paul Kauffman, but it seems as though Eshanti's story checks out. We even uncovered a manifest linking him to a flight from New York to India about eighteen years ago. Both his parents and his sister were on the flight as well."

Patrick didn't bother to hide his disappointment, cursing loudly. "What else do you have?" he said, ousting one of the team members from his seat at the main computer so he could take his place. "I'm assuming there's something or you would not have called me down here."

"Yes, of course." Raul scrambled to his computer. "Take a look at this painting here, of the mountains."

"What about them?" Patrick's patience was wearing thin. "Do you know where they're located?"

"I believe I do." He pulled up another photograph on the screen beside Eshanti's mountain painting. "The photograph on the left is of the Cordillera Real mountain range in Bolivia, taken from a vantage point close to La Paz by a noted photojournalist. You'll notice each of these peaks match the ones in Eshanti's painting, down to the layered snowcaps."

Patrick leaned forward in his seat, examining both mountain ranges. "They certainly appear to be the same."

"Yes." Patrick detected an eager quality in Raul's voice. "And given the angle of the mountains in Eshanti's painting, we surmised La Paz might be worthy of some investigation. This painting of the storefront is reminiscent of Bolivian architecture as well." Raul pursed his lips.

"And?"

"And we found this." Raul handed him a printout. "Rolando Velarde is a life-long resident of La Paz. He was born on February 7th. He's twenty-six years old. He's been arrested several times by the local authorities for petty theft. I think you might be especially interested in this online video we found of him at a nightclub a couple of months back. The quality's not great because it was taken by another patron's phone, but it's enough for you to get the idea. Thank god for YouTube," he added. "Sure makes our lives a hell of a lot easier."

Raul nodded for one of the other researchers to pull up the video onto the largest of the screens. A shadowed, grainy clip appeared before them. There was a strobe light flashing in the background behind a sea of faceless, dancing figures. Patrick was, for a moment, mesmerized by the hypnotic undulation of the group, drawn into their world of carefree imbibement. And then, he noticed a glimmer in the corner of the screen. It was barely noticeable at first but a second later there was another glint. And another. And another. And then it became clear what he was seeing.

An empty wine glass passed in front of the camera lens close enough so that Patrick could make out what it was. As the video continued to play, he realized dozens of beer steins and tumblers of every shape and size had begun sailing around the room. Some of the people closest to the onslaught had stopped dancing and begun to flee. Others stood in rapt awe of the spectacle. Finally, the photographer zoomed in on what appeared to be a bar brawl on the far side of the dance floor where an inebriated young man was verbally berating another individual. The angrier he got, the more glasses took to the air, as if controlled by the depth of his fury. Patrick leaned forward toward the screen hoping to see the man's face more clearly but was startled back into his seat when a moment later the man was sucker punched, knocking him off his feet. There was a beat of motionless silence as he hit the ground just before every suspended glass shattered against the floor with a resounding crash.

Patrick continued to stare at the screen even after the clip came to an abrupt end, trying to make sense of what he'd seen. "He's telekinetic," he said at last.

Raul nodded. "It appears so."

Between Eshanti's painting of Bolivia, the man's birthday, and this evidence of his psychic ability, Patrick felt a spark of hope ignite inside of him. "Do we have any sort of confirmation that the man in this video is Rolando Velarde?"

Raul scrolled through the comments written below the YouTube video. Although many of the remarks were unintelligible since they were written in Spanish, he didn't need an interpreter to recognize the name Rolando mentioned time and time again.

"Surely there's more than one Rolando living in La Paz," Patrick said.

Another member of his team spoke up from the computer terminal to his left. "We cleaned up the video as best we could and got two relatively good stills of the man's face. We compared those to a mug shot we were able to procure from one of his arrests six years ago. It's not perfect, but we think it's a pretty good match. See for yourself."

The YouTube video feed was replaced with a side-by-side comparison of the two images – one of Rolando Velarde's mug shot and the other of the grainy still from the nightclub footage. There was no mistaking that the two men had the same narrowly-set eyes, broad nose, and thin lips. The heavily-gelled hairstyle was the same in both photographs, as were the thick sideburns.

"We have a call into the nightclub to see if they still have video surveillance from this particular night, but we haven't heard back from them yet."

Patrick considered Raul and his expectant posture. "Why didn't this man come up in any of our previous searches?"

Raul's gaze shifted. His focus turned to the rolled-up paper in his hands. "His name was on the birthday registry, but when we investigated him over a year ago, there was no indication that he possessed any psychic powers. This video is relatively new. It wasn't available when he was initially considered."

"So he was ruled out simply because you didn't have evidence of a known ability?"

"Correct." Raul rocked uncomfortably on his feet. Patrick enjoyed watching him squirm.

"But now it appears he's telekinetic?"

"Yes, sir."

"And he was born on February 7th?"

"Yes, sir."

"Do we have an exact location for him? His current address?"

Another member of the team spoke up. "No, sir. He's no longer at the address we had for him, but we're working on finding his new location. It's possible he's living with friends which would mean there'll be no tracible record of his whereabouts. We'll find him, though, I'm certain. With your permission, we'll send a search party to La Paz to track him down."

Patrick considered this possibility. "That won't be necessary," he said at last. "I'll take my own team. We'll find him ourselves."

CHAPTER

29

JOSE

Friday, November 11
Phoenix

There was something calming about having Thomas
and Salomon staying at his apartment. Being something
of a recluse his entire life, Jose had never really felt
close enough to any of his friends to consider sharing
the same living space and had always chosen to live
alone. He hoped, of course, to eventually move in with
Andrea when she was ready, but he had always secretly
harbored the suspicion that he wasn't going to take well
to another person living in his space. If the ease he felt
with Thomas and Salomon was any indication,
however, he wasn't going to have any problem at all.

He wasn't surprised to see Thomas already dressed
and at the dinette with a bowl of corn flakes when he
emerged from his bedroom Friday morning. Although
the three men had stayed up late discussing strategy the
night before, he already knew Thomas well enough to
understand that he wasn't going to stop until the man
responsible for his mother's death was dealt with

properly. Salomon, however, was still racked out on the floor beside the couch.

"D'you sleep at all?" Jose whispered to Thomas as he slid into the seat beside him at the table.

Thomas shook his head. "Not a lot. I'm exhausted, but my mind won't shut off. Not to mention I just keep feeling for indications that we're in danger. Us or the girls. I worry if I sleep that I'm gonna miss something, you know?"

He did know what it was like to worry over someone. He'd worried over Andrea every time she showed up in the emergency room. He understood that like himself Thomas was a man of action. It wasn't enough to stand by and wait for something to happen. He wanted to be proactive. He reached for a bowl off the counter and poured himself some flakes. "I was up quite a bit myself," he told Thomas quietly. "Trying to figure out how to cover our tracks now that we're buying six plane tickets to La Paz."

A groan sounded from the living room. "I'm awake," Salomon called groggily. "You do not need to whisper."

"Sorry," Jose called to him. "We were trying not to disturb you."

Salomon padded into the kitchen, his eyes bleary, his t-shirt askew. "It's quite alright." He looked at the bowls of cereal on the table and screwed his face into a grimace of contempt. "Where is the other breakfast? Why aren't we having those round things again?"

Jose couldn't keep from laughing. "Are you talking about the doughnuts Andrea brought?" he asked. "Because we ate the entire box yesterday."

"We ate them all?" Salomon lifted himself onto the counter. "Can we get more?"

Even Thomas cracked a smile. "I'm sure there's a Dunkin Donuts on the way to the airport. But don't come down too hard on the cornflakes. These are frosted. And they're grrrreat."

Salomon dipped his hand into the box and pulled out a fist full. "They're pretty good," he said after taking a bite. "Not as good as doughnuts, though."

The men crunched in contemplative silence, and Jose knew they were all thinking about the same thing.

"What if I open a bunch of credit cards in all of our names. Maybe two or three each. And then later this morning I'll use those cards to purchase a bunch of airline tickets for all different flights to a few different places over the next week or so. If they're tracking us via the credit cards it'll force them to pursue a dozen different leads to figure out where we're actually headed."

Thomas swallowed a mouthful of cereal and tapped his spoon against his bowl. "That's not a bad idea as long as they're tracking us through conventional methods. I'm just afraid Patrick might be using his psychic ability. Dalton told Mia there are rumors that he's got some sort of sixth sense, but who knows. Either way, how are we gonna afford all those tickets?"

Jose grinned. "I already thought of that. I'll just spend the extra for refundable tickets. We already know we're not gonna use them all so I just need to make sure I cancel the flights we don't use during the termination window. By that time, we'll be to La Paz and will hopefully have a plan for what we're going to do there. It'll buy us some time to get our heads together if nothing else."

"You're very smart," Salomon said through a mouthful of frosted flakes. "I say we do it. Hopefully, it will help cover the girls' tracks out of Belize as well." He scoffed then and regarded Thomas. "As far as Patrick Meyer's supposed abilities are concerned, I don't think we need to be all that worried. After all, if he was really that good, don't you think he would have tracked us down long before now?"

Jose drank the remaining milk from the bottom of his bowl and pushed up from the table. "Exactly. So I should get started on those credit card applications."

"No. Wait," Salomon said, grabbing Jose's arm as he placed his bowl in the sink. "There's something else that's still bothering me from last night. I think we need to finish our discussion about Rolando."

Jose poured himself a second cup of coffee and sat back down beside Thomas at the dinette. "Okay. You're the one who talked to the old woman about him. What's your gut say? I thought we decided he had to be dark. And when we get to La Paz we're gonna figure out how to hide him from the rest of the baddies."

Salomon nodded, his eyes narrowed deep in thought. "I know that's what we decided, but I can't stop thinking about the last thing Kamila said to me. She wanted me to know there's still a way."

"Still a way to stop the dark psychics?" Thomas asked, leaning his chair back on two legs.

"That's just the thing. I think she's telling us there's still a chance for the light psychics to fulfill the prophecy. She's a clairvoyant. I think she's seen the end. Knows how it all plays out. But like Lanying's grandfather told her, the keepers aren't supposed to interfere. I think she knows too much, though. I don't think she can stop herself."

Jose took a sip of his coffee, trying to follow Salomon's line of reasoning. He'd been told about Kate. About how she was the seventh light psychic and that the prophecy could no longer be fulfilled by them because she had died. "Do you think this Rolando guy might be light?"

"If he is then that would mean that Kate wasn't," Thomas said.

Salomon shook his head. "I was able to use the hairpins Kate gave Mia to see into her past. I saw her ability. She could control people. Get them to do what she wanted. And Mia confirmed she was light. She was definitely one of us."

"Unless she wasn't." He paused. "Unless I'm not." His place in the prophecy was something Jose had been considering since his return to Phoenix. That maybe instead of being a light psychic of the Sevens Prophecy, he was just a guy with a strange ability in the right place at the right time. "I mean, think about it. Lanying's a slam dunk. Her grandfather was a keeper. She's the one who saw the two of you and Donescia in her visions. And Thomas, you and Mia are obviously connected. I'm the odd one out here. Maybe this Rolando guy is a light psychic, and I'm just Jose, the overqualified candy striper."

Thomas glared at him. "That's crap. You're one of us. You showed up in Baltimore outta nowhere and landed at Mia's police station under her direct assignment." He rolled his eyes. "As if that's pure coincidence."

"If you're nervous about coming with us, you're welcome to stay behind," Salomon said. "I don't think any of us would blame you, especially since I get the feeling from Kamila that things are going to get ugly, and…"

Jose couldn't believe what he was hearing. "No. That's not it at all. I'm not opting out. I'm coming. I wasn't ever *not* coming. You think I'm gonna let the five of you go into this thing without me? Without my abilities?" The anger in his voice prevented Thomas and Salomon from being able to look him in the eye. He saw in that moment just how tired, anxious, and lost they all truly were and decided immediately he needed to let this one go. He sighed. "I'm sorry. It's just that I'm trying to make sense of this by playing out some different scenarios. If you guys were wrong about me maybe you were wrong about Kate too and that's how there's still a chance. I'm trying to think outside the box, but maybe there's not enough caffeine in the world for that type of thinking at this point."

Thomas raised his mug in a gesture of solidarity. "To caffeine."

"And doughnuts," Salomon added with a nod.

"And figuring out what the hell we're supposed to do next," Jose finished.

With all the necessary information at his disposal, setting up credit cards for everyone in the group proved to be astonishingly easy. Even Salomon, with his lack of income, was approved for an immediate low-limit, high-interest card. Just before lunch, he purchased six flights, three from Phoenix and three from Belize City, to El Alto International Airport located eight miles southwest of La Paz. He also purchased two dozen flights to various other locations scheduled for the coming week. Even still, as he clicked accept on the travel website, he worried that his efforts wouldn't be enough to help them outmaneuver the dark psychics.

With the final purchases made, he grabbed his car keys and called over his shoulder to the others on his way out the door. "Gonna go say goodbye to Andrea and my folks. And don't worry, I know not to tell them where we're going."

He found his parents in the kitchen of the restaurant, overwhelmed by the Friday afternoon lunch crowd.

"You're going where?" his mother asked as she sliced peppers for the fajitas.

"On a trip with Thomas and Salomon. I don't know how long I'll be gone. A couple weeks maybe."

"And these are the boys you met in Baltimore?"

It was all too much to explain so he decided to keep it simple rather than risk starting a conversation he wasn't ready to have. "Yeah. It's gonna be a guys' thing. I'll have my cell, though, and I'll be in touch."

"You've told Andrea?"

The screen door slammed in the rear of the kitchen. He turned to see Andrea laden with grocery bags entering the room. "Told Andrea what?" she asked, setting the bags on the counter beside the prep station.

"He's going out of town. With those boys you met in Baltimore."

She raised an eyebrow at him and something between sadness and confusion crossed her face. This certainly wasn't how he planned to tell her, and she obviously wasn't thrilled about the method of conveyance or the message. His leaving should not have come as a shock, however, as she knew about the prophecy and the reason for Thomas and Salomon's presence. "This is news," she said briskly, unloading a head of lettuce from the bag.

He crossed the kitchen to help, following her into the large walk-in refrigerator with a stack of freshly cut steaks. "I'm sorry," he said when they were out of earshot from his parents. "Maybe I should've called, but I wanted to tell you in person. I had no idea you'd be out at the store when I got here. I planned on telling you first."

Her back was to him as she rearranged produce on a shelf to make room for the lettuce. "It's fine," she said, her chin lowering. "It's just that if you're going where I think you're going, then I'm scared for you, that's all. And I honestly didn't think you'd be leaving so soon. Don't you need time to plan?"

He set the steaks on a shelf and gathered her into his arms. She immediately folded herself into his chest, shuddering against him. He wasn't sure if her reaction was due to her emotions or the chill of the refrigerator, but he relished her warmth just the same. "Probably," he told her. "But there's an urgency surrounding all of this I can't really explain. I know the others feel it too, like we're being pushed forward by something we can't see. It's like a nagging feeling in the back of your mind that won't leave you alone. Picking. Picking. Picking. I just know if we have any chance of stopping the dark psychics, we need to get there soon. So we're leaving tonight, after dinner."

She slid her arms up under his shirt and his skin prickled at her touch. She traced his ribs with her fingertips, her face still pressed against his chest. "I know you don't want to tell me where you're going, and that scares the crap outta me because I'm smart enough to know why. If the dark psychics come here looking for you, you want me to be able to honestly tell them I don't know where you are. Plausible deniability. But if these people are that dangerous, Jose, how do I know you'll be safe?"

He took her chin in his hand to lift up her face, forcing himself to answer for his actions. He couldn't lie to her. He also couldn't tell her the truth. "Andrea, I have the ability to heal. So promise me you'll try not to worry. I'll call you when I can, and hopefully, I won't be gone for very long." Tears pooled in the corners of her eyes. She looked wholly unconvinced. "Seriously. I'll be fine."

She pursed her lips into a tight line before saying, "You have the ability to heal. But who's in charge of healing you?"

She was right, of course. He could heal any number of living things, from houseplants to pigeons to other people. What he couldn't do was heal himself. "It's not going to come to that. Please don't cry. I promise nothing bad is going to happen." He said the words without thinking, before considering whether it was the sort of oath he could keep. But she responded before he could take it back.

"Ask me again," she said, holding him tight.

He had no idea what she was talking about. "Ask you what?"

"That question you asked me after my first culinary class, the night I took the job here at the restaurant."

He remembered the occasion, of course. It was a night of many firsts. Her first class. Her first job as a line chef. The first time she stayed overnight at his place. "I asked you a lot of questions that night," he teased her now, encouraged by the direction of the conversation.

229

A small smile played at her lips. "You know which question I'm talking about." She pinched him gently on the chest. "Ask. Me. Again."

There was no mistaking the desperation in her voice. "You're serious?"

She nodded.

"You want me to ask?"

She nodded again.

He almost couldn't believe what he was about to do, but he'd spent enough time around people in the emergency room to know desperate times often resulted in desperate acts. He certainly wasn't going to deny her.

Without another word, he pried her from under his shirt, taking a step back before lowering himself onto one knee. He recalled what he'd said to her on that night of firsts and did his best to repeat it, word for word. "Andrea Morillo, I love you. I've loved you since the day I first saw you, bruised and broken in the ER. I knew then I would do whatever it took to heal you. What I didn't realize at the time was how determined you were to heal yourself. I know you want the time and space to do that, and I will continue to give you as much of both as you need. But when you're finally whole, I would like to know if you'd make me the happiest man on earth by being my wife?"

Her arms were drawn across her chest, and she shivered without his body to keep her warm. Her expression was soft, wistful even, and he was certain this time she wouldn't ask for more time to make her decision.

"Yes," she whispered. "Yes, I'll be your wife." She took his hand, pulling him up off the floor. "But now you don't have a choice. You have to come home.

You have to be safe. Because now you have a very important engagement to keep."

CHAPTER
30

PATRICK

Friday, November 11
London

Wesley's veins bulged down his neck. "What do you mean Eshanti's gone? Where the hell did she go?"

"More importantly, why did she leave?" Lillian added.

The six remaining dark psychics were gathered around the study in preparation for the evening meal. In the past, Patrick enjoyed this gathering time. It gave him an opportunity to decompress from the events of the day before dining. Tonight, however, there would be no repose. The others were at his throat.

"She left this morning," he told them matter-of-factly. "Of her own accord, I might add. She's returned to Mumbai. Good riddance, I say."

Wesley paced the room, stomping around like a wild beast. "You're the reason she left, Patrick. It certainly wasn't 'of her own accord' as you suggest. You drove her away with your inquisition and invasion of privacy. You made her feel unwelcome. Another

232

roadblock on the road to fulfillment courtesy of you and your control issues."

Patrick made a show of rolling his eyes in disgust. He certainly wasn't going to be reprimanded in his own home for something as inconsequential as Eshanti's departure, but he was loathe to defend himself, especially to Wesley, who, quite honestly, wasn't worth the breath. "She's not one of us. She's not part of the prophecy. She never was. But there's someone else who is. I'm certain of it. And I've already found him."

Wesley quit pacing, stopping directly in front of where Patrick was sitting in his favorite wingback, brandy sniffer in hand. "Here we go again," he said, crossing his arms to his chest. "Can't wait to hear this load of crap."

Patrick refused to let Wesley ruffle him. He still needed the bastard, if only for another day. He only needed to retrain himself until they arrived in La Paz. Until they found Rolando. Until they fulfilled the prophecy.

Then he would shut Wesley up once and for all. Eshanti would be second in line.

"Now, now, Wesley, let's display a little more couth, shall we?" He took a sip of the brandy. It burned the back of his throat. He relished the heat. "Thanks to my dogged perseverance to the cause, I have located the seventh dark psychic in La Paz, Bolivia. We're all leaving first thing in the morning. Five o'clock sharp. With any luck, tonight's dinner will be the last under the old regime. Perhaps by this time tomorrow the prophecy will finally be fulfilled."

Javier cleared his throat from where he sat on the edge of an adjacent settee. "Bolivia? Are you sure?"

"Yes. Quite," Patrick said, setting down his glass on the sideboard. "His name is Rolando Velarde. He shares our birthdate. He has a psychic ability. He has a criminal record. He's the one we've been searching for." He leaned forward for dramatic effect, capitalizing on their anticipation. "In fact," he continued, "one of Eshanti's most recent paintings was of a storefront. I've traced it to a location in La Paz. The prophecy is as good as fulfilled."

There was a beat of silence while everyone considered his revelation. Then Wesley let out a snort. "You've gotta be kidding. You've had this sort of certainty about everyone. I remember you saying the same thing about Eshanti, what a perfect match she was, and we all know how you feel about her now."

Patrick felt his face flush, heat rising to his cheeks. "Rolando is different. He's not a fraud like Eshanti. And once we get to Bolivia, he will help us fulfill the prophecy once and for all."

Javier coughed uncomfortably. "Do you think it might be prudent for us to bring her along with us to La Paz? Just in case."

Patrick couldn't believe what he was hearing. After all the work. All the long hours. All the dedication to their cause. Now Javier was questioning his judgement about Eshanti? It was nothing short of offensive.

"I've made my decision about Eshanti. She isn't one of us. She never was. Her inclusion in our group was a mistake from the beginning. I don't want any of us to speak her name again." He gazed around the room, making eye contact with each of them. They needed to understand. "We don't need her in La Paz. She's not welcome."

Lillian crossed the room, perched herself on the arm of his chair, and draped her legs across his. She was in seduction mode. Her default setting. It made Patrick sick.

"Now are you positive about this, Sugar? Have you felt her disloyalty with your ability?" Her Southern drawl was like honey and it stuck to his brain, muddling it. "Because from where I'm sitting she's never done wrong by us. I personally think we should bring her along."

Thankful that she was actually physically present instead of just a mirage, Patrick pushed her off his lap, spilling her onto the floor. She landed with a thump, heels to the sky. Javier ran to her defense and helped her to her feet.

"What the hell?" she said, smoothing her skirt as she took a step back. "Have you gone mad?"

"Well, now you're not sitting anymore," Patrick said through gritted teeth. "So maybe you'll see things differently. Maybe you'll see things my way, at least if you know what's best for you."

Her eyes narrowed. Seductive Lillian was gone. He liked her better this way. "Are you threatening me, Patrick?"

He smiled. He couldn't help it. Seeing her angry was just too satisfying. Was he threatening her? Probably not. She posed no real danger to his future endeavors. She was like a lap dog. All bark, no bite. Just the same, he wasn't going to give her the satisfaction of a direct response. "You're excused, Lillian. You're obviously in no capacity to strategize. Let's let the men discuss the details of how we're going to find Rolando, shall we? I'll have one of the staff take your dinner up to your room."

She surprised him then, holding her ground, even taking a step forward. "I have as much to gain as you do from the fulfillment. And I sure as hell won't be sidelined by the likes of you. So if you're ready to strategize, let's strategize. How do you plan on us finding this Rolando?"

Patrick had to admit he was impressed. Lillian standing up for herself was something new. Something unexpected. It was sort of a turn on. He'd need to file this image of her away for later. But in the meantime, she was right. They needed to discuss the specifics of locating Rolando.

He took a calculated sip of his brandy. "We'll leave in the morning. Head to the store straightaway. I'm quite certain that's where we'll find Rolando. Meanwhile, I've called in a couple of favors from some cartel connections in South America as a precautionary measure. They know how to find people. Even ones who don't want to be found."

Lillian let out an exasperated groan. "So it's okay to use Eshanti's paintings to locate Rolando even though you're certain she's not a prophetic psychic? That's wildly hypocritical, Patrick. You know that, right?"

In that moment, looking at Lillian standing in the middle of the room, hands on her hips in abject defiance, he knew what he was going to do to her once the prophecy was fulfilled. He would do to her what she feared the most, and he would make her beg him to stop. Because it didn't matter what she thought about him. And it didn't matter what she thought about Eshanti. He hated the Indian woman. And that alone was enough to exclude her going forward.

CHAPTER

31

DONESCIA

Saturday, November 12
Belize

Donescia folded the last of her skirts into the only travel bag she owned, the one she used to carry her belongings from the mainland to the island and back again each month. It was also the bag she used when she traveled to the United States to speak to congress about the effects of climate change on reef ecosystems. While there'd been absolutely no trepidation associated with that trip, to say that she was unconvinced that she was making the right decision about this trip, traveling with the two strange women to Bolivia, was an understatement.

It was outlandish enough that they would ask her to go back with them to the United States, but when they arrived this morning to tell her they'd be going to South America instead, she'd almost changed her mind altogether. It was insane, leaving her job and her family behind to follow these strangers into what sounded like a dangerous situation. That she was being hunted by dark psychics was terrifying, but when she overheard the women discussing what happened to their friend Thomas's mother, she almost told them she wasn't going to go.

But then, she considered the alternative. If bad people were coming after her, the same bad people who murdered Thomas's mother, she owed the women a huge debt. She certainly had no way to protect herself on the island, and so perhaps it was better that she left with them. She knew about the strength of numbers. It had saved her more times than she could count. She just hoped putting distance between them would be enough to protect the other inhabitants of the island. She couldn't stand the thought of anyone accidentally getting hurt because of her.

She fastened the zipper on the top of her bag and worried again that she would be cold in Bolivia. Mia had assured her that they would purchase whatever warm clothing she needed, but she didn't like the idea of someone else having to take care of her. The warm breeze blew through the window of her modestly furnished room, and she paused beside the now empty dresser to look out beyond the small breakers to where she knew the reef lay hidden on a shallow sandbar. She couldn't help but think back to what brought her to the reef in the first place. The reef she hoped would survive a short time without her.

The summer before her eleventh birthday, Donescia had learned of her ability to control water; it's movement, form, location, and most importantly, temperature. The discovery of her gift had been quite accidental, and now, as she checked her purse for her passport and identification for what seemed like the hundredth time, she smiled, thinking about the day when her family's ancient refrigerator died in the middle of a blistering summer heat wave. Her mother had just bought a large cut of beef from the market which she intended to cut into smaller portions and freeze for later. Without a working refrigerator, however, she lamented that the roast would go to waste. While Donescia and her father washed dishes together, he had commented that he wished they had a way to make ice, and with the innocence only a child can possess, Donescia had placed her hands in the sudsy dishwater and tried. Immediately, the water froze into a solid block.

Her family had never questioned her strange powers, and although they were quick to use them to their benefit, they cautioned her about showing off her abilities to others. Sadly, this counsel fell on deaf ears, and it wasn't long before she was branded as a purveyor of black magic. Initially, she was only verbally ridiculed and harassed by strangers. But after several weeks, even her friends started throwing trash at her as she walked to and from school. She couldn't blame her siblings for avoiding her after that.

Her father, however, tried his best to protect her. On one occasion, he took her to an ice cream shop in the tourist district for her birthday. It was a tradition, something they had done together every year for as long as she could remember. This was the first time, however, that her best friend Paulita hadn't tagged along. It had been a somber occasion, despite the celebratory milestone, and they walked back home in silence, her ice cream barely touched, melting down the side of her cone.

She hadn't noticed the group of boys waiting on the stoop at the far end of the street. She hadn't known they were waiting for her. She didn't realize how much hatred some people held for her simply because she was different. Simply because there was something about her they did not understand.

She'd been unprepared for their attack and so had her father. But as she closed her eyes now, inhaling the salty, humid sea air, she knew she'd made the right decision all those years ago, escaping the mainland in favor of the peaceful isolation of the atoll. She'd made a life for herself, with the help of her abilities and the Oceanic Society, but life on the island wasn't perfect. She was alone. A lot. Which is probably why when Mia and Lanying showed up out of nowhere and offered her something resembling friendship for the first time in fifteen years, she jumped at the opportunity instead of allowing skepticism to prevail.

She hoped now, as she took one last look at the room which had served as her home for over a decade and shut the door behind her that this decision to follow the other psychics to Bolivia would also prove to be the right one.

She found Mia and Lanying waiting for her at the large table in the center of the palapa, bags at their feet, worried expressions on their faces. Mia stood when she saw her enter the room.

"All ready to go then?" she asked. Her voice carried the same trepidation as her eyes. They thought she was going to change her mind. They thought she was going to back out.

"Yah," she told them, placing her own ratty bag in the pile with the others. "Ah made mah peace wit it. An afta talkin wit yah friend Thomas an hearin bout his momma, ah can't risk stayin here."

"You're making the right decision," Lanying said kindly. "I know how unbelievable all this is. And I know how hard it is leaving home to do something so unimaginable. But Mia and I and all the others... we support you. And we need you to be a part of this with us."

The sound of a pot being dropped in the kitchen echoed through the space, and they turned toward the sound. Donescia caught a glimpse of one of the research assistants through the door. "Yah think all ah di others ah gonna be safe?" she whispered.

Mia nodded as she got to her feet. "Yes. Jose's concocted a plan to steer the dark psychics in other directions. He's opening credit cards in each of our names and purchasing refundable flights with them to several different locations. Let's hope they track you leaving the island and don't bother to come here at all."

"But we all goin tah Bolivia?"

Lanying took up Donescia's bag with her own. "Yes. They'll figure it out eventually so it probably won't buy us much time, but hopefully it'll be enough to get us through to the next step."

"And wat is di next step?"

She saw an apprehensive glance pass between the women as they headed out of the palapa toward the dock. Mia shrugged. "We don't know exactly. But six heads are better than five, so hopefully you'll be able to help us figure it out."

There was a sincerity in the woman's voice that put Donescia at ease. Here she was, leaving the only life she'd ever known to go on some ridiculous journey in the hopes of keeping the world from falling into darkness. With people she'd known for less than a week. To a city she'd never even heard of until this morning.

And yet, something deep inside compelled her to step onto the boat. Three hours later, the same surreal sensation of peace lured her onto the plane. She sat in the window seat as the wheels lifted off the tarmac, the sky rose up to meet her, and for the first time in her life, she felt as though she was exactly where she was supposed to be.

CHAPTER

32

LANYING

Saturday, November 12
In Route to La Paz, Bolivia

Maybe it was the altitude. Maybe it was the hypnotic hum of the jet engines or the dim cabin lighting. Whatever the reason, for the second time at 30,000 feet in the air, Lanying was unexpectedly spirited away to another location while watching her in-flight movie.

As the cheesy chick flick and surrounding passengers faded away, she found herself in a dank back alley, complete with the requisite trash bins and sewage runoff. The surrounding buildings were squat with adobe roofs and crumbling plaster walls. They were so unlike the modern high rises of Shanghai or the brick facades of Baltimore, she was certain she wasn't anywhere she'd visited before, in real life or otherwise. Like always, she waited for the person she'd been sent to observe to appear, but when no one emerged in the alley after several seconds, she got impatient and began looking around for more clues regarding her whereabouts. She craned her neck following the alley's sightline out to where it met with a larger, cobblestone street and was shocked to see a snow-capped mountain range guarding the city like a sentient defender.

I'm in La Paz, she thought to herself as she turned her attention back toward a door which was opening at the back of the closest building. Three boorish-looking men tumbled into the street, shouting at each other in Spanish. Although she knew they couldn't see or touch her, she recoiled, an involuntary reaction to their aggressive behavior. Within moments, it became obvious that two of the men were in clear opposition to the third as they were forcibly removing him from the building. The evicted man was of medium build with a broad nose, thin lips, and narrowly set eyes which glared viciously at his assailants as he continued to shout. The other two men were far larger than the third, but despite the considerable size advantage, still seemed wary of their target. Lanying wasn't surprised when their raised voices drew the attention of pedestrians out on the street, but when a Caucasian woman turned into the alley, camera in hand, to inquire about what was going on, she was met with the barrel of a handgun.

"Sal de aquí!" one of them called to her, his voice echoing off the surrounding structures. The eyewitness scurried back onto the street without any further provocation.

Alone again, the three men stared at one another. The presence of the weapon seemed to suppress the third man, whose eyes darted nervously around the space. Lanying watched as a loose brick lifted off the street behind them and sailed into the air, cracking the gunman in the back of the head. He fell to his knees, dropping the gun as another brick launched itself at the second man. The smaller man dove for the gun, snatching it off the pavement just as the first man returned to his feet. He pointed the pistol at his attackers, who raised their hands in a show of submission as they back toward the door.

"Ve adentro. No vuelva a salir," he told them, brandishing the gun in their direction, motioning them back from where they'd come.

In one smooth motion, the men disappeared into the building, leaving the third man alone in the street. She watched him eye his surroundings, nervously checking over his shoulder at the street beyond and the closed door as he tucked the weapon in the waistband of his jeans and hurried to the back corner of the alley. He slid a trash bin to the side and crouched down, feeling along the edge of the wall for something. He cursed under his breath, his face red with frustration as he pushed a stack of crates over, jostling for more room to maneuver. Finally, after another minute, he cried out, and in addition to a void in the wall where he'd removed a loose brick, she could see a box about the size of a dictionary in his hands. He set the box aside as he replaced the brick and returned the crates and the trash bin to their original locations. Then, after another wary glance at the door, he opened the box to inspect its contents, lifting a plastic baggie of what appeared to be white powder from within.

The man pocketed the contents of the box, and Lanying's mind spun with possibilities. If she was indeed in La Paz as she suspected, she could only assume, given the paranormal nature of the soaring bricks, that the man standing before her was Rolando. Since learning of the prophecy, her visions had all been related to its fulfillment in some way. The only psychics she'd ever seen, however, had all been light. Thomas was light. Salomon was light. Donescia was light. Perhaps this vision indicated Rolando was light as well. If so, what would this mean for the fulfillment? She suddenly wished she had Mia's ability to see the state of his soul. Then she would know for certain.

As she watched him bury the box in the bottom of a trashcan beneath a pile of rubbish and make an awkward attempt to fix his hair with his hands, she searched her own intuition for an indication about his allegiance. The entire episode implied a dark nature. The physical confrontation with the other men. The ease with which he held the firearm. His knowledge of the hidden box. The drugs inside. But as she forced herself to see beyond the obvious indications, she acknowledged that it was possible he was light. Perhaps the men who cast him from the building were criminals. Perhaps there was a justifiable reason he knew the location of the box. Perhaps he was delivering the drugs to the authorities.

Perhaps, like Mia, he was an officer of the law, working undercover in some capacity.

Rolando made his way to the end of the alley where it bled into the street. He paused at the corner, glancing to his left and right as if he was looking for something or someone. He took a phone out of his pocket and placed a call. The conversation was in Spanish, of course, so she was unable to understand any of what he was saying. What she recognized with conviction, however, was the tone of his voice and his body language. He sounded angry. Flustered.

And beneath all of that, scared.

If he was a cop, he wouldn't sound scared, she thought to herself. He'd be relieved at finding the drugs and escaping unharmed.

When he finished the call, he disconnected and turned the corner, disappearing from sight. Seconds later, the alley faded away and the interior cabin of the plane returned. To her right, Donescia sat wrapped in a colorful sarong with her chin resting heavily on her chest. Her breathing was slow and shallow, sound asleep. To her left, Mia was typing frantically on her computer. She appeared to be catching up on paperwork from her caseload.

"I think I was just in La Paz," she whispered to her, leaning close enough that their shoulders were touching.

Mia looked up from her screen in alarm. "Just now? You had a vision?"

Lanying nodded. "And I think I may have gotten our first look at Rolando." She proceeded to explain to Mia what she'd seen and shared her thoughts about his possible ulterior motives.

"It's got to be him," Mia said when she was finished. "The flying bricks are proof enough for me. God how I wish I could've seen him, though. One quick glance is all I'll need."

"I had the same thought," she said. "I also wish I had the ability to move around inside my visions like Salomon can. I would have loved to have followed him or even gotten out of the alley to get a better idea of where I was in the city. All I have to go on is the view of the mountain range. Once we get there I can probably orient myself with them and get a general idea, but it definitely won't be anywhere specific enough to do us any good."

Mia closed out her computer file and shut the laptop as a flight attendant came by with the beverage service. They took their plastic cups and ordered a water for Donescia when she finally woke.

"Regardless of Rolando's affiliation, I think we're going to have to count on Salomon's keeper Kamila to help us find him," Mia said once the attendants were passed. "Let's just hope Salomon knows how to find her outside of a vision. If he can't, it won't matter if he's dark or light, especially if Patrick Meyer and his crew get to him first."

Lanying took a sip of her cranberry juice. "What'll we do once we find him?"

Mia closed her eyes as if the weight of their burden made it too difficult to even keep them open. She rubbed at her temples with the pads of her fingers and sighed. "I don't know exactly," she said at last. "I wish I did. The good news is what you saw him with was probably cocaine. Bolivia has powerful anti-drug laws, specifically with regard to the manufacture and sale of cocaine. The box probably contained a sample hidden for him by a cartel operative. If he's bad, he might be one of their go-betweens."

"And having drugs in his possession would be enough for us to have him arrested, effectively sheltering him from Patrick?"

"Maybe. If we could prove it. But like you said, he might be good. Maybe he's undercover, trying to bring down the operation." She shrugged. "Either way, it's a start."

Lanying considered her friend, impressed as always by her wealth of knowledge. That she knew of Bolivian regulations and drug cartels in addition to American law enforcement spoke not only to her intelligence but also to her dedication.

"You really think Rolando could be light?" she asked.

Mia sipped her soda. "Stranger things have happened. And since we have no way of knowing definitively until I see him with my own eyes, I think it would be prudent to keep an open mind. Besides, you said yourself you've only ever had visions of light psychics." She adjusted herself in her seat, crossing and recrossing her legs, trying to find a comfortable position. "Salomon said the keeper told him there's still a way. Maybe Rolando is that way."

Lanying leaned back on her headrest, remembering the first keeper in her life – her grandfather - the man who'd believed in her before she knew there was even something to believe in. As she had so many times since his passing, she called to mind his final words, when he asked her to promise that she would never lose hope. Had he known a sense of pervasive hopelessness would overwhelm them by the end? Or had he found something in his years of research to indicate the light would eventually prevail?

She felt for his presence now in the airspace above Central America and was surprised when a sense of calm washed over her. It was almost as if she could feel his hand on hers, his gentle voice encouraging her to go on, no matter what. And with a sudden, certain understanding, he knew she could face whatever obstacles lay ahead in Bolivia.

CHAPTER

33

SALOMON

Sunday, November 13
La Paz, Bolivia

Although they'd procured separate sleeping accommodations for the men and women at the rustically affordable Hostal Republica in the heart of downtown La Paz, the six light psychics had voluntarily sequestered themselves together in the women's room. Salomon was certain the others felt much the same way he did; now they were finally all together, none of them wanted to be apart.

Mia had procured a pack of Post-it notes from the check-in desk of the hostel and had begun slapping them on the wall with great efficiency. Little squares of yellow already covered most of the space between the door and the only piece of framed art in the room — a burro with a collar of orange lilies. "We need to write down everything we know. All of our leads. All of our loose ends. We can't just wing it tomorrow so we need a plan going forward." The enthusiasm in her voice was infectious, and she smiled around the room at them - to

Thomas and Jose sprawled out across the sagging mattresses, Lanying and Donescia sitting opposite one another at a small wooden table on the other side of the door, and Salomon perched atop a rogue stool they'd discovered in the hallway. "Who's first?" she asked.

Thomas spoke up, straightening himself on the bed with his back against the headboard. "We know Patrick Meyer and the dark psychics are coming after us. Back in Phoenix, I didn't feel any danger. Not even a twinge. Now that we're here in La Paz, though, it's growing in intensity. But I haven't had any auditory hallucinations like I did back in Baltimore, so I'm taking that as a sign that we still have some time."

Mia scribbled notes onto a Post-it.

"If he's coming here he must be tracking us. I guess the decoy flights weren't enough to deflect his attention," Jose lamented.

"Maybe," Mia said, still writing feverishly with her pen. "Or maybe he knows about Rolando. He might be coming here for him, not us."

"It doesn't matter why he's coming," Lanying added, sounding slightly exasperated. "Only that he is. He's hunting down dark and light psychics. Which means, if Thomas is starting to feel the danger already, we need to track down Rolando right away. I saw him with drugs. We should go to the police and let them know. Maybe we can have him arrested before Patrick gets here."

Mia chewed on the end of her pen. "Unfortunately, we're going to need more information about him before we're able to do that. We don't even know his last name or where it is that you saw him with the drugs. The local authorities will laugh us out the door if we go to them with a first name and a story about a psychic vision. We need to find him first."

All eyes turned to Salomon.

"I've already told you everything Kamila shared. His first name. That he's part of the prophecy. She didn't tell me if he's light or dark or where he lives. I suppose we're going to need to figure that part out on our own."

Lanying picked at her cuticle as she scrolled furiously on her tablet's screen. "There are hundreds of Rolando's listed as living in La Paz. We don't have the time or manpower to trace down every lead."

"We need to find Kamila. She's the only lead that matters," Thomas said, turning to Salomon. "And you're our only connection to her. I think, now that we're here, there's only one thing to do."

The weight of this responsibility rested heavily on Salomon's shoulders. But he was a man who was experienced with the stress of hefty burdens. He'd spent his entire life being responsible for other people - his siblings, wife, and extended family, not to mention the well-being of his entire tribe. He was chosen to attend university. He was chosen for the coveted position at World Vision. He was the one his people turned to when they needed nourishment, financial assistance, and medical intervention.

In all these tasks, however, he had ultimately failed. He no longer held his job at World Vision. His entire family perished in the rebel attack. He thought of them now – his sister Manu, blind to the truth of her unfulfilled potential; how much life she had ahead of her, stripped away in the blink of an eye. His wife Keicha, a Women for Women International Program graduate whose zest for life and thirst for knowledge made her his perfect life partner. He would never again lay awake beside her in the stillness of the night, whispering secret aspirations, afraid, if spoken too loudly, they would never come to pass. But of course, she was gone too, and in her absence, all that was left was the prophecy and the five other people sitting in the room with him. He knew he could not fail at what he was now called to do.

He grabbed his bag from where it lay on the floor beside the door. He knew exactly where the relic was hidden, at the very bottom beneath his stack of folded clothing, wrapped protectively in a thick linen cloth. He felt for it now and brought it into the light.

"I'll see if I can find her. See if she can tell me where we can find him."

The others nodded at him in silent recognition of this pivotal moment. He saw the truth mirrored in their eyes, that he was the only one capable of getting the information they needed in the hopes of continuing on. Without him, they were at the mercy of fate. And Patrick Meyer.

He let the cloth slip away and held the carving in both hands.

Instead of materializing near Kamila's shop, on the familiar market street with its merchandise-lined storefronts, he found himself in a large public square anchored by an imposing-looking cathedral on one side and wide ascending steps on the other. He could imagine the space as a gathering place for the locals, where they could congregate for celebration and protest, trade and barter.

On this occasion, however, the plaza was strangely empty, completely devoid of life. Not even a lone pigeon could be seen searching beneath a nearby bench, hoping to find a morsel of food in someone's abandoned lunch wrapper. Instead, what he saw forced the air from his lungs and brought him to his knees.

Enormous pits marred the façades of the cathedral and surrounding buildings where chunks of brick, mortar, and plaster had been eradicated by some unknown force. The resulting burn patterns suggested a fire or surge of electricity was responsible for the catastrophic damage. Flames still smoldered in several buildings around the perimeter of the square, and the air was thick with the acrid stench of consumption. Salomon heard sirens wailing in the distance, but it was quite obvious they would arrive far too late to be of any assistance to those who remained. Although the entire area was submerged in almost a foot of water, he could still make out the outlines of the six bodies lying just beneath the surface.

He knew instinctively whose faces would be staring wide-eyed at him as he gathered the courage to venture closer to where they lay, forcing himself to take step after agonizing step in their direction. He had to know. He had to be sure.

Donescia was the first, her floral skirt floating weightlessly atop the shallow pool in which she laid. Her hair was singed, her hands charred into unrecognizable nubs. The sight of her brought back images of his family, of his tribesmen, and the scorched aftermath of the rebel attack on his village. His stomach churned angrily, but he suppressed the urge to be sick and continued on to yet another body floating just beyond an overturned food cart to his left.

He found Thomas and Lanying. Jose and Mia. But at the sight of his own broken body, which appeared to have been cooked from the inside out, he dropped the carving, releasing him from the vision's painful display.

The others were immediately at his side, talking over one another and helping him to the bed where they forced him to lie down. Lanying disappeared from view while the rest stood fretting over him, and he was relieved when she returned quickly, placing a damp washrag gently across his forehead. "Take deep, slow breaths," she instructed him. "We don't want you to hyperventilate."

Out of the corner of his eye, he could see Jose pacing alongside the bed, shaking his head with a deeply furrowed brow. "That was the craziest thing I've ever seen," he said. "And I've seen some crazy stuff walk into the ER. It was like the most bizarre seizure ever."

"I know. I couldn't get the damn thing outta his hand," Thomas was saying to Jose. "He had a death grip on it."

Lanying was on the bed beside him now, her face just inches from his, cooing at him the way his mother had when he was a child. He was grateful for both her proximity and the calm of her voice. "It's okay," she said, as much to everyone else as to Salomon. "You're here with us now. You're safe."

"What the hell happened?" Mia asked from her position at his feet.

What had happened? he thought to himself. For a moment, he could barely remember, as if his mind was trying to protect him from the horror of the experience. It was all very fuzzy. The smell of smoke. The memory of water. A crumbling façade. But slowly, with great concentration, as if coming out of a fog, an image of his own ashen face bubbled to the surface.

"We all die," he sputtered.

Everyone fell silent.

"Eventually?" Lanying breathed. "Or in the immediate future?"

Blood pulsed inside his ears and temples. He worked to steady his breathing. "Here. In La Paz. In some plaza or square. There was a big church. A bunch of steps. Fire. Electricity. Water."

No one spoke. No one moved. A car horn blared on the adjacent street.

"Were the others there? The dark psychics?"

He shook his head.

"Kamila?"

"No," he said.

"And you're certain we were dead?" Thomas asked, his voice close to breaking. He saw Mia steady his body against her own.

"Yes. All six of us," he said, pushing the vision of their corpses from his mind to focus on a pleasant memory instead - the softness of his wife's skin. At night, in sleep, he dreamt of her. Of a time when they would be together again, side by side, as partners. Of a time when he needed only to reach out his hand to feel the comfort of her warmth. But that time was not now. Now was the time for redemption and healing. Now was the time to be the man he was destined to be. "But we cannot lose hope," he continued, pushing himself up on the bed. "Because my gift is limited. I channel visions from objects, but I'm no clairvoyant. I do not predict what is to come, only what the lifeless thing would have me see. And so maybe I've been shown this vision as a warning. As a way for us to avoid this destructive end. Let us not despair but celebrate this insight as a gift. If we want to survive, we need only to choose a different path."

CHAPTER
34

LANYING

Sunday, November 13
La Paz, Bolivia

"So we're up against fire and possibly electricity." Mia was talking more to herself than the others, her pen at the ready in her hand. She locked eyes with Thomas as she continued, a look of anguish contorting her face. "The fire isn't a surprise, given the tragedy in Baltimore, and is something we can hopefully protect ourselves against. But the electricity is scary stuff. I don't have a solution for how to fight it."

From the wall between the beds, a clock ticked off the seconds both too quickly and too slowly for Lanying. On one hand, the threat of confrontation loomed over her, causing time to drag. Was it wrong for her to simply wish to get on with whatever was coming regardless of the outcome, just to have it done? The waiting and not knowing were enough to drive anyone mad. On the other hand, while they were still without a viable plan, each passing moment was a precious commodity. She knew if they were going to stand a chance against the dark psychics, they needed as much time to conspire as they could possibly get.

"From what I could tell from the vision, Donescia used her water to battle the fire and did so quite effectively. I suppose we weren't counting on the electricity…"

"Which conducted through the water we were standing in and electrocuted us all," Thomas said, finishing Salomon's thought.

He nodded. "Our feet were singed. Bodies bloated. As if we cooked from within."

"So how dah wi put out di fire wid out di wada?" Donescia asked from where she'd been listening at the table. She'd been so quiet throughout their discussions, Lanying had assumed incorrectly that everyone's accents had prevented her from following along. It was clear now that she was thoroughly engaged.

She thought for a moment about the significance of the question before replying. "Would it be possible for you to hold the water off the ground? Could you extinguish the fire and keep the water away from us at the same time?"

Domescia nodded. "Yah. Suppose I cud."

A smile tug at the corner of Mia's lips. "Yeah. Of course. We didn't know about the electricity so it would make sense that Donescia just let the water fall to the ground. If she holds it at bay or redirects it away from us, we might stand a better chance."

"Or better still," Lanying said. "She could submerge the dark psychics with water so they electrocute themselves."

"Good thinking. But I bet they'd be smart enough not to try to use the electricity if they're wet," Mia said, jotting down their ideas on the wall. "It might not be a way to stop them, but it might be enough to keep them from killing us."

Salomon chuckled gruffly. "Well, that's a better outcome than we had ten minutes ago."

Donescia cleared her throat from the corner. "Don't mean teh sound stupid, but watta bout di man here. Rolando? Iffin hees wunna dem, maybe wat Salomon sees is di end. Di end ah di world."

The room was silent, everyone considering the possibility. Lanying wished for the hundredth time that her grandfather was there to counsel and advise. *What should we do?* she thought to herself.

And then, just like that, she knew.

"In my last vision, I saw Rolando near the mountain range from a specific vantage point. Let's start using the three-hundred-sixty-degree street feature on Google Maps to pinpoint his location and go from there. Salomon, you should do the same with your visions of Kamila. We have the technology. Let's use it to our advantage."

She slipped her laptop out of her bag and booted it up while Mia did the same for Salomon. "We'll head out to whichever location one of you feels the most confident about first," she said. "A friendly competition."

It felt strangely comforting to be beside Salomon, back in front of their respective computer screens searching for a way forward. She picked a random location in the center of the city to place her icon and let the screen shift to the street view. She moved the cursor to the right, panning the camera as far to the east as it would go before scanning left in the opposite direction. It was clear from the image of the mountain range that she was nowhere near her intended location.

What she did surmise, however, was that she had chosen a location which was too far outside the city. The place she was looking for was more densely populated.

She tried again, placing the little yellow figure slightly to the north.

And then to the west.

And then a little further west.

Slowly she began closing in on an area that resembled the location of her vision.

"I've got it!" Salomon cried out from the bed beside her, nearly knocking the computer off his lap. "This is the place I found Kamila. Here is the shop."

Everyone, including Lanying, crowded around Salomon, peering over his shoulders at the computer screen. Sure enough, the street appeared as Salomon had described it, with cobbled pavers and wind-beaten flags leading to each of the merchants.

"Adivino? What does that mean?" Thomas asked, pointed at the signage.

"It means fortune teller," Salomon explained.

Mia tapped her pen against her thigh. "And you're sure this is where we can find her?"

He nodded.

Mia turned to her. "How close are you to finding the alley where Rolando recovered the drugs?"

Fifteen more minutes would have probably been enough time for her to have pinpointed the location. But time was of the essence, and they had a better chance of uncovering Rolando's whereabouts through Kamila than they did through her lead. "Not close enough," she said. "Let's go."

Without a car, they were at the mercy of public transportation. They all agreed the minibuses, which buzzed up and down the streets like swarming bees, looked petrifying and opted for two taxis instead, men in one, women in the other. Lanying gave the driver the address Salomon procured from Google Maps and let her head fall against the headrest. She didn't know what they would find when they got there, but she worried she wouldn't have the strength to face another dead end. She worried none of them would.

From the middle seat, she leaned around Mia to look out the window at the commotion of city life speeding past. At its core, La Paz wasn't so different from Shanghai, sustained by busy people just trying to get by. The corner grocer. The curbside vendor. The deliveryman. The streets of La Paz pulsed with their good intentions. Intentions Lanying was determined to protect.

She tracked their location on her phone and was surprised when the taxis stopped abruptly several blocks away from their destination.

"No hay coches en la calle de la bruja," the driver explained in Spanish. "Camina de aquí."

"No cars on Witch's Street," Mia translated. "We need to walk from here."

Lanying was still contemplating the coincidence of Kamila's shop being located on a road called "Witch's Street" as she slipped the driver a handful of coins.

"Where do we go?" Mia asked her after they'd all reunited on the far side of the street.

Lanying glanced down at her phone, but Salomon was already heading up the hill. "This way," he said with obvious purpose in his step.

She lagged behind the others, distracted from their purpose by the explosion of color and texture in every direction. Layer upon layer of handwoven tapestries blanketed the exterior walls of the buildings and the ground beneath her feet. Burlap sacks of crimson peppers and chili powders rich as a sunset lined the walkway causing her nose to itch. There were yucca roots and plantains proudly displayed by their shopkeepers who kept watchful eyes over their goods as both locals and tourists bustled past. It was all she could do to keep up with Salomon whose long legs and purposeful stride carried him out of sight.

She forced herself to forge ahead, plodding along to the top of the hill where the street narrowed and the lines of patrons pushing in opposite directions converged. After losing sight of Salomon for a third time, she panicked, fearing she'd lost them for good, but a moment later someone accidentally shoved her into Jose's back.

"Sorry," she said, visibly shaken as he pulled her to the side. "Are we here?"

"Yeah," he said. "But Salomon says something's not right."

She glanced at him now, and he nodded up to the space above the door. Two empty hooks hung rusting in the wall. "No one responded to our knocking, and the sign for the shop is gone. Not to mention the door is closed. Before now it's always been open."

Mia pushed forward, running her hand along the length of the jamb. She stopped at the knob and tried it. Of course, it was locked. "Do you remember seeing a back entrance?"

Salomon pursed his lips. "No. But that doesn't mean there isn't another way in."

Lanying led the way this time to the end of the street where they rounded the corner and circled the block into an alley which ran behind the buildings. "I counted 211 steps between Kamila's shop and the turn off. If we count back, we should be able to figure out which one is hers."

At the 200th step, she stopped and was disappointed to see there was definitely no back door. Instead, there was a fire escape of sorts which led to a window on the second floor. Without hesitation, Mia began her assent.

"Mia," Thomas said, his voice tight and thin. "You can't break in."

She didn't turn back. "It might be unlocked."

"What if the dark psychics are here, lying in wait?"

She chanced a glance over her shoulder at this. "Are they lying in wait, Thomas? Can you feel them?"

He sighed. "No. But this is illegal, Mia. You can't just bust your way in there."

She took two more steps up the ladder and pulled herself onto the landing. "I'm not busting my way in. I have finesse."

They watched from below as she tapped on the window. Lanying held her breath, waiting for Kamila's face to appear at the glass. When no one materialized, Mia tried shimmying up the sash. It was locked.

"She's not here, Mia. We should go," Thomas called out, but Lanying could hear the resignation in his voice. He knew she wasn't going to stop until she found a way inside. They all knew.

Even though Thomas could alert them to any impending danger, she couldn't help checking over her shoulder as Mia stripped off her jacket and, after balling it around her fist, broke out the lower pane of glass.

She reached inside to flip the latch and daftly opened the window.

"Gimme a sec," she called down.

Lanying didn't realize she was holding her breath until Mia reappeared several minutes later. Her face betrayed nothing of what she found as she poked her head out the window.

Was Kamila inside?

Was she injured?

Was she dead?

"There's nothing here. Like nothing." Mia motioned for the rest of them to join her inside. "Just the same, Salomon, I think you need to check it out since you've been here before. Make sure we don't miss anything that might be relevant."

Lanying and Donescia were the first ones up, with the men following close behind. Once they'd all squeezed through the tiny window they milled around the empty room, their footsteps echoing off the adobe walls.

"There was a table here," Salomon said pointing. "And a few tapestries on the walls where the holes are now."

Mia nodded, kneeling down to run her hand against the knotty plank floor. "There's no indication that there was any sort of confrontation. But then again, the place has been recently mopped so there's no dust to reveal any footprints. Just some water spots from the rag. It's the same downstairs."

They split up, searching both the upstairs room and the lower retail space for some indication that Kamila was still around. A rune. A map. A note. Perhaps even something written hastily on a wall.

But there was nothing, just as Mia had said. Absolutely nothing.

Once they regrouped in the second floor living space, Salomon looked directly at Thomas. "Do they have her?" No one needed to ask who he meant.

Thomas stammered, his expression betraying his regret. "I just... I can't..." He raked his hands through his hair. "I don't feel anything, but because I'm not connected to her in any way I don't know if I'd feel anything even if there were something to feel."

"So the dark psychics might have her already. We have no way of knowing."

Thomas lowered his chin.

"You never saw her anywhere else? Just here at this shop and out on the street?" Mia was grilling Salomon now, in full police mode.

He shook his head mournfully, as if he felt personally responsible for her somehow. Lanying understood his anguish and reached out to take his hand, squeezing it gently, letting him know he wasn't alone.

"Okay. Then I don't think there's anything more for us here. They either have her or they don't. If they have her, we're probably screwed. Either way we should probably go back to the hostel and regroup. It might be time for Plan B."

CHAPTER

35

THOMAS

Sunday, November 13
La Paz, Bolivia

Back at the hostel, Thomas started blankly at the sea of yellow Post-it notes tacked to the wall. His gaze fixed on the word 'fire.' In the days following his mother's death, he'd attempted to hold himself together for the others, for the prophecy, and for Mildred herself. He knew she wouldn't want him to lose sight of the important work they were doing, but seeing the word written before him in black and white, he couldn't keep himself from imagining what her final moments must have been like. The only comfort he took was in Carlos' assurance that she hadn't suffered. According to the fire department and medical examiner, the heat of the blaze had been so extreme, her death had been instantaneous.

He thought now of the house they'd shared together, with its stoop for a porch and window boxes Mildred tended with great care. He thought of the meals full of laughter, eaten at the kitchen table with

Howard and Mildred in the early days when he was certain they would eventually decide he was too much trouble and return him to the system. They hadn't though, and the modest, two-story clapboard had become the first true home he'd ever known. But it was gone now. The building and the family. If he survived the confrontation with the dark psychics, he and Mia would have no home to return to. He would need to start again.

This realization washed over him, a rushing wave of despair, as it had done so many times over the past days. That his inclusion as part of the prophecy had cost Mildred her life was too great a cross to bear. And yet, he was surrounded by others who were counting on him to keep them safe, to warn them of impending danger.

On the drive back from Witch's Street his apprehension increased. Now, he picked absently at his cuticle, concentrating on Kamila in an attempt to determine if she was in peril. Unfortunately, his mind kept wandering, worrying that his warning for the rest of them might be too late, just as it had been with Mildred.

"So what now?" Jose asked, breaking the uncharacteristic silence that had fallen over the group.

Lanying glanced up from her computer where she continued to search for Rolando's whereabouts, but the rest of them, including Mia, remained in an almost catatonic state. Kamila's absence should probably not have been a shock to them, but somehow it was, and Thomas could sense that the others were taking the setback as poorly as he was.

He locked eyes with Lanying. "Any luck?"

She shrugged. "Maybe. I think I may have found the spot. The alley is behind a bar. But what am I going to do? Walk in there and ask if they know where I can find a guy who I saw get kicked out recently? And oh, by the way, he can levitate objects."

"Why not? We literally have nothing to lose." Thomas didn't add that if they were going to go they needed to head out sooner than later as his anxiety was growing by the minute.

A beat passed. And then another. No one seemed thrilled by the prospect of another dead end. And then there was a knock at the door.

He shot a look at Mia and could tell she knew exactly what he was thinking. Her hand instinctively flew to her sidearm which was holstered to her hip. He gave her a quick nod to indicate he didn't feel any threat coming from whoever it was on the other side of the door, and she cautiously turned the knob.

"Mia!" a voice cried from beyond the threshold.

A moment later she was pinned in a formidable embrace, thrown backwards into the room by a diminutive-looking woman of similar height but substantially more girth. The woman was smiling broadly over Mia's shoulder from beneath her bowler hat, displaying a row of teeth which reminded Thomas of a Jack-o-lantern at Halloween.

"And Thomas," she cried out glancing around the room. "You're here too. And Lanying and Donescia and Jose." She released Mia from her grasp and took another step into the room toward Salomon, arms outstretched. "Oh, Salomon! You made it. I knew you would."

He took her hands in his and greeted her warmly. "I can't believe it," he said, tears pooling in the corners of his eyes. "Everyone, this is Kamila. Kamila, you obviously already know the other light psychics."

An uneasy relief spread through the group as Thomas took Kamila's coat and offered her a seat at the table. He should have guessed that as a clairvoyant, she'd have a means of tracking them down. As she settled into the wooden chair, they began barraging her with questions.

"Where is Rolando?"

"Why weren't you at your shop?"

"Can you take us to him?"

"Are we all to perish at the hands of the dark psychics?"

"How do we secure the prophecy for the light?"

She waved a finger, admonishing them like naughty schoolchildren. "First things first. Thomas, how strong is your instinct to flee?"

He considered it, the constant nagging which had been pulling at his gut since their arrival in La Paz. "On a scale of one to ten, it's probably a six," he told her.

She nodded thoughtfully. "Good. We still have some time. You let me know when you reach an eight, though."

What did she know that he didn't? "Why?"

"Because the dark psychics are already here in La Paz. I didn't see exactly when they got here, but I know they intend to go to my store. After that, my vision got fuzzy, so until I see something more, we're going to need to use your sense of danger to keep us safe."

"So that's why your store was empty," Lanying said. "Did they already raid it?"

Kamila smiled mischievously. "Of course not. Once I knew they were coming I cleared the place myself. I couldn't leave them any clues as to our whereabouts. They need to figure things out on their own. And besides, I'm not going to need the store anymore after today. I'm taking you somewhere else instead."

"Is it a plaza?" Salomon asked. "A town square?"

"Yes. Plaza San Francisco. How did you know?"

The others listened patiently as Salomon described for a second time what he'd experienced in his latest vision. "We assumed the relic would lead to you again. But it didn't. It gave me a glimpse into our disastrous end at the hands of the dark psychics. What I can't understand is why you would bring us here to die?"

She noticeably flinched at his final accusation, her smile long gone from her lips. She folded her hands in her lap and tucked her chin to her chest. "I would never have hastened you here if I thought all was lost. But don't forget that you're here because you have a destiny to fulfill, with or without my intervention. It was only my intention to help tip the scales in the right direction."

Mia lowered herself to her knees on the floor beside the crone. Thomas had seen this Mia before. This was the Mia who tended to children and abuse victims, the broken and estranged. This Mia, more than any of the others, was the Mia he loved the most. Sure, there was something to be said for the woman who could hit the center of a bullseye downrange at two hundred yards or take out a man twice her size with her bare hands, but it was her compassion that drew him to her time and again.

"None of us believes you brought us here to do us harm. But if we have any chance of stopping the dark psychics, we need to know about Rolando. If he's light or if he's dark."

The old woman lifted her head and took Mia's hand in hers. "I cannot tell you specifically. But what I can share is this – not all who feel called to the prophecy are worthy. It takes more than an impressive ability or a willing heart…"

Lanying interrupted, scrambling to her feet. "'To seal the fate of the world.' I read that line in one of my grandfather's journals."

"Yes, yes," Salomon agreed. "I remember it too. Is it Rolando who's unworthy?"

Kamila glanced around the room, making eye contact with each of them as she went. When her gaze met Thomas, he saw the regret residing there. "Again, I cannot say. But maybe there's still time to see for yourself."

At Kamila's suggestion, everyone put on their coats and shoes and packed their pockets with everything they thought might be useful in the hours to come. Thomas packed a bag of bottled waters and he saw Salomon place the carving in the cargo pocket of his pants.

"You never know," he said to Thomas when he noticed he was being watched.

Less than thirty minutes later, Thomas locked the door behind him and followed the rest of the group down the stone staircase to the courtyard below. Kamila motioned for them to follow her to the other side of the narrow street where there was a sign indicating the location of a bus stop.

"How much to ride?" Lanying asked Kamila as she foraged in her jacket pocket for cash.

"Two Bolivianos. Or about twenty-five cents US."

"That's it?"

"Si," Kamila told her with a broad smile. "It would be more for a first-class bus, but that's not the bus we're taking."

As Lanying passed out two silver coins to everyone, Thomas watched down the street for an oncoming bus. He thought of his first bus ride in Baltimore, to Howard and Mildred's, when he'd ventured off without the social worker to stake out the house on his own the day before his official placement with the Pritchetts. He remembered how much anxiety he'd carried along with him on that trip. How he'd silently prayed he would find what he was looking for at the end of the line. He recalled looking through the back window into the family room where the glow of the television was enough to illuminate the warmth of Mildred and Howard's smiles as they laughed at a cheesy sitcom, and the realization that the Pritchett's was a place he could call home.

He bit his bottom lip and swallowed back the memories, forcing himself to remain present in his current situation. He still had Mia. He still had his fellow light psychics. He still had a prophecy to fulfill.

A moment later, a small chirp of excitement escaped Kamila's lips, and she took a step forward toward the street in obvious anticipation of their ride. Sure enough, there was no mistaking the old school bus, decked out in blue and green stripes with colorful tassels hanging in the front window, ripping along the street in their direction. "This is us," she said brightly.

She told the driver where they were headed, and they each handed the cheerful-looking man their coins as they boarded the bus. Thomas was taken aback by the sea of faces before him. Women in vibrant coats and shawls chatting together across the aisle and surrounding seats. Men in simple jeans and quilted jackets with straw hats and worn edges. These were sturdy people. Proud people. And it occurred to him as he took a seat beside Mia in the back of the bus that he was fighting for their futures as much as his own. If the dark were allowed to take power, there was no telling what would happen to the people of La Paz. Or the any of people in the rest of the world.

He took Mia's hand, squeezing it tightly in his own, and she returned the gesture before resting her head on his shoulder. She knew all too well what was at stake, and although he knew it meant she was also in danger, there was no one else he wanted by his side.

They sat wordlessly together for several minutes, bouncing along the pitted street, until the moment the bus turned a particularly sharp corner and his urge to escape ratcheted up another degree.

"Mia," he said, his lips brushing the top of her head. "Regardless of what happens today, I'm glad you're here."

CHAPTER
36

PATRICK

Sunday, November 13
La Paz, Bolivia

Patrick thought nothing could destroy his optimism more than schlepping through the filthy streets of La Paz, with its annoying granola tourists and impoverished locals.

He was wrong.

"There's not a damn thing here," Wesley said after kicking open the door to the store where they hoped to find Rolando.

Patrick pushed past the brute into the open retail space which was, in fact, empty. *This isn't possible,* he thought to himself. *He has to be here.*

"There's a staircase in the back," Javier called over his shoulder. "Maybe he's upstairs."

Patrick led the parade across the room and up the stairs to the second floor. It was similarly vacant. He cursed under his breath.

"Looks like somebody else had the same idea about gettin' in here," Lillian said, sidestepping the shards of glass beneath the broken window. "Maybe whoever it was already got him."

"Maybe it's the light psychics," Javier said, fingering a piece of glass from the floor.

Patrick had been so certain they would find him here. So positive that Eshanti's painting of the store would lead them straight to Rolando, he hadn't allowed himself to consider other outcomes. Even still, he couldn't stomach the notion that the light psychics had somehow gotten to him first. That was utterly preposterous. By what means? With what resources? There had to be another explanation. Rolando was still out there and he intended to find him. Now, however, they had only one option left – he needed to call in his favor.

Without bothering to leave the room for the sake of privacy, Patrick reached into the astral plane to feel for the emotional markers of his contemporary – the head of one of the largest drug cartels in South America. He'd done business with the man over the past several years and their partnership had been an amicable one. He wanted to make sure, however, that his call would be welcome. It would do him no good to fuel his accomplice's volatile nature by disturbing him at an inopportune time. He found, however, as he located him nearby, that he was in good spirits and would be receptive to his inquiry. He pulled his phone from his pocket.

"Yes, this is Patrick Meyer. I wish to speak with Mr. Ramirez. Yes, thank you. I'll hold."

A moment later, Sergio Ramirez took the line. "Mr. Meyer, I assume since I'm hearing directly from you that you were unable to discern the whereabouts of Rolando Velarde on your own."

There was an air of superiority in his voice, a subtle smugness Patrick forced himself to ignore. "Yes, well, my lead did not pan out quite the way I'd hoped, and I was calling to find out if you'd made any headway regarding his current location."

"I have."

There was a long pause. Ramirez was going to make him beg for it. Although it infuriated him, Patrick couldn't help but admire the bastard.

"I would be most appreciative if you would share any information you have with me."

Ramirez chuckled. "I bet you would. But that information is gonna cost you."

Patrick glanced at his watch. He didn't have time to dicker. "You're welcome to use the restricted off-shore account for this month's purchases."

"And next month?"

"Yes. Yes. Next month as well."

Ramirez cleared his throat. "I'll give him a call and tell him to meet you at the food market, Mercado Lanza. Maybe you can have a chat over a nice plate of silpancho, huh?"

"When?" Patrick asked, hoping Ramirez couldn't hear the desperation in his voice.

"I'll tell him to be there in half an hour. Hope you can make it by then."

The line disconnected, and Patrick turned to the others. "We've got him. Let's go.

CHAPTER

37

MIA

Sunday, November 13
La Paz, Bolivia

When his anxiety ticked up another notch, Mia sent Thomas to tell Kamila. She knew it was all he could do not to bypass her for the front of the bus where he could force the driver to stop. She knew his ability was telling him to jump off the moving vehicle and proceed on foot in the opposite direction. But he wouldn't. He'd changed in recent months. Grown stronger not only in his ability to control what he felt but in his determination to move past his instinct. She was proud, not only in him but in herself for looking beyond the timid behavior he initially exhibited to the reality of his potential all those years ago. At the end of the world, he was the perfect partner, and she was glad to have him by her side.

As he returned to his seat beside her, his face was ashen. "Kamila said to let her know when the anxiety increases again and also that we're almost to Rolando's.

I guess we'll know whether he's light or dark in the next couple of minutes."

She pulled her jacket closed across her chest, chilled by the thought. Perhaps he would be light and the seven of them would unite as one and fulfill the prophecy, ending a millennia of uncertainty. Or perhaps his aura would reveal him as a dark soul, casting him to the other side. In which case, she only hoped their small but willing army would be powerful enough to detain him and remand him to the authorities. Keeping him from the other dark psychics was their last hope.

"I have a good feeling about today," she told him at last, forcing herself to be positive. The look on his face indicated he knew the truth, though, that she was petrified about what the day held in store.

"Me too," he replied, draping a protective arm around her shoulders. "We've got this."

If they were both going to continue lying to make the other one feel better, Mia decided just to keep her mouth shut for the rest of the trip. She didn't have to remain silent for long, however, because moments later the bus lurched to a stop, and Kamila motioned for everyone to follow her onto the street.

"We're here," she said, nodding up at a three-story walk-up on the other side of the street. "This is where Rolando lives. This is where we should find him." She glanced around the group at each of them, studying their faces, her brow furrowed into a tight line beneath the brim of her hat. "Whatever happens from here, know that you were born for this."

They followed her across the street and halfway up the stairs before she froze mid-step, bracing herself against the railing. Mia reached out to take her arm which was shaking. "Kamila? What is it? Is something wrong?"

The woman's eyes glazed over and lost focus. She appeared to be in some kind of trance.

"What's happening?" Jose called from the landing below. "Is she okay?"

"I don't know," Mia replied as she steadied Kamila from behind. "I think she might be seeing something."

A moment later, Kamila sucked in a deep breath of air, shaking her head as she came out of the daze. "He's not here," she announced, without turning around. "They already have him."

A solid pit formed in the hollow of Mia's stomach. If he was dark, they'd just lost their opportunity to have him arrested. If he was light, they would need to find a way to get him back, assuming the dark psychics hadn't already killed him. "Please tell me," she implored. "Is he one of us?"

Without responding, Kamila pushed past Mia on her way back down the steps. "Follow me. We don't have much time."

Mia was impressed by the pace the woman kept as the group scurried along the crowded street behind her. She heard Salomon and Donescia's worried voices to her left and Thomas and Jose's heavy footfalls to her right. Lanying raced ahead in an attempt to keep up with their guide, pleading for information along the way.

"Where are we going? Are they all together? Kamila, please tell me! We need to know what we're getting ourselves into."

A nearby clock tower chimed, signaling the beginning of the afternoon siesta, and the already crowded street grew thicker with hungry pedestrians heading purposefully in every direction. As the throng of people grew, it became more difficult for their little group to stay together, and it was all Mia could do to keep sight of the crone's slumped shoulders as she continued along the winding street. With her diminutive stature and bowler hat, she looked like every other Bolivian woman in La Paz. Worried about becoming separated, she called over her shoulder for Donescia and Salomon to keep up, and when she turned forward again, caught a glimpse of Kamila rounding the corner of a particularly ornate looking building. A moment later, she rounded the corner herself and was met with the sight of an open plaza.

"Oh, God," she heard Salomon cry out from behind.

She turned to him. His eyes were wide. Frantic. "Is this the place? Is this Plaza San Francisco?" she asked.

A single nod confirmed their location, and she watched desperately as he scanned the crowd of people from his elevated vantage point. "Where's Kamila? I can't see her anywhere."

Before she could set out to look for herself, someone pulled at her arm nearly knocking her off her feet. She turned to see Thomas's flushed face beading with sweat. "This is it. Whatever is happening, it's happening right now. I've never felt the urge to flee so strongly in my entire life. I want you to run, Mia. Get away from here. I need you to be safe."

She grabbed his arm, locking it firmly around her own. She was shaking and so was he. But it didn't matter. "I'm not going anywhere, Thomas. We're sticking together. All of us. And we're getting out of here alive."

She caught movement out of the corner of her eye as Lanying approached with Jose. "I can't find Kamila," she said warily, "but I'm pretty sure that's Patrick Meyer standing right over there." She pointed across the plaza about fifty yards away to where a discernable group of foreigners was forming a circle in front of the cathedral's steps.

Mia craned to see above the taller civilians, trying to catch a glimpse of the group's auras. When a short break in the crowd allowed her to finally identify their allegiance, her breath hitched. "They're dark. All of them. Even the man who is clearly Bolivian. He must be Rolando."

Forming a small cluster of their own, the light psychics eyed each other reverently, knowing not only the risk they were all about to take but also the significance of what was at stake. Thomas cleared his throat before beseeching the others. "If any of you would like to walk away, there will be no hard feelings. We know how Salomon saw this playing out. We can try to stop them here and now from ushering in the darkness, but there might be nothing left for us to do."

A beat passed. The voices and bustle of the plaza fell away, and all that remained were the six of them.

"Watta we waitin' fah?" Donescia asked. "Go now ta dem!"

Mia glanced at her friends. Friends who were now family. She nodded. "Let's go."

They pushed their way through the crowd to where the dark psychics now stood, hands linked, in a perfect circle. Although their eyes were closed, there was no mistaking the confidence pulsing from their ranks.

"We're too late," Lanying said, her voice trembling.

They waited for an indication that the prophecy was being fulfilled. For a darkness to spread across the plaza or a clap of thunder to rumble from the sky. But there was nothing. Aside from the gawking onlookers with their cellphones pointed at the bizarre looking ritual, nothing seemed out of the ordinary.

And then Mia heard Kamila's voice echoing clearly over the commotion of the square. "Dark psychics of the Sevens Prophecy, you have an imposter in your ranks. No fulfillment will come for you today."

Seven sets of eyes blinked open, their heads turning in unison toward the sound of Kamila's voice. Mia searched for their guide and found her high atop the church's steeple in a stone framed opening, megaphone in hand.

"Go away, old woman," Patrick called up at her. "You have no business here."

"Oh, but I do. Like you, I've spent a lifetime studying and preparing for this day, only I am not here under false pretenses as you are."

Mia watched heat spread across Patrick's face, his hands clenching into fists at his sides. It was obvious that he wasn't used to being confronted, especially by someone like Kamila.

"What should we do?" Jose whispered.

Something told her Kamila had a plan. "Watch and wait," Mia replied.

She noticed a spasm playing at Patrick's cheek causing his left eye to twitch ever so slightly. For all his worldwide connections and corporate domination, he was certainly having difficulty composing himself in the face of this seemingly insignificant Bolivian grandmother.

Patrick began speaking to the man beside him in an obvious snub at Kamila. After a brief exchange, however, he appeared unable to ignore the reality of what was happening. Or more to the point, what wasn't happening. "Everyone here knows who they are and what they represent," he called to her. "We are the seven dark psychics of the Sevens Prophecy."

Kamila cackled in spite of herself, deep and throaty, which almost made Mia smile. How brave the woman was in the face of such dangerous adversaries. "Six, Mr. Meyer. There are only six of you."

"Eshanti isn't here," he spat. "And now that we've found Rolando, the true seven are together at last to usher in the end of days."

Mia had spent her entire life surrounded by criminals. Between a childhood watching her father with them at the precinct and a career pitting herself against them on a daily basis, she'd learned to expect certain behaviors from people who deep down, despite their tendencies toward the dark, knew they had done something wrong. She loved observing them from behind the one-way glass of the lineup room, oblivious to her scrutiny. Although she trusted her abilities implicitly, she'd also learned to trust her instincts when it came to reading people's body language.

As she watched the six dark psychics standing alongside Patrick, it was clear there was dissension among their ranks. To Patrick's left, a blond bombshell picked at the cuticle of a perfectly manicured thumbnail. She'd twisted her shoulders away from him, a clear sign she found something about him offensive. On his other side, a small-statured Spaniard shifted nervously on his feet. Unwilling to meet Kamila's gaze, he stared at the ground, appearing quite interested in a discarded bottle cap. Mia continued to assess the other dark psychics, noting an enormous hulk of a woman, a Middle Eastern man, and Rolando were all fully engaged in the conversation between Patrick and Kamila. The seventh, a broad-shouldered brute with a thick head of hair and impish smile, seemed bemused by the entire ordeal. She considered all of this as Kamila responded for the third time.

"You fool!" she laughed. "Not all who feel called to the prophecy are worthy. It takes more than an impressive ability or a willing heart to seal the fate of the world. You alone are the one who isn't a psychic born into the prophecy. No one else is to blame. It's your narcissistic blindness which prevents the dark fulfillment. You are the one who has no involvement in this matter."

Mia reached beside her to take Thomas's hand. Without provocation, Lanying took her other hand. They held her up, preventing her knees from buckling in the wake of Kamila's revelation.

"Did she just say what I think she said?" Jose said.

Lanying replied. "That Patrick isn't part of the prophecy after all?"

"Yeah. That."

"So do we still try to have Rolando arrested?" Salomon asked.

Before Mia could respond with the plan that was quickly formulating in her mind, she saw the enormous Amazonia step out of the dark psychic's circle and stretch her arms toward the cathedral. Thomas must have felt what was about to happen because before she could cry out, he was already screaming for Kamila to move.

"Get down, Kamila!" he cried.

In less time than it took to blink, a raging inferno exploded in the alcove of the bell tower, obliterating Kamila where she stood. The crowd around them rushed like a tidal wave from the plaza, a cacophony of shouting and wailing, people gathering belongings and children in a mass of hysteria.

Mia heard a whimper escape her lips before she realized the dark psychics were now turning their attention on Thomas. His ill-fated warning to Kamila had conveyed both their location and their allegiance. There was nothing left to do but confront them where they stood.

"Run," Thomas said calmly as the Amazonian woman raised her hands again. "And be careful with that water, Donescia."

Although only a split-second glance of acknowledgment passed between Mia and Thomas, it was enough time to convey everything she wanted him to know. She loved him. She believed in him. She was proud of the legacy they would leave behind if they didn't survive.

She turned to run just as a flash of heat exploded behind her, throwing her to the ground. She willed herself not look back as she scrambled to her feet, her hands bloody with embedded gravel. She could hear water splashing and the sound of someone gasping for air.

And then she stopped midstride. She couldn't do it. She couldn't run away from the battle.

She turned to see Lanying and Salomon huddled together behind a nearby retaining wall which served as the supporting structure of the enormous plaza steps. Beyond them, Jose crouched beside Thomas, who was soaking wet and covered in third-degree burns. He hadn't run as fast as the others. He'd hesitated and obviously, Donescia had too. The hydrokinetic was now holding a wall of water aloft, shielding them from the dark psychic's fiery assault while Jose worked to repair Thomas's scorched flesh. A hard knot formed in her throat, and she couldn't swallow. She couldn't breathe. She couldn't move. She'd listened to him. She'd run away. And now because of her poor judgment he lay dying on the ground.

The external blaze of Patrick's psychic puppet couldn't compare to the internal firestorm which burst forth inside of her.

"Give me cover," she called to Donescia as she removed her handgun from its holster. A wall of water would protect her from the fire but its permeability would allow her to shoot through. Mindful of her worrisome lack of ammunition, she squared her shoulders toward her closest target, Patrick Meyer and, after accounting for the water's effect on the bullet's trajectory, pulled the trigger only once.

She watched through the liquid screen as Patrick fell to the ground, grasping at his thigh. "One of you get over here and help me!" he cried. "And the rest of you, find a way to get rid of that water!"

Mia smiled to herself before taking aim at the flame thrower. Her perfectly placed shot had immobilized Patrick without killing him outright. She knew she wouldn't have the same benevolent luxury with her next target. She chanced a brief glance at Thomas to check on Jose's progress and was relieved to see the burns retracting. Donescia just needed to protect them from the flames a moment longer.

But that's when she noticed the blond standing right beside her, seemingly out of nowhere. Her police instincts kicked in, and she leveled her weapon at the woman, firing off two direct shots.

When nothing happened, she clicked off a third round, this time aiming at the blonde's chest. She smiled at Mia before disappearing into thin air.

"What the hell?" Mia wondered aloud, frantically reaching into her pocket for additional bullets to reload her sidearm. After wasting precious bullets on the phantom, she mentally calculated how many remained, a number that was regrettably low thanks to the airline's restriction on the amount of ammunition she was allowed to carry on a commercial flight.

"Salomon, duck!" she heard Thomas call in a weak voice just seconds before a softball-sized chunk of concrete exploded into the wall above Salomon's head. Before she could react, Thomas was calling again for them all to take cover against a sea of shrapnel being hurled in their direction. The group converged on Thomas, who was almost well enough to stand on his own, and with a strength that only pure adrenaline can produce, Salomon lifted him from the ground and slung him over his shoulder as they rushed into the cathedral.

The moment Donescia released her wall of water into the sky as weightless vapor, the Amazonian's flame attack resumed, with firebolts pummeling the exterior of the building. The ground shook with every hit, and the room quickly filled with smoke from the burning wooden door.

"I supposed it's too much to hope that this is the part where they leave us to escape," Jose said sarcastically, bending over Thomas in an attempt to complete the healing process.

"They'll only stop once they've killed us all," Lanying said.

CHAPTER
38

PATRICK

Sunday, November 13
La Paz, Bolivia

Akantha let her hands fall to her sides, and even over the chaos around them, Patrick could hear her labored breathing. She'd defended them to the best of her abilities, but it hadn't been enough. He couldn't believe the light psychics managed to get away.

He was still applying pressure to his leg wound, considering their next move when he was kicked from behind, thrown across the pavement onto his hands and knees. His bullet hole throbbed with a searing white heat. He closed his eyes and ran his tongue over his teeth, immediately recognizing the metallic taste of blood. He righted himself, wiping the blood from his wounded lip. He hoped he hadn't bitten through.

"This is all your fault, Patrick!" Wesley screamed at him from behind. "You're a liar and a scam artist!"

He saw Akantha and Saif lift their hands, coming to his defense, but he waved them off. He wasn't afraid of Wesley.

"I did everything I said I would," Patrick said, rising shakily to his feet. "I found all seven dark psychics."

"You made us leave Eshanti behind," said Lillian. "You're the reason the prophecy isn't already fulfilled."

Patrick tried to ignore the pain in his thigh. Tried to concentrate on what they should do next.

"There will be time for the prophecy, but at this moment, another matter is more pressing. The light psychics. We should kill them now while we know where they are, and then we won't have to worry about them anymore. We can go to Mumbai and meet up with Eshanti tonight. Everything is still going to work out in our favor. We will fulfill the prophecy once and for all."

Flames illuminated Patrick's face as he and Javier watched the door to the cathedral burn. He saw a gleam of something in Javier's eyes. Trepidation perhaps. "I think it might be better if we just head straight to Mumbai now. We can't guarantee our own safety if we stay," he said, confirming Patrick's suspicions.

Javier was spineless. He had always been spineless. Patrick had never found this shortcoming to be a hindrance, however. Quite the opposite, in fact, as his vacillating nature assured that he was easily led.

"We have a very unique opportunity before us in that our enemies are here; the only people in the world with the ability to prevent our destiny from being realized. Right behind those doors. Cornered animals just waiting for us to initiate the slaughter." He paused, shifted his weight off his leg, noting the incredulous faces staring back at him. He wasn't leaving without a fight. The light psychics needed to die. It was only a matter of convincing the others. "I know that crone has convinced the three of you that Eshanti is the seventh dark psychic. But what if she isn't? What if there is someone who still needs to be found? We'll need time to find them. Time we might not have if we allow the light psychics to live."

"'*We'll* need time to find them?' Who is this *we* you're speaking of, Patrick? You heard the old woman. You're the reason the prophecy isn't already fulfilled. It's been you all along." Wesley took a step closer, his hands balled into tight fists at his sides. Seeing them forced Patrick to acknowledge the other's believed the old woman's lies. They now saw him as expendable.

But they couldn't fulfill the prophecy without him.

They still needed him.

It was only a matter of reestablishing his worth.

"Akantha's allegiance lies with me. As does Saif's. They won't leave the country without me and you know it. So I'm going inside the cathedral to get the light psychics. I'm taking Akantha to smoke them out. Hopefully it won't take any more than a few minutes, and we can be on our way with one less thing to worry about."

Lillian, Wesley, and Javier exchanged glances. If he could show them how valuable he was to the cause perhaps they would realize the truth.

He wasn't just a member of the prophecy. He was the prophecy.

CHAPTER

39

MIA

Sunday, November 13
La Paz, Bolivia

Everyone got on their hands and knees as smoke billowed from the wooden door and accumulated near the ceiling of the church's narthex. Mia lifted her head, chancing a glance out a small, blown-out hole in the side of the building. Through the smoke, she could make out the outlines of the dark psychics huddled over their leader across the square.

"They're going to come for us," Thomas said, feeling the danger she couldn't yet see with her own eyes. "We need to find a way out. Otherwise, we'll be trapped."

Mia crawled into the sanctuary. The tile under her hands felt cool to the touch compared to the warmth of the flames at her back. An ornately gilded altar lay before her; gold carvings covered the wall from floor to ceiling. Along the nave, rows of wooden pews lined the aisles, but she noted that in addition to a handful of smaller secondary altars, they appeared to be the only flammable objects in the space. The structure of the cathedral itself was crafted of pure stone and brick which would be detrimental to their enemy's fiery threat.

If they could only entice the dark psychics to use electricity instead of fire, perhaps there was still hope.

She knew Donescia needed a source of water to protect them from the flames. And if they wanted to fight back against the threat of electrocution, they'd need water for that as well. Outside, Donescia had channeled the water from a nearby fountain, but there was very little water to be found inside the cathedral. To her left, she spied the requisite holy water font and further ahead, near the altar, there appeared to be a larger baptismal font as well. In preparation for what she suspected was to come, she peeled off her coat, her sweatshirt, and the cotton t-shirt she was now thankful she'd decided to wear as a base layer at the last minute that morning. After pulling it over her head, she began ripping it into six equal strips. She dipped each strip into the font and wrung it out, whispering a silent prayer for God to protect them, and after redressing returned to the narthex.

"Take these," she said, handing everyone a strip of wet fabric. "Tie them around your head and cover your nose and mouth to protect your lungs from the smoke. Once they come inside they'll probably burn the pews, hoping to smoke us out. Those pews are the only flammable objects around, though, and with the strength of that woman's flames, they won't burn for long. They won't be expecting us to go high because of the smoke, so if we can hide out of sight in the raised, gallery pulpit while protecting our lungs with these strips long enough for them to get frustrated, they might resort to using the electricity. And I think I have a plan for that."

"That plan is gonna have to be good enough," Salomon said scrambling up from his position on the floor by the hole to the outside. "Because they're on the move, and it won't be long before they'll be busting down that door."

Mia was relieved when Thomas didn't need help getting up off the floor. The solid mahogany door of the cathedral sizzled and popped behind them, splintering as she led everyone to the interior of the cathedral and up the spiral staircase to the pulpit. It was tight quarters, with everyone circled up, crouching on their heels in order to keep their heads from being seen from below. She could hear the ragged breathing around her, saw her own fear mirrored in her friends' eyes.

"Wat d'yah be needin' me tah do?" Donescia whispered through her mask.

Mia took Donescia's hand across the pulpit. "There's some holy water in the font at the door and in the baptismal font just below us. It's not a lot of water. Definitely not enough to extinguish any fire they might set. But it might be enough to use against them if they try to electrocute us. The trick is going to be forcing their hand. I think I can do that, though."

"Di wahta conducts di power."

"Exactly," Mia replied. "When the time comes, I'll let you know. You're going to have to douse whoever is responsible for the electricity at the exact moment they begin their assault."

"We know it's not Rolando," Salomon offered. "Or Patrick."

"Or the fire woman," added Jose.

"Or the blond woman," Mia said, remembering her disappearing act. "That leaves the other three." Donescia's jaw was set, her eyes narrow. Mia could feel her determination. "Just make sure you keep the water away from yourself and the rest of us, no matter..."

Mia's final words were cut off by the sound of the charred remains of cathedral's door being smashed to the ground. Slow footsteps echoed off the stone tile.

"I know you're in here hiding like the cowards you are," Patrick bellowed. "I can feel your fear. It's oozing out of you."

Mia stifled the urge to cry out. To confront him, face to face. But she knew it wasn't in anyone's best interest to be so bold. She needed to stay safely tucked away until the opportunity to strike presented itself.

"Rolando, the pews, if you will, to the front of the sanctuary."

The sound of wood splintering and collapsing echoed throughout the cavernous chamber. Beside her, Lanying covered her ears with her hands and closed her eyes. The others startled each time another pew crashed into the ever-growing pile of debris. Mia imagined the mountain of rubble atop the altar - unusual kindling for an enormous bonfire - and just when she thought there couldn't be any remaining wooden objects to add to the pile, the room grew silent once again.

"Akantha, if you will..." Patrick said.

As the fire erupted, Mia felt a whoosh of oxygen being consumed by the flames. Smoke immediately began to build in the rafters, and it wasn't long before tears burned from her eyes. After a minute, she heard footsteps retreating out of the church. She reached for

Thomas's hand as it became more and more difficult to see.

"Can you still feel the danger?" she whispered to him. "Are they still down there?"

He suppressed a cough and whispered back, "There's a good chance we're going to die from smoke inhalation, so yeah, I can still feel the danger."

This wasn't the answer she was looking for. "Do you think they're still down there?" she asked again.

Jose lifted off his heels and peered over the top of the pulpit for a split second before returning to the floor. "She's still down there. The fire woman. And Patrick. Dude's got a mask."

Mia knew immediately what they needed to do. The roar of the fire below was beginning to subside. If they were going to act, they needed to do it now.

"Come out, light psychics," Patrick called through his respirator, making him sound like a British Darth Vader. "Suffocation is such a horrible way to die. My way will be far quicker. I promise."

Mia blinked back stinging tears and wiped away the ones which were already running down her cheeks with the sleeve of her jacket. Her friends' faces were blurry. Donescia coughed.

"I need one of you to go downstairs. Quietly. I need you to create a distraction. Not a big one, just enough to draw their attention to the other side of the room. Then I'm…"

"I'll do it," Lanying said before Mia had finished speaking. "I'm the smallest which means I'm the smallest target." She pushed past the others toward the staircase before anyone had a chance to object. "Give me thirty seconds starting now."

Mia watched as her friend disappeared down the spiral steps. The crackling fire smoldering at the altar was enough to mask the sound of her descent. She counted the seconds as they ticked past and removed her handgun from her holster to check the cylinder for ammunition. Six bullets were loaded. She hoped at least one of them would hit its mark.

Twenty-eight, twenty-nine, thirty…"

The sound of something large and metallic hitting the ground echoed off the cathedral walls. Mia took it as her cue to stand and take aim at the two figures below. Although the smoke remained the thickest in the rafters, the thinning layers of haze between them prevented her from having a clear shot. She pulled the trigger anyway. Once. Twice. Six times.

Ears ringing, she could only imagine the resounding thud the fire thrower must have made as she fell to the ground. Mia watched as Patrick did nothing to attend to his fallen comrade but instead turned his attention toward the pulpit. Although she couldn't hear what he was saying, she caught sight of movement near the entrance, and it became obvious that he had beckoned for the others to return.

She lowered herself to the ground and motioned for everyone to pay attention, overly enunciating her words and using exaggerated hand gestures, hoping to adequately convey their mission. "They're coming. We need to spread out and take cover. If he's going to use the electricity, he'll do it now." Everyone nodded in agreement. "Let's go."

She loaded her last four bullets into the gun's cartridge while everyone else scrambled down the stairs. When she looked up, Thomas was still beside her. He brushed the tips of his fingers across her cheek and mouthed 'I love you.' She gave him a weak smile. "Love you too," she said. She couldn't imagine what she would do if he somehow didn't survive.

Shaking the thought from her head, she followed him down the stairs to where the main altar once stood. Now all that remained were the smoldering ashes of the former pews, a scorched carcass of rubble. The smoke continued to dissipate, seeping out the open windows of the attached belfry. Since they were no longer able to use the smoke for cover, they clustered in two groups behind the enormous columns on the right side of the church. Salomon, Donescia, and Lanying closest to the altar; Mia, Thomas, and Jose closest to Patrick.

Although a mild ringing remained, a result of the gunfire, her hearing was beginning to return. She listened as the other dark psychics returned down the center aisle. Thomas tensed by her side.

"Is she dead?" one of the men asked in a thick Spanish accent.

"Perhaps. But she's not my concern." It sounded as though Patrick had removed his mask. "Rolando, bring one of them to me."

Mia drew her gun, ready for the man to appear around the corner. She peered over her shoulders in both directions, listening to hear from where he was coming. But there were no footsteps. Instead, she watched in horror and amazement as Lanying's feet lifted off the floor, and she began floating out from behind the column. Salomon reached for her, missing the tips of her outstretched fingers by less than an inch before she disappeared around the corner. He started after her but Donescia held him back. Salomon thrashed wildly, crying out after her, but ultimately remained behind the cement pillar, protected from the dark psychic's assault.

Mia waited to hear Lanying scream, but she remained strangely silent. It was an ominous feeling, not being able to see what was happening. Her imagination was running wild with possibilities, each one more terrifying than the next, so when she heard Patrick call for someone named Saif to 'take care of the Asian,' she couldn't stop herself. Her training took over.

As she stepped into the nave, beyond the protective shelter of the buttress, the scene before her was not what she'd expected. She assumed the dark psychics would be focused on killing Lanying and that she would have an opportunity to fire off at least one good shot. Instead, the dark psychics ignored Lanying entirely and stared at Mia as if they'd been expecting her to appear. As if they knew she wasn't capable of standing by while they slaughtered her friend. Her brain registered to pull the gun's trigger, the barrel leveled at Patrick's head. She felt the sensation of the metal sliding backward toward her palm just as she was overtaken by the brightest light she'd ever known.

And then everything went dark.

40

DONESCIA

Sunday, November 13
La Paz, Bolivia

"They're going to kill her! Do it now!"

Donescia didn't know Thomas well, but when she saw the way he was trembling and heard the desperation in his voice, she knew instinctively that she was born for this precise moment. All the ridicule she had endured. Her friends and family calling her a witch, accusing her of black magic. She had suffered it all so she could help fulfill the Sevens Prophecy. Without thinking about the possible consequences or her own safety, she stepped out from behind the pillar and rained the gathered water from the baptismal font onto Saif.

Three bodies dropped to the floor.

Holy water bathed the surrounding tiles.

She was relieved to see Saif, the electrocutioner, had been overwhelmed by the current reentering his system. Her water had the desired effect, rerouting the voltage from the apparent safety of his palms to the rest of his body where he was wholly unprotected. Now, he twitched on the ground involuntarily, the spastic motions of the remaining energy leaving his singed corpse.

Beside him, Rolando lay eerily still. His proximity to Saif had resulted in an errant stream of water connecting them, and he'd become caught in the crossfires of her attack. If any life remained inside of him, she certainly couldn't see it.

She was aware of the commotion to her left, where the others had converged upon Mia. Her water took a split second too long connecting with Saif and as a result, his bolt struck Mia squarely in the chest. But she had seen how Jose cured Thomas's burns and prayed silently that he would be able to do the same for poor Mia. She wanted to race to her side, but her feet remained cemented to the ground. She was unable to tear her gaze away from Saif and Rolando, telling herself again and again that she had killed them in self-defense. It was kill or be killed. And she had the prophecy to protect after all. She had only done what she was born to do.

Still, taking another man's life ripped at her conscience.

"Stand down," Salomon called out, wrenching Donescia from her thoughts. He had Mia's weapon drawn at the four remaining dark psychics. At his feet, Jose's hands worked frantically over her heart, willing it to beat again. Thomas cradled her head in his lap while Lanying held her hand and whispered quietly into her ear.

As they tended to her, the church bells in the belfry above began to toll a slow and steady hymn. At first,

Donescia could only hear the chimes, but then Lanying began to hum along. Finally, she began to sing.

> "Soft as the voice of an angel,
> Breathing a lesson unheard,
> Hope with a gentle persuasion
> Whispers her comforting word:
> Wait till the darkness is over,
> Wait till the tempest is done,
> Hope for the sunshine tomorrow,
> After the shower is gone.
>
> If, in the dusk of the twilight,
> Dim be the region afar,
> Will not the deepening darkness
> Brighten the glimmering star?
> Then when the night is upon us,
> Why should the heart sink away?
> When the dark midnight is over,
> Watch for the breaking of day."

As the bells fell silent, tears spilled down Lanying's face, and Donescia discovered she needed to wipe her own eyes as well. Looking around, she wasn't surprised to see every light psychic affected by the hymn. She was, however, surprised to see one of the dark psychics step forward.

"Can you save her?" the short Spaniard asked with a tentative voice.

"Javier!" Patrick spat, his voice laced with venom.

Although the other light psychics ignored his query, focusing solely on Mia, Donescia saw Javier take another step forward, entreating them further. "Please. Is this what you do? Do you heal the injured?"

She watched the man dubiously as he took another hesitant step away from what remained of his group. She could tell by the softness of the lines around his face there was something more than curiosity at work inside of him. "He di psychic healer," she told him.

"And he can bring her back from the dead?"

"I'm warning you," Salomon bellowed. "Don't come any closer."

Javier stopped. The three dark psychics standing behind him held their positions.

And then the cathedral echoed with the sound of Mia taking in a huge breath of air. Compelled into motion by her friend's return, Donescia hurried to the others who cried out with excitement as Mia coughed and sputtered back to life. Having only known her fellow light psychics for less than a week, she was surprised by the joy she felt watching Thomas and Mia's tearful reunion. These were her people. The people she'd been waiting for. She crouched beside them, ignoring the hard tile against her knees, and wondered in amazement of all she'd born witness to over the past days and hours. Jose reached his arm around her shoulders, gathering her into his embrace, and she hugged him back.

They'd done it. They'd stopped the dark psychics.

And thanks to Jose, they'd all survived.

The Spaniard's cracking voice interrupted their revelry. "I'd like to join you, if I may."

"Javier, what in god's name..." Patrick said, his brows pinched into a tight V.

Thomas and Salomon began to voice their objections, but it was Mia who silenced them. "What's your name again?" She sat up, resting her weight on her elbows. "Javier?"

"Yes. Javier Delgado," he stammered, approaching them slowly, his hands raised above his head in a show of submission. "I... I'm having trouble understanding what just happened. How it is that you just brought her back from the dead?"

Beside Donescia, Jose cleared his throat and straightened his jacket across his shoulders. "I didn't bring her back from the dead any more than I would have had I performed CPR. I can't bring people back to life. I can only heal damaged tissue. Luckily, I was able to repair the electricity's damage to her heart muscle fast enough to save her life."

An uneasy calm settled over the cathedral. The smoldering remains of the wooden pews continued to hiss.

Mia broke the silence with a small, measured voice. "Javier, do you feel different than you did an hour ago?"

"Different?" He stared directly at her, unflinching. "Yes."

Mia drew her legs under her body and, bearing her weight on Thomas and Jose's arms lifted herself to her feet. Donescia watched as she reached out to Javier who was now only steps away.

"Does it feel like an understanding?"

"Yes."

"An awakening?"

"Yes." Javier's responses were coming more fervently now.

"Does it feel like you can appreciate what it means to be someone other than yourself?"

When he didn't answer immediately, Patrick responded instead, grabbing him forcibly by the arm. "Javier! We're leaving. Come with us now."

"No," Javier said pointedly. He ratcheted out of Patrick's grasp, throwing himself at Mia who caught him just before he fell to the ground.

"Mia?" Thomas said, one eyebrow raised in disbelief as he helped Mia steady Javier between them.

She winked at him. "Take his hand," she said.

"Huh?"

"Take. His. Hand," she repeated. "And Lanying's too."

Donescia saw the circle forming and took Jose and Salomon's hands before being asked. Mia was smiling now and she had a feeling she knew why. It took a bit of convincing but after some coaxing from Mia about their safety, Salomon eventually set the gun on the floor and took Lanying's hand.

The circle was complete.

The resulting peace was instantaneous.

CHAPTER
41

JAVIER

Saturday, April 29
Baltimore

In his twenty-seven years, Javier had never attended a wedding. Today's would be his first. As he stood beside Salomon under a sprawling elm tree, assembled with the other groomsmen on Thomas and Mia's special day, he considered the journey that led him to this place and these people.

The afternoon sun was to their backs, illuminating the tree-lined aisle which the bride and her attendants would soon walk. The warmth on his shoulders reminded him of his home in Marbella on the Mediterranean coast. The city where he'd met Patrick.

The place where he'd first learned of the prophecy.

He'd never known his father. His mother came and went as she pleased, often leaving him in the care of neighbors or strangers depending on the urgency of her personal agenda. It didn't take long for him to expect being left. It took well into his teens before he finally accepted it.

He avoided school. There was nothing for him there. By the time he was nine, he'd learned there was money and far more esteem to be made on the streets. With his ability to make objects disappear and reappear in other locations, he'd mastered what others described as 'sleight of hand.' Now you see it, now you don't. His abilities drew in crowds. Tourists tossed coins at the young magician on warm summer evenings as they strolled under the palm trees of the promenade before dinner and drinks. Most days he earned enough for food. Some days he did not.

He was introduced to the ball and cup trick by an elderly local who happened to be resting on the bench beside him during one of his performances. As the crowd dissipated, the man pulled three cups and a tiny red ball out of his pocket and proceeded to show Javier the trick, demonstrating how to palm the ball to effectively hide it from the audience. Javier was able to replicate the trick immediately, much to the old man's delight, but the boy's conscience got the better of him, and he eventually confessed the truth, that he was able to move the ball from under the cups with his mind.

As Mia came into view behind the procession of bridesmaids with her own father linked to her arm, Javier thought of this man, Matías, and the role he played in his life. Mia's cheeks bore the flush of radiant happiness, and her father beamed with pride. Javier had never known the warmth of that pride, despite being taken in by Matías. In his own way, the old man had become the only father-figure he had ever known. He provided food. Care. Companionship. He also introduced him to the seedy underbelly of Marbella, where gangsters and the mafia gambled in back alleys and smoke-filled pool halls. Javier became the golden child, Matías' pride and joy, winning thousands of dollars from unsuspecting marks. Life was good.

Until the night Javier found Matías dead in his bed. He never learned what took his mentor – a heart attack or maybe a stroke. It didn't matter. He was gone. And because fourteen-year-olds aren't known for their good sense, he'd struck out on his own, leaving the tiny apartment they shared over the corner market without looking back. Three months later, full of hatred and fearful of the world, he met Patrick.

Patrick filled a void for him. A hollowness his absentee parents created and which Matías satisfied with a conditional alliance instead of love. As long as Javier provided for Matías' needs, he remained relevant. It proved the same with Patrick. Their bond was forged under the same clause of expandability. He was disposable to both men and this understanding grew inside him like a cancer, hardening his heart. Without Matías, Patrick, or the prophecy, Javier would surely fade into irrelevance once again.

Consequently, Javier lived under the philosophy that if he couldn't be loved, he could at least be connected to someone. He did what he was told. Followed the dark psychics rules. Believed with all he had that he was one of them.

Mia smiled broadly through her lace veil at him as she joined Thomas and the minister at the end of the aisle. It was Mia who'd recognized the change in him back in La Paz; who saw the external manifestation of his internal struggle. She told him later, as they stood together in the ticketing line at the Bolivian airport that although his aura had been dark in the plaza, she'd noticed that it was brightening at the edges. She'd explained about her gift and about how she'd never seen a person's aura change from light to dark or vice versa which is why his was so confusing to her. She also confessed that after her heart was coaxed into reanimation, the first thing she'd noticed was that his aura was no longer dark. That was the moment she realized he might be capable of fulfilling the prophecy for the light.

Thomas and Mia exchanged their vows. Professed their love. Promised to stand by one another in sickness and in health for as long as they both should live. It was this love, this commitment he'd seen between the light psychics which had ultimately softened his heart. He'd watched Jose protect Thomas' burnt body without regard for his own well-being. When they were forced to seek shelter, he saw Salomon hoist Thomas off the ground and carry him to safety. Out of the corner of his eye, he noticed Lanying risking her own life to create a distraction for Mia. And finally, he watched the tenderness between them when they thought they'd lost one of their own.

The contrast between the light psychics and the people who comprised his inner circle was so striking, it was as if he himself had been hit by Saif's electricity, shocking him into awareness. This was what love looked like. This was what family looked like. This was something worth fighting for.

Now, as the officiant pronounced them husband and wife and introduced Mr. and Mrs. Thomas Pritchett to the assemblage, Javier fought to hold back tears. He was still growing accustomed to this new set of emotions – joy, compassion, faith – all of which were unknown to him before the fulfillment. Since the moment their hands connected inside the Basilica of San Francisco he'd felt overwhelmed by a sense of peace and astounded by a strange and unexpected state of being.

In addition to the new, however, something old had slipped away.

It had taken over a week for him to figure out what he'd lost in the transition. He'd just finished putting his affairs in order back in London and was en route to Marbella where he intended to find his mother, wherever she was, and forgive her when he realized what the prophecy had removed from his life and everyone else's.

Fear. He was simply unable to be afraid.

And without the fear, there was no worry. No dread. No anxious feelings to keep him awake at night.

No fear also meant he had lost the ability to hate.

Mia and Thomas floated down the aisle, arm in arm, the fading sunlight casting shadows through the newly budded trees. After the reception, they were headed back to Parkville, where thanks to a construction team hired by Meyer Enterprises, their home had been rebuilt in record time exactly as it had been before the fire. Sadly, no amount of money or resources could return Mildred to them, but Patrick had worked above and beyond to make honest reparations for his past transgressions. There hadn't been acceptance, but there had been forgiveness.

Behind the newlyweds, Mia's maid-of-honor, Chelsea, and Thomas's best man, Jack, joined the procession. Lanying and Salomon followed closely behind. Both had returned to their native countries after leaving La Paz – Salomon back to the Congo, where he took a position at the University of Kamina in Katanga teaching history, and Lanying back to Shanghai, where she had reconciled with her parents and resumed her studies in pursuit of becoming a certified nutritionist.

Jose and Andrea fell into step behind the others, a precursor of their own impending nuptials which were planned for the fall. Javier had already received his invitation and knew he wouldn't miss the opportunity to share in their special day. He was thankful that despite working against the light psychics for so many years, they not only welcomed him into their ranks but into their family without hesitation. He was one of them. And it was as if he always had been.

The last to walk the aisle were he and Donescia. She winked at him as he took her arm and fell into step beside her. Although he was in regular communication with the other members of their group, it was Donescia who he spoke to on a daily basis. After spending four hours together stranded in the La Paz airport due to delayed flights, they'd discovered a lifetime of commonalities. He cried at her stories of how she was tormented for being different as a child. She'd laughed as he described the tricks he would play on his teachers, making objects disappear and reappear in different places around the classroom. They'd bonded to one another over cold airport sandwiches on the floor of the international terminal. Looking at her now, a wreath of baby's breath woven around her head like an angel's crown, he knew his life was finally just beginning.

THE END

Dearest Reader,

When I decided to write the *Sevens Prophecy Series*, I knew I wanted to give a voice to some of the larger issues in our world which are difficult to discuss - the thousands of women and children who have been forced into sexual slavery, the pain and indignity of domestic violence, the tragedy of third world poverty and first world body shaming. Please know that although I've written works of fiction, there's nothing fictional about the real-life anguish actual men and women facing these issues experience each and every day. Here are some of the facts:

"An estimated 2.5 million people are in forced labor (including sexual exploitation) at any given time as a result of trafficking, the majority of these trafficking victims are between 18 and 24 years of age, and 98% of those used for forced commercial sexual exploitation are women and girls.

Worldwide, almost one third (30%) of women who have been in a relationship report that they have experienced some form of physical and/or sexual violence by their intimate partner, and globally, as many as 38% of murders of women are committed by an intimate partner.

Some 795 million people in the world do not have enough food to lead a healthy, active life. That's about one in nine people on earth. Sub-Saharan Africa is the region with the highest prevalence of hunger. One person in four there is undernourished. However, if women farmers had the same access to resources as men, the number of hungry in the world could be reduced by up to 150 million.

In the United States, 20 million women and 10 million men suffer from a clinically significant eating disorder at some time in their life. The best-known contributor to the development of anorexia nervosa and bulimia nervosa is the body dissatisfaction (40-60%) of elementary school girls (ages 6-12) who are concerned about their weight or about becoming too fat. This concern endures through life."

I implore you to learn more about what you can do to increase awareness or help put an end to these issues by taking a few minutes of your day to read the information on the following websites which served as my fact sources:

www.ungift.org   www.who.int
www.unodc.org   www.wfp.org/hunger/stats
www.unglobalcompact.org   www.nationaleatingdisorders.org

In the words of the great 18th century abolitionist William Wilberforce:
"You may choose to look the other way but you can never say again that you did not know."

Sincerely,
Amalie Jahn

About the Author

Amalie Jahn is the author of the *Sevens Prophecy Series*, *The Clay Lion Series*, and many, many to-do lists. Visit her online at www.amaliejahn.com.